Echoes Along the Sweetbrier

James D. Yoder

This is a work of fiction. Names, characters, places, and incidents either are the product of the author's imagination or are used fictitiously. Any resemblance to actual events or locales or persons, living or dead, is entirely coincidental.

ISBN 0-7414-2143-7

Published by:

1094 New Dehaven Street, Suite 100
West Conshohocken, PA 19428-2713
Info@buybooksontheweb.com
www.buybooksontheweb.com
Toll-free (877) BUY BOOK
Local Phone (610) 941-9999
Fax (610) 941-9959

Printed in the United States of America

Printed on Recycled Paper

Published August 2004

To all those who persisted
through the rocky paths and seas of life
until they found the Pearl of
Great Price.

A NOTE FROM THE AUTHOR

Echoes Along the Sweetbrier is a historical novel set in the latter part of the nineteenth and first two decades of the twentieth century. The plot emerged from the experiences of real persons and actual events, though set in a fictional Pennsylvania community. I have used the novelist's tools to develop the story, attempting to reflect some aspects of the conservative Mennonite culture of the turn of the century and the conflicts experienced by protagonist, Susanna Steiner.

Any similarity between the characters in this novel and persons living or dead would only be coincidental.

I hope this novel stimulates readers, and conveys the life and meanings of the characters caught in the painful conflicts.

ECHO OF SORROW

1

Eighteen-year-old Susanna Steiner plunked the sadiron on the range top and slipped the housing around a hot iron. Tightening the clasp with a calloused finger, she turned back to the sturdy oak ironing board stretched in front of the open window where the tops of the late blooming beauty bush nodded.

Her left hand clutched her pale chin as the words burned in her brain. No! Reuben Maust, what are you doing? No, no....

Nausea crept upwards to her throat at the mingling smells of the freshly laundered and sun-dried overalls she pounded with the iron. Surely the morning sickness was over now that it was ten o'clock.

"I'll have to confront Reuben Maust again tonight," a part of her whispered to the other trembling portion. Startled by the thud of her mother Anna's heels on the threshold by the east kitchen door, Susanna turned. She realized she was unable to shove the fear back down into her heart. She knew it leaped from her dark brown eyes.

"Susanna, two pairs of brother Aden's britches and your Father's Sunday broadcloth shirt, then enough for the morning. Let's sit on the east porch and listen to the cardinals as we snap beans to can this afternoon." The strings on fifty-year-old Anna Steiner's white prayer cap drifted back as her black-stockinged legs carried her matronly form across to the willow laundry basket resting on the green bentwood chair.

Susanna thought of her people who'd settled in these Pennsylvania valleys since the late eighteenth century. Mennonites. Their very own sixty acres on the fertile north bank of the Sweetbrier. Swiss and German were her people.

"Susanna, you look weary. Sweat's beaded on your forehead. Let me iron these overalls and this shirt while you rest. You must have stayed out too late last night at the gathering over at Hostetlers." She smiled tenderly at Susanna.

Susanna noted the smile and felt her mother's unfailing love. How can I tell her? Her stomach tightened. "No, Mother." Susanna lifted a hand to push in a hairpin that had worked its head out from the thick braids wound around her head. "Aden and I got home about eleven o'clock, Mother." Susanna tried to steady fingers that automatically stretched up again, this time to mask a twitching upper lip.

The memory scratched at her heart like branches of the wild plums by Sweetbrier Creek. Should I try to see Reuben again? She pondered. Dear Lord, dear Lord. What am I going to do? Her heart pounded against her rib cage. Susanna gasped, breathing in the air blowing off the sweet clover field.

Her mother jerked a ladder-back chair from its place at the oak dining table. "Sit, Susanna, you're paler than one of my Buff Orpington hens." Anna lifted the sadiron from its cast-iron trivet parked at the wide end of the ironing board and shoved it down the denim overall leg as skillfully as the Chinese laundry man over at Blessing did.

Steam circled toward her rosy cheeks and graying hair. "You must have played outdoor games last night, tired as you are today, Susanna. Was it *walk a mile*? That game can wear out any young one...believe me...." Anna chuckled. "That's how I got to know your father, Susanna. Yes," she added, "one can meet new people while playing *walk a mile*, and, it's especially nice when the full moon is shining."

***

Suddenly Susanna's brain was assaulted by an onslaught of echoes--echoes from along the Sweetbrier where Reuben Maust had insisted they walk over two months ago after the singing. They encircled her heart like an iron hoop long forgotten and grown into the bark of an oversized oak.

"Let's look at the little waterfall by Metzler Bend where the wild roses cascade down. It's moonlight, too..."Reuben's voice liquid, warm as pancake molasses.

Susanna hesitated, "It's too late, Reuben, and..." then there'd been that uncertainty about it. She had turned at the sound of an approaching buggy, noticing that it was Bishop Weaver's son, Isaac, and his new bride, Reuben's sister, Rachel. Isaac and Rachel had raced past their halted buggy, Rachel's loud laughter rippling in the cool April evening.

Reuben had grabbed her hand, squeezing it until it hurt, though she'd said nothing as she skipped, trying to keep up and avoid entangling her feet in the buck brush alongside the trail. She could still feel the heat of his hand. Entangling her foot in the loop of a wild grapevine, Susanna staggered and would have fallen, but Reuben reached out and caught her.

"How do I know you didn't do that on purpose?" His deep laughter rolled up his throat. Then, he'd held her with one arm, but just for a moment.

The voices still circled in her head. "You're lucky to be going with Reuben Maust, Susanna. Those onyx eyes of his could charm a courthouse judge to change a burglar's sentence," Sadie Swick had said, unable to hide the jealousy in her own voice.

"Make you a splendid living, Susanna. Fine carpenter, too, Reuben Maust is," Beulah Byler added. "Besides, his sister, Rachel, is married to Bishop Weaver's son, Ike. Marry Reuben and you'll be the same as in Bishop Weaver's family."

Suddenly Susanna realized that Reuben had led her off the main trail. His hand slid from her hand up her arm. She could still feel it, tight, like a blacksnake coiling around an unfortunate rabbit.

"Reuben, the falls are over eastward, you're going away..." but she couldn't finish. Reuben thrust his face into hers kissing her forcefully with his hard, firm lips. His sandpaper jaw and face chafed her cheek.

Susanna remembered hearing the nervous murmur of the falls behind her shoulder and the rattle of the leaves in the burr oak as the great tree shuddered in a swift gust. She even remembered the whippoorwill's call. Now she recognized it was a ghostly, sad song, a portent of her heart-wrenching shock. Susanna wanted to put her palms up over her ears as the cries echoed in her head: "Whip poor Willa, whip poor Willa...,"only her name wasn't *Willa*, it was *Susanna*.

"Reuben, what is it?" Her own voice, fear-laden as he forced her to the mossy ground by the hazel bush. "Reuben, I have to get home, Mother, Father..."

"Susanna, hush." He placed a big, calloused hand that smelled like walnut planks over her face. Near panic, she reached out with one palm to try to shove him back, but she couldn't breathe with his hand smothering her.

"Susanna, you're my girl. I only want to show you my love. Susanna...." Reuben's rough bungling in attempting to partially disrobe her added other sounds to the night, ripping organdy, and tearing undergarments.

Overpowered and fear-stricken, Susanna realized then that there was nothing she could do as a splitting pain stabbed her body and pierced the encircling waves of echoes along Sweetbrier Creek.

***

Relieved to get off her feet, Susanna dropped onto the oak-stained chair and clasped her hands in her lap. She drew back her high-topped button shoes and hooked her heels behind a lower chair rung. She made herself look up to her mother's gentle face.

"No, Mother, it wasn't...it wasn't the games." She realized her voice quivered and wondered if she could hold back the tears. "I, I haven't been feeling well mornings, Mother, I..." Susanna didn't want to tell her mother that she'd not needed the flannel rags she so patiently placed in the little basket in her bottom bureau drawer for "that time of the month."

Anna turned and strode briskly to the stove to retrieve a hotter iron. She licked her finger and touched the bottom of the heavy iron. It sizzled. She glanced again at Susanna's face. She let the iron drop back to the black stove top and her plain mauve skirt brushed her shoes as she stepped to Susanna's side and placed her berry-stained hand on her shoulder. With her right palm and fingers, she felt Susanna's sweating brow.

"Maybe you need a tonic. Dr. Hershberger over in Rosefield makes a tonic that's good for late spring or summer fevers."

"Mother, I, I don't need a tonic." Susanna dared to focus her aching eyes upon Anna's gentle face, meeting her gray-blue ones. Even the mention of "tonic" made her stomach heave.

Anna ignored the ironing, drew up another ladder-back chair to Susanna's right. She reached out and clasped Susanna's hands. "Something's bothering you, Susanna, what is it? You haven't been yourself. Sadie Wenger mentioned it to me after services two weeks ago, 'Your daughter Susanna's not herself lately, Anna.' A daughter can always tell her mother, no matter what it is, Susanna."

Susanna felt a quiver race up her backbone. Her tongue stuck to the roof of her mouth, dry as the back porch step in blazing July, as the scene from two months ago slid through her brain. It was if the wind in the giant chestnut by Sweetbrier Creek now wailed her sorrow.

A muscle spasm twitched Susanna's shoulder as, even now, she could feel the rude shove to the small grassy hillock. She'd thought that surely Reuben, rough as he'd pressed her down, was only teasing. And he was strong. A carpenter. Hard muscles, bulging biceps. His handsome hair had fallen over his forehead as he pressed his dark-skinned face into hers. His hand grasped at her bodice as, again, she heard her dress rip, the one she'd hung on the nail behind her closet door and covered with her winter coat. Try as she did, Susanna could not keep back the tears.

Then it started. Welling up from a bottomless pit somewhere at the farther end of her soul, spilling out to her mother, whose warm hands clasped hers in loving security.

But those hands would pull away, wouldn't they, once she's known? Mother's face would collapse, then tighten in hard horrified lines like Magdalene Sutter's had when she heard that her first-born son, Eric, had eloped and married a Catholic.

Susanna knew that her tongue had loosened, maybe even unhinged by an angel, for the flood poured out like a spring deluge over the dam on the Sweetbrier.

"Mother, I'm going to have a baby," she heard someone say. It seemed as if there was a rushing wind, a hot dry wind of sorrow blowing in the room, coiling above her head, then funneling itself into her bruised soul.

She heard her mother gasp and saw her hand close over her shocked face. "Susanna, what are you saying? No..."

"Mother, what do you call it when a man forces you?" Susanna heard someone ask in a voice rusty as old corrugated iron.

"No, my child. You--you weren't...?"

The word leaped. An ugly word, a fear-ridden, ripping word with its rolling r sound. "Mother, Reuben Maust raped me!"

PAPA, OH, PAPA

2

Anna led Susanna, weeping and bent double, into the living room where the green shades, half-lifted, cast a soothing light. "Here, Susanna, take your time. Try to get your composure while we sort this out." Anna swallowed, while silently praying, "God, grant me understanding." The ugly word with the r sound tangled in her brain.

Then she heard Joseph pull open the kitchen screen door. "Anna, Susanna, Mary Zook sent over a three-gallon pail of her garden peas. You and Susanna'll..."

"Joseph, step in the room." Anna clutched the varnished oak parlor door. She knew the pain in her eyes betrayed her. "It's Susanna. Susanna needs us. Needs us more than she ever has needed us before, Joseph."

Joseph, with a nod of his head and shoulder, stepped across the linoleum onto the blue rag carpet to Anna's side.

"Susanna? Well, Anna, what is it? Has Bishop Weaver asked Susanna to start a singing class for the Willow Bend girls? I always said, Susanna, with her music ability..."

Then Joseph, who had removed his straw hat, revealing his pink and white forehead and salt-and-pepper hair, which sprang into loose curls when damp, focused his brown eyes upon his daughter, bent over on the horsehair sofa, weeping, head buried in both hands.

"Joseph, Joseph." Anna struggled to say more. Her tongue failed her, leaving her eyes to convey her desperation.

Joseph slid to Susanna's right on the mauve sofa, his blue broadcloth-covered arm stretched behind her. Susanna, nestled beneath his arm, lifted her face, streaked with tears. Her eyes pled for mercy.

"Papa, oh, Papa, something terrible happened to me, Papa...." Susanna gasped, her bosom heaving.

Joseph Steiner focused his eyes upon Anna's pale face and sorrowful blue eyes. "Anna, what's she trying to tell me? Has she already told you? What is it? Maybe you'd better run and send Aden for Dr. Bowman over at Mt. Blue."

"I must tell him myself, Mother. Papa, Reuben Maust raped me."

"Susanna, no." His shoulders arched back, his eyebrows lifted and his eyes widened, round like the bottoms of two Smith Cough Syrup bottles. "How could this happen, Reuben Maust?" Then Joseph collected himself, forcing his mouth shut as a deeper part of his being seemed to realize this was no time to scare Susanna by more display of shock than what was already on his face."

"Listen to her, Joseph. Just give her time." Anna sagged to the other side of Susanna and scooped her daughter's hands into her own. On the opposite wall, Susanna's grandparents, Ezra and Fanny Steiner, looked down from their oval frame, eyes focused upon her, straight line mouths clamped shut according to the proper piety of their generation.

"Two months ago, after the gathering at Hostetlers'. On the way home Reuben wanted me to stroll down Sweetbrier Creek in the moonlight and listen to the falls." Susanna looked at her father, then found the handkerchief in her apron pocket and blew her nose and mopped her eyes.

"He forced you? Reuben Maust forced you, there in the woods, in the darkness?" Joseph's voice trembled.

"That's what Susanna told me too, Reuben. Oh, God give us all grace from heaven. Bishop Weaver'll have to know soon, and...Susanna, does Reuben Maust know? Have you told him?"

"Yes, Mother. I made myself climb in the buggy with him at last week's singing. Somehow God gave me the strength to tell him, confront him. I could not have done it, Papa, Mama, in my own strength."

"God, have mercy." Faith in his daughter and admiration for her strength vibrated in Joseph's deep bass voice. "I'm going now, Susanna. Reuben Maust will answer to me." Joseph's face flushed, his lips drew down and his eyes narrowed as if he was about to step out into a winter blizzard. He rose and grasped for his hat which had fallen from the stand table with the brass eagle claws clutching the crystal balls at the leg bottoms. He swept his hat up off the rag carpet floor.

"No, Papa, no. You go, I go. What's said before Reuben Maust must be said in my presence. It's my life, Papa, it's my life." At those words, Susanna broke into uncontrollable sobbing.

After Susanna had composed herself, Joseph headed toward the barn to dip oats for his team. Anna, her face tear-streaked, sliced the pork roast for dinner, but her hand trembled so she had to lay the knife down.

Fifteen-year-old Aden stepped into the kitchen. His eyes searched their faces. Susanna could see the bewilderment creep across his face. Then he looked down at the floor, cheeks red. He would not look up at her. What had Aden heard? And he, her own brother under Reuben Maust's eye and arm every Thursday and Saturday mornings in his cabinet shop.

"Reuben Maust is more than a friend to me, Susanna," he'd said. And his eyes had reflected no uncertainty about his admiration for his cabinet-making tutor. "When I grow up, I want to be just like Reuben Maust," Aden had said just last week.

REUBEN, LISTEN TO ME

3

Twenty-one year-old Reuben Maust reached out his husky arm to hang his rip saw on the pegs on the carpentry shed wall. It was one of his father, Abe's, tools and whenever Reuben used the tools, he thought of his father who'd died from a stroke two years ago. Sawdust and sweat beads glistened in the dark hair on Reuben's arms. Perspiration stained his blue cotton shirt. He placed both strong hands into his hip pockets, turned and arched his aching back at the sounds of horse hooves clopping down the lane. He reached into his front pocket to feel the two dollars Ezra Helmuth had paid him that day for building two hog houses over at his farm.

Reuben recognized the Steiner buggy hitched to their smart strutting roan, nodding his head as they turned past the climbing roses at the gate. Susanna and her pa. Reuben's angular jaw dropped as his lips spread across his white teeth into a charming smile.

Joseph brought the buggy to a halt, wrapped the reins around the whip post and leaped out. Reuben saw Joseph pat Susanna's arm and mumble something like, "Stay in the buggy for now."

"Evening, Joseph," Reuben said. He stepped over a rut in front of the shed and out of the glare of the western sun on the horizon. Reuben started to extend his sweaty arm even if he did notice Joseph's face twitching as if he might be having a stroke.

"Reuben Maust, I need to talk to you and I prefer to talk to you alone." Joseph ignored the extended hand.

His voice had a determined edge to it, and Reuben noticed that his face was set, mouth as straight as one side of his carpenter's square. "Why, all right, Mr. Steiner. Sure. Ma's finished milking and she's in the kitchen cooking up smothered steak. Sure. Right here, Mr. Steiner. What is it?" Reuben flashed a smile, which he hoped would be disarming, as he was quite aware that Susanna's father had not extended an arm to shake hands.

"Evening, Susanna." Reuben, straw hat in hand, nodded to Susanna over in the buggy, bonnet tied under her chin. She nodded her head and he heard her faint, "Evening, Reuben."

"Reuben, it's about--it's...."

Reuben noticed that Joseph Steiner looked as if he was going to choke as his sun-spotted hand rose up to his throat to steady his jaw.

By this time Susanna, who'd slid out of the buggy and edged herself next to her father, clutched his arm. Reuben grinned as he swept his eyes over her pink-clothed bosom.

"It's about me, Reuben, or, I should say, us, Reuben." Susanna drew back her shoulders and focused her dark eyes into his even darker ones as if to make certain she had contact. "Reuben, it's true, what I suspected two weeks ago, I'm going to have a baby." She stood, black shoes together, the wind catching her prayer veiling strings. Her eyes lowered.

"Susanna tells me you forced her, Reuben. Forced her. Before God and in this community you know that is a grievous sin, Reuben Maust. You've put a shadow over my Susanna that'll take years to sweep away. Change her life forever. Yours, too, Reuben. And, I...Susanna and I trusted you."

Joseph took out his handkerchief and wiped the tears that'd crept to the corners of his eyes.

"Forced her? Susanna, is that what you're telling your folks? Forced?" Reuben lifted his chiseled face, dark whiskers showing through on his jaw. He laughed, startling the meadowlark on the garden fence by the trumpet vine. The breeze halted and the sun hid its face behind a cloud bank. Suddenly the wind started again, colder, whipping the edges of their clothing.

"You know it's true, Reuben. I have the dress, ripped down the front, and," her voice faltered, "the--the other garments, too."

"Joseph Steiner, surely you don't believe I'd do something awful as that, do you? Force myself on Susanna? Why, it was Susanna herself suggested that moonlight walk, she willingly hiked up her skirt and climbed through that gap."

"Reuben, Reuben, listen to Father and..." Susanna leaned forward, entire body pleading.

"All you have to do is to check it out with your brother, Susanna. He's like a brother to me. Think I'd violate his sister?"

"Reuben, Aden's confused. Leave him out of..."

"Well, I see what you've done, Susanna, poisoned your pa against us Mausts. Sure, we only got a forty acres and not as prosperous as you folks. Course, your pa, Susanna, had his farm given him by his pa." Reuben spit out the cold, hurtful words.

"Reuben. Listen to me, I--" Joseph extended both hands.

"And, Mister Steiner, if you only wait a few weeks you'll see that your hysterical daughter, old enough to know better, is just having some female problem. She'll be regular in a few weeks, you'll see. Give her a tonic." Reuben's eyes narrowed. "Then you'll be racing back over here begging my pardon." Reuben dug a shoe toe into the dust, let his mouth fall as his eyes shifted down, hands in his pockets like a little boy freshly accused of stealing cookies.

"Hush, Reuben. Be still." Joseph stepped in front of Reuben, whose black-haired head rose six inches above his own.

Reuben could feel the heat of Steiner's body, the old man's work brogues nudging his own shoe toes.

"We'll have to take this to the Bishop and to the church, Reuben. You're a member over at Edenvale. They'll have to handle it there. That doesn't let you off at Willow Bend Church, though. I'm going to insist to Bishop Weaver that you be ordered to give a public confession there. Susanna and I both want to hear the words." Joseph Steiner seemed to realize that he'd stepped too close to Reuben. He edged back.

All at once Reuben's cheeks flushed. A vein pulsed on his forehead. His eyes widened at the threat. "What's the problem, Mister Steiner? No problem here. You and I both know that when the young couples stand before the Bishop, more'n one of the brides got a belly swelling up with a young one. Soon's Susanna comes to her senses, I plan to make an honorable woman out of her. I've got seven hundred dollars saved."

"Reuben, now you know that happened only twice in this community in twenty years, how could you--"

"I can't marry you, Reuben," Susanna said. "Not now. Maybe never. At least not until we take this to the church. I'm innocent. Before God you know that, Reuben, and I did have a high regard for you, but now--"

"I don't like your attitude, Reuben. Not serious enough for a situation like this we face, changing everything." Joseph shifted his legs, feet wider apart now for a more certain foundation. "Susanna's reputation smirched. Our Susanna is a Christian and we are going to Bishop Weaver over this. We've got to have his admonition and see how the church will handle all this, your situation, too, before I ever hear you talk of marriage to my Susanna." Joseph Steiner wiped his eyes again with his handkerchief. He stepped back further. Susanna stepped back with him.

Reuben could not ignore the cold silence when Joseph stopped talking. But, what the sweat? He planned to make an honorable woman of her, didn't he?

YOU DIDN'T HEAR SUSANNA

4

Solomon Weaver, bishop of the five-hundred-member Willow Bend Church, was surprised when he stepped to the dining room screen door to find out whose arrival Teddy happily announced with his barking at the hitching post. "Serena, it's the Joseph Steiners. Susanna and her parents. Looks like the boy, Aden, isn't in the carriage."

Serena Weaver dried her hands on her coarse homespun apron and looked out the curtainless window across the expanse of bluegrass where the mock orange bowers, heavy with white blossoms, swayed in the wind. "Why, won't that be nice. I've been wanting to show Anna that new yellow rose I got up at Mt. Blue Nursery. Couldn't be a more perfect time. It's in full bloom." Serena Weaver reached behind her back to check her apron strings bow.

"It's not like Joseph Steiner to take time off from his early corn cultivating to pay us a visit. Important--yes, it must be important. Bishop Weaver ran his thumb up his front suspender straps to straighten them, relieved too, that his shirt was still clean. He noticed, as the Steiners headed up the limestone steps and onto the wide painted porch, that all three of them looked down. Something serious on their minds. He opened the screen door. "Why, Joseph and Anna, Susanna, too. Come on in." He extended a warm and farmer's hand. Yes, it must be a funeral.

"Morning, Brother Weaver." The Steiners all shook his hand as they stepped into the spacious dining room, well lighted from the wide-open eastern windows. The mid-morning sun cast a warm light into the room with its large but plain handmade china cabinet. A marigold carnival glass fluted vase sporting yellow roses and white mock orange graced the extended dining room table. The savory smell of onions in a pan on the kitchen range drifted into the room.

"Why, Susanna and Anna. What a pleasant surprise. I can shove a chunk of smoked ham in my oven, boil up some of those new potatoes in my garden and you folks stay for dinner." Serena Weaver smiled. Anticipation of a good visit showed on her face. Her eyes shifted to survey Susanna's dull brown dress.

"Brother Weaver, we, we..." Joseph lowered his head, eyes cast upon the variegated rag carpeted floor, then back up to the Bishop's gray eyes. "Brother Weaver, we have to talk something over with you. All three of us. Susanna, Anna, and I. Could we see you in the room?"

Of course Bishop Weaver knew when anyone said "the room," they meant the seclusion of the living room where the sliding doors were opened for Sunday guests.

"Why, certainly. Step this way, Anna, Susanna..." he cast an uncertain look at Serena, who turned to check the onions frying on the stove.

Anna and Susanna seated themselves on the leather and oak couch against the west wall facing the bay window with its potted mother-in-law's tongue and angel wing begonias. Bishop Weaver drew back a library table chair for Joseph, then pulled up a second one with an ornate pressed-wood back for himself. "Well, ahem, uh--what is it, Joseph?" He clasped his work-worn hands and leaned forward. A lock of white hair fell over his forehead.

"Brother Weaver, we have a serious matter to discuss with you. A grievous matter that has already brought us to prayer. It's hard to begin, but it has to do with Reuben Maust and Susanna." Joseph lifted his eyes to focus upon Bishop Weaver's face, which looked as if it were sliding down into his beard. Joseph straightened his shoulders and noticed how Susanna stared at him as though wanting to protect him.

Susanna turned and faced Bishop Weaver, eyes red and swollen. “It’s about me,” Susanna said. “Yes, and about Reuben Maust, too, but he is a member over at Edenvale. I have to tell you,” her voice wavered as if it might fail her, but she gained strength, lifted her eyes again, and continued. “You know I’m still a single girl, Bishop Weaver. You know Reuben Maust has been seeing me--taking me to the gatherings and singings. I, uh--.”

Anna, who sat with tears in her eyes and hadn’t taken off her black bonnet, reached across and placed her palm over Susanna’s hands.

“Susanna’s trying to say...,” Joseph said.

“Father, I have to say it. Bishop Weaver, I’m going to have a baby. Reuben Maust forced himself upon me over two months ago. I tried to--to. He was too strong, he tore my clothes and took advantage of me.” Tears streamed down her cheeks as her eyes searched Bishop Weaver’s face as if to read, what next?

“Not a stalwart young man like Reuben. Oh, Heavenly Father, not another one of these cases. So much pain--goes on for years. And Reuben’s mother, Bertha, a widow now, too.”

“Bishop Weaver, we look to you for guidance,” Anna said, her voice wobbling.

“Maybe you’d better give me more details about it, Susanna. Serious charge. Very serious words, ‘A man *forced* you.’ Do you mean--” he coughed and brought his fist to his lips, “Do you mean rape?”

“Yes, it was rape. After the gathering at Hostetlers in late April. Reuben wanted me to walk down to the Sweetbrier and listen to the falls. That’s when he took advantage of me, and though I tried, I couldn’t get away. Reuben Maust is a very strong man, Brother Weaver.”

Bishop Weaver straightened his shoulders. His face muscles tightened. Thoughts of his large flock circled in his head. A weight pressured his heart. Rifts. Agonizing confrontations. Deacons involved. Families torn. Forgiveness?

Yes, a Christian leader was obligated to usher such a catastrophic situation toward full reconciliation.

His mind whirled. Reuben Maust. Where was he? Why wasn't he here to give account for himself? How would one know if Susanna's charges were...? And Reuben Maust's very own sister, that comely Rachel, married to my oldest son, Isaac, too. Dear God, what an entanglement.

The Steiners waited patiently as the ceiling-tall grandfather clock clacked a desperate rhythm. Bishop Weaver realized if he hesitated too long, he might appear incompetent as a guardian of their souls.

"Joseph, Anna, Susanna, this, this will involve the whole congregation, won't it? Yes. But, one thing, and I'll say it plain out. Where is Reuben? Why isn't he here to answer these charges? Surely," he looked at Joseph, "you know I have to hear Reuben's side of this account, painful as it is. Only fair way. We do have to be just." He tried to put his left leg over his right, but because of his short legs, the maneuver failed.

"But you know Reuben is a member at Edenvale Church. His accountability rests there." Joseph rearranged his hands in his lap. "We asked. I even insisted that Reuben come today, Brother Weaver."

"He wouldn't come," Susanna said, "he refuses any acknowledgment of what he did to me. He said it was only..." Susanna looked at each one for a moment, then lowered her eyes. "He said it was only...you know, that ugly word St. Paul uses in Corinthians, forn..., fornication." Her cheeks turned crimson.

"Fornication? Then if that's what it is," the Bishop looked in sequence at all three Steiners, beginning with Joseph, "then the blame should be equally shared." Bishop Weaver felt considerable relief. Big difference between what the Bible calls fornication and rape.

Bishop Weaver noticed that Susanna's body had grown rigid as if she was somehow going to assert herself, refuse to be pliable and submissive as according to St. Paul. Then he remembered. Attire. What was the young woman wearing on the night of such events as she described?

"Why, I must ask you, Susanna, since you have uttered such serious charges against Reuben Maust, just how were you attired the night in question?" He noticed she drew back and her brown eyes grew darker, her eyebrows drew together slightly.

"Attired? Bishop Weaver, are you questioning the way I was dressed?" She sat straight, dark eyebrows raised.

"Women, that is, especially young women, don't often realize how, through carelessness and maybe without due regard. they invite young men to approach them and express their passions, they--"

"Brother Weaver. Are you suggesting that I went to the Hostetler gathering immodestly dressed? Why--"

"Did you forget your instruction before baptism, Susanna? First Timothy, Chapter 2, verses 9 and 10" 'In like manner also, that women adorn themselves in modest apparel, with shamefacedness and sobriety, not with broidered hair, or gold, or pearls, or costly array.'"

Then Brother Weaver realized he'd better hone in closer to an important issue, embarrassing though it might be. "And, your bosom, Susanna. Was your bosom properly draped? You know you're still a growing girl and when clothes get too tight they--"

"We have instructed our son and daughter according to the plain teachings of our church, Solomon." Joseph left out the *Bishop Weaver*. "Susanna dresses modestly according to the instructions in First Peter, Chapter 3, *modestly*, the inner adorning of the heart. You yourself, Solomon, gave her communion Easter Sunday."

"I would have been negligent in my duty if I had not brought it up, the matter of attire, Joseph. But, I must say we face a grave situation. God have mercy on your soul, Susanna, and Reuben's too. No doubt you will want your marriage banns read in church soon as possible under these conditions. I wouldn't put off a wedding. Not at all under these circumstances. Not at all." He cleared his throat and surveyed the Steiner's faces "You'll need to make a public confession, Susanna. Reuben will have to do it over at Edenvale Church. I'll speak to Preacher Heatwole over there. We must all pray that the congregation will forgive..." He wiped his brow with a large linen handkerchief pulled from his back pocket.

"But, Bishop, you, you don't..." Joseph turned his bewildered eyes upon the stressed churchman.

"We wouldn't want to fail to pray to the Heavenly Father right now. Let us pray." Bishop Weaver's knees thudded on the homemade carpet as he kneeled and turned facing his wooden chair.

With such exhortation, the Steiners all followed his example. Their knees creaked and thudded as they found positions before couch and chair.

"Merciful and loving Father," Bishop Weaver's voice rose to a wavering moan. "We beseech you to look down upon this young couple who have fallen so grievously into the paths of Satan. Their purity blown by hot winds of fleshly urges. Help Susanna Steiner, here on her knees feel your love through her guilt, a gift to propel her back into your everlasting arms."

On and on he prayed. Fervently, unctuously, ignoring Joseph's groan of disbelief and Susanna and Anna's gasps. For ten minutes the words rolled, like Ezra Bowman's wagon load of potatoes on the way to market, as Bishop Weaver shifted from one knee to another in his pleadings. Finally, like a mockingbird who had reached the last song in his repertoire, he stopped.

All four heaved and struggled, bracing themselves and rose to their feet.

"You didn't hear Susanna, Bishop Weaver." Joseph leaned closer in toward the Bishop, his face drawn. Sweat broke out on his forehead. Anna had her handkerchief over her mouth.

Susanna interrupted as she stood by the stand table, back straight. She stared straight at Bishop Weaver and with an unfaltering voice said, "I said that I was innocent, Brother

Weaver, regardless of what Reuben Maust says to others of our community, or anywhere for that matter. I am blameless. I see no need of any confession on my part before the congregation. To do so would be lying. I was wronged." Susanna turned to her mother. "Mother, don't we need to go?"

"Yes, daughter, yes. Come, Joseph. Give the Bishop time to think it through. It takes time." Anna wept openly into her handkerchief.

HOW CAN WE GO TO CHURCH ANYMORE, SUSANNA?

5

Reuben Maust's mother, Bertha, hung her head in silence as their spirited bay, Duke, drew their buggy down into the little glen past an ancient orchard on Redbud Road. Young corn flashed deep green leaves on the left slope of the hill.

A self-satisfied smile on his face revealed Reuben was working through his dilemma. In a couple of days his mother would come around. Loosen up. Sure, a shock to see her son step forward in front of the Edenvale congregation and confess his indiscretion. Preacher Heatwole there, a forgiving man. Could tell by the way he nodded his head, and his eyelids slid down over his sad eyes when he had to mention Susanna's name and the carefully selected words describing how we both overstepped the boundaries.

Too bad Susanna takes on so about this. She's like feisty Duke swishing his tail up ahead. Testy. Susanna likes to buck the traces now and then. Reuben flashed a smile to the wide world in general, leaned back, lifted his shoulders, his handsome legs wide apart. Blood surged in his veins as he reveled in being alive.

Get the corn laid by, cultivator put away by Saturday and head over to Blessing to Glick's Hardware where that little clerk, Roxanne Spitz, takes off in the afternoon. He liked it, too, that she wore rouge on her cheeks and her curly hair defied her combs and pins. The way the wisps circled on her neck made the heat flash through his body. If the carnival, down by the river, hadn't left town yet, Roxanne would be more than happy to ride on the Ferris wheel with him.

Reuben slapped the reins and clicked his tongue at Duke, hurrying him across the wide bridge boards over Sweetbrier Creek. Water gurgled and rippled as if giving approval to his morning ventures.

"Son," his mother mumbled, "it--what you had to do this morning in church, made me feel sad."

Reuben noticed she was still weeping about it, but after a few days maybe she'd take some pride in a son as stalwart as he who actually publicly confessed an indiscretion. Why, when one thought of what that salty old Amandas Schrock did, fathering a son by the hired girl and lying about it, his own actions this morning were right manly, weren't they?

"Ma, I know." He reached across with his left hand and placed it on top of her clasped ones. "But I know you prefer a manly son, not a wimp like Phenias Fretz who doesn't even have the courage to ask Goldie Ann Showalter to go to the singing. I'll make an honest woman out of Susanna Steiner. You'll see." He shook her hands, emphasizing the point, then let go. "Two or three grandchildren running around in your front yard fighting to pluck your prize tulips." He grinned.

"The folks at church, they...they were so forgiving, Reuben. So forgiving." She wiped the tears from her eyes and straightened her gray-clothed shoulders. "Why, they stood in line to shake your hand afterwards. Some of the brethren even gave you the kiss of peace." Her work-worn hands clutched her Bible as if they sought security. He noticed that she had a faint smile on her lips at the mention of the "kiss of peace."

Have to do something special for Ma. Reuben hated painting, but he knew his mother had been pleading for him to whitewash the yard picket fence so her irises and her tiger lilies would show off better. Hated it. But there would be time to slap some whitewash on it before Duke and he headed for the carnival. Reuben hummed in self satisfaction.

***

The spring wagon rolled down the dusty road toward the Rosefield Creamery.

"Is it true, Susanna, what the young people are saying about you?"

Susanna looked across at her brother whose yellow hair spilled out from under his straw hat. She wanted to reach out and pat his shoulder, but refrained. What had he heard? Yes, Aden probably knew. No telling what Reuben had told him. It'll soon be obvious. She remembered Aden's angry outburst when Father stopped him, last Thursday, from going down to Reuben's carpentry shop.

"There is a problem that has to be sorted out, son," Joseph had said, one firm hand on the lad's shoulder.

"Pa, Reuben Maust is my friend. What are you doing? What are you saying? This has to do with Susanna, doesn't it? All these secret conversations." Frustrated, Aden stalked out of the house and slammed the back porch screen door, then headed down through the pasture and into the maple woods.

Susanna realized that Aden already had questions about why the two deacons, accompanied by Bishop Weaver, strode up their walk last Thursday evening like three Old Testament prophets, Bibles squashed up under their arms, and after closing the parlor doors, sat with her in the room while the clock ticked, instructing her according too Matthew 18: "If thy brother shall trespass against thee, go and tell him his fault between thee and him alone; if he shall hear thee, thou hast gained thy brother."

A weight as heavy as the iron rails of the bridge over the Sweetbriar ahead bore down on her soul as she reflected on how she and her parents had gone first to the Bishop to share the shameful violation she'd experienced. They came, the deacons and Bishop, because of the second part of the admonition. "But if he will not hear thee, then take with thee one or two more, that in the mouth of two or three witnesses every word may be established."

"What are they saying, Aden, the young folks?"

Aden turned his face toward her. His blue eyes sad, face drawn, lips pouting. He shifted his body. A shoulder twitched. "I hate to say it, Susanna, but it's getting around among the young folks that you--that you...." Aden looked down at his scarred boots, slapped the reins on Nell's broad side more than required as her hooves dug in the soft sand and gravel.

"What happened to you, Susanna? It can't be true, what they're saying, can it? What's going on? You throwing up yesterday morning. Ma looking like there's been a funeral in the family. Pa, hardly ever saying a word. Face set like that Great Stone Face in Nathaniel Hawthorne's story."

Susanna stared at Nell's nodding head in front of her, her eyes following backwards along her satin coat. Her favorite horse, Nell. Nursed from a colt by her hands. If she could only unhook Nell now, leave the spring wagon here by the bridge and jump on her back and ride...

Susanna realized Aden was waiting for her reply. "Aden, I have to tell you something very painful." Her heart pounded, then seemed to skip a beat. "Aden, I know how much you admire Reuben Maust and I know that for now Father forbids you to go down to his shop. I can see the hurt in your face."

"It's unfair, Susanna. What have you done to Reuben?" His voice cracked and trembled. "Why doesn't he drop in to see you anymore? Why does everyone look like someone died?" Aden yanked back on the reins. His forehead furrowed. The spring wagon rattled. The two cream cans in back clanked together. Bridge boards shook under Nell's feet. Then Nell's hoofs hit the sand where the primroses stretched themselves alongside the ditch and a sudden wind blew sweetness from the honeysuckle on the fence to their noses.

"Aden, you've already heard about Reuben Maust and what happened to me. Aden, I'm going to have a baby." Her dark eyes focused upon his face, mouth open, hurt and confusion in his eyes.

"You, you didn't, Susanna? Not what they are saying?"

"I'm innocent, Aden. Reuben Maust forced himself on me over two months ago. Only God knows what steps I shall take in the months ahead."

Aden halted Nell under the shade of the tall locust. He turned. Tears filled his eyes. "I don't believe you, Susanna. I mean, I don't believe he forced you." He stared, face contorted, his eyes opened wide and blazed with heat.

"You will have to believe me, Aden." A cold hand reached from unknown depths and squeezed her heart. Oh, God, not this. Not Aden turning his back on me.

"Isaac Weaver said Reuben had to make a confession in front of the Edenvale congregation, and he mentioned your name, Susanna. Your name. It involved both of you." Aden shrank back as if to distance himself.

"It did. You're right. It involved us both. But, Aden, Reuben Maust overpowered me. Took advantage of me. I couldn't..."

"Don't tell me you couldn't run away." His adolescent voice split with strain. "What did you do?" His voice scraped the depths of his anger. "What did you do, Susanna, flaunt yourself before him? Bathsheba and David? Is that what you did?"

Hurt seared her soul. Her knuckles turned white from locking her fingers together, straining to control her voice and her face. So this is the way it is. Isaac and Reuben's sister, Rachel. They saw her going through the gap into the woods along the Sweetbrier. They probably said she went willingly. Oh, my God! What were they telling Aden?

She saw that Aden was crying as he shifted his buttocks away from her to the farthest edge of the spring wagon seat. "Bishop Weaver wouldn't lie. He knows the truth. Everything's broken and messed up. How can we go to church anymore, Susanna?" He sobbed.

Susanna reached over and took the reins. "Get up, Nell." Her own voice grated in her ears like a withered old crone calling her ravens on the roof-beam. Emptiness. The world, a cold void. Silent. Gray, no color at all. For the rest of her days, the wind would only moan.

Her heart ached at the memory of last week when she and her mother were purchasing three yards of organdy in Polson's Dry Goods in Lynn Valley. She'd seen her old pals from the gatherings, Sadie Swick, Beulah Byler, and Dorcas Hershberger. When they'd spied her, they shifted away. Nothing very obvious. But, clustering and turning away from her and her mother. She caught a glimpse of Dorcas Hershberger staring at her, then looking back to Sadie and Beulah. Words drifted when the cash register had stopped jingling, "Reuben Maust had to get up in church and make a confession."

Susanna turned to Aden who was trying to stuff his red handkerchief into his back pocket, but his hand trembled too much. She attempted once more. "Aden, I'm asking you to believe in me. God knows my innocence." She reached over to clasp his arm, sheathed in blue oxford cloth, but he jerked it up and away. "Last Thursday night, Aden, Bishop Weaver and the deacons told me that unless I had a witness to verify my 'story,' that they were forced to go along with Reuben Maust's account. And since he made a public confession of...." Her mouth worked to say the word in front of her brother, then her lips formed the word, "fornication."

"I know that. I'm surprised you even say an ugly word like that. Don't tell me." Aden's lips curled. Susanna struggled to endure the silence. She felt as if the buggy wheels crunching the gravel below now rolled across her heart. Could her soul take any more bruises?

"That's why we stayed home from church Sunday, wasn't it, Susanna? I expected something. Bishop Weaver read your name from the pulpit, didn't he?" Aden's voice echoed in her brain, hard as nails.

"That's what happened, Aden. Though I haven't received a full account of it yet, Sadie Swick's mother, Louella, dropped by yesterday to buy new potatoes. She told Mother out in the garden." Susanna wiped the tears that streamed down her cheeks.

Silence hung like miasma. How could she expect Aden to believe her? All the boys, the way they gathered behind the barns, legs spread apart, laughing, hooting, sharing. God only knew what, from their adolescent experiences. Reuben. What had Reuben told Aden?

In her heart she began to quote the words of Jesus: "Blessed are ye, when men shall revile you, and persecute you and say all manner of evil against you, falsely..."

And though they said not another word as they approached the creamery ahead, peace suddenly flooded Susanna's heart. Aden, too, had lived through the storm. What of tomorrow? Had she lost her brother along with everything else?

MY NAME IS DESPAIR

6

Susanna stared out the bedroom window overlooking the front lawn where the graceful cedar and the hard maples nodded and dripped after the slow rain.

Three months. Soon everyone would know. Susanna pushed the Bissell brush-sweeper back and forth across the rag carpet of her bedroom floor, oblivious to the fact that she had already swept that portion twice.

Gray gloom outside. Gray gloom shadowing the room. Though she'd raised the green roller blinds to let in more light, it hadn't helped. A sudden thunderclap warned of an approaching downpour. Wind howled at the back eaves of the stately eleven-room house with the dark slate roof.

Susanna sagged on her bed. She thought of Hagar, thrown out of Abraham's tent by old Sarah. Her name, Disgrace, through no fault of her own.

Susanna pondered. Was there more she could have done? What made Reuben think she led him on?

She wished her Papa hadn't bought those lightning rods. Then if lightning struck the house during the storm, she could hunch here in her bedroom until it would all be over.

Excommunicated. The word, sharp and cold. Bishop Weaver and preachers, Elias Wise, and Protus Byler. How could they so easily give in and side with the bishop and the deacons? Why? How did such men gain their power? Where were the church sisters? Would not even one of them come and put her arm around her?

But wasn't she taught from St. Paul... "let your women keep silent in the church?" Where were the voices of the women? Outside. She was an outsider, in limbo, and would be until she give birth to the child in her womb, and even after that. Maybe then, over at Blessing...would they receive her into membership there? How could people live without a church?

What was Reuben going through? Could she find the nerve to face him again? Did he feel any guilt at all? What if he came over and asked her to marry him? Insists on it? She heard her own words creep from her throat: “Oh, Papa, oh, Mama.”

Susanna wrapped her arms around her shoulders and held herself in the dampness and gloom. The odor of the polish she'd swished over the great walnut bed headboard with the oak leaf and acorn carvings mingled with the old rag smells from the homemade carpet. She felt her shoulders sag as she sighed. She sat on the bedspread with the antique quilt of dark velvet, odd-shaped pieces sewn together in a haphazard pattern. She always thought of the quilt as bright with its rich gold splotched here and there, but today the quilt depressed her, dark, heavy--the women who made it, old grandmothers, whiskers on their chins, Mother's ancient aunts, long moldering in their graves in Sweetbrier Cemetery. Pain seeped from Susanna's heart as outside the eaves dripped summer rain upon her large-sashed window.

Next, her eyes focused across to the west wall and lingered on the ancient old green chest that her great grandmother Rebecca Steiner brought from Germany. Susanna’s hope chest. Over half-filled with linens, crocheted runners, and doilies. The words, "Rebecca Steiner," painted in black still visible on the wide, front boards.

"When you marry, Susanna, it goes with you, my great grandmother's chest," her father often said. But now there was no cheer. The chest lumbered, oversized and disproportionate, against the wall, reminding her of the undertaker's parlor when the lights were turned down around an ugly coffin. Today it was the chest of "no hope." No hope at all.

Her mind searched for the name of the old woman beyond Leek's Hill. Lived in that fallen-down shack. Pigs in the pen at the side. Vulga Polnaski? Desperate women sneaked to her place. Hazel Lou told her once. What did she do to the girls who sneaked in? Mumble ancient chants? Spoon out vile purges? Wires? Coat hangers?

Susanna shuddered at the account in the newspaper of a girl from Staunton, Molly somebody-or-other, who had sneaked out to old Vulga's place, braved her fierce hounds, deep in the night. Constable found Molly next morning dead in the road ditch. Legs drenched with her blood.

Or, old Annie Overholt and her powwow magic, sanctioned by the church. Would old Annie have a secret formula? Some mysterious mumbled prayer?

Trapped. She was trapped. Imprisoned in a tiny cell. Susanna tried not to think of tomorrow, another month, six months ahead. "Oh, God." She groaned as her body rocked back and forth. The squeak of bedsprings beneath her and the rattle of the corn husk mattress only made her feel more deeply the racking pain inside her soul. "Lord Jesus, what am I to do?"

She thought of Ruth of the Land of Moab and her mother-in-law, Naomi, and how when Ruth's husband died, she'd packed her garments and hiked up the hills with Naomi toward Bethlehem, pleading with Naomi, "Your people shall be my people."

Who were her people now? Mama and Papa had changed too. No, they wouldn't admit it. Faces drawn into those long, serious shapes calves have when they lower their heads in a burnt-up pasture. Downcast eyes. Not that they didn't believe her, but changed, anyway. Her burden, their burden. Aden's scorn.

Would her old school pal and cousin, Rosella Meyers, disown her, too? Hadn't Rosella heard of her misery? Tied down with her invalid grandmother living with her papa and mama over on the eastern side of the community--would Rosella listen to her? A shroud of despair enveloped her as she buried her face in her hands, bleached from the lye water she'd used to mop the kitchen floor. "Despair." She croaked the words. "My name is Despair."

***

It had taken Susanna an hour and a half to travel the six miles toward Mt. Blue. She felt guilt from leaving her mother alone to can the red beets, but surely her mother recognized her need to visit Cousin Rosella. She even overheard her mother talking to Papa last evening on the back porch while she dried the dishes. "The girl needs someone besides us to talk this over with, Joseph. No one can live through this alone. I'm afraid I'll have to admit, folks at Willow Bend Church have turned their backs on Susanna. I can't understand why Bishop Weaver wouldn't...." Then Mother Anna had broken down weeping.

***

Rosella Meyers fluffed a pillow, then placed it beneath her bed-ridden grandmother's head. She checked the window, making sure the white curtain didn't blow over into her grandmother's face, then stepped back into the living room. She drew up a rocking chair facing the bay window where Susanna sat sipping a glass of cold mint tea she'd served a few minutes earlier.

"It's refreshing, Rosella, thank you." Dear Rosella, herself suffering so when her old Aunt Martha died, leaving one-half of her estate to her, her favorite niece. Having to endure her Aunt Willa's rebuke and scorn, even lies when she accused Rosella of manipulating the old woman to gain favor.

"Yes, water from our deep well at the side of the house." She smiled at Susanna, leaned back in her rocker.

"You already know, don't you, Rosella?" Susanna placed the pressed glass tumbler against the palm of her left hand and held it with her right.

"I'm afraid I do, Susanna. Dear Susanna. I was there when Bishop Weaver read your name from the pulpit." Rosella pulled her handkerchief from an apron pocket and wiped her eyes.

"I'm innocent, Rosella. Reuben Maust took advantage of me. Rape. Did you ever hear an uglier word? No one but my family seems to believe me, that is, except Aden. We're suffering, all of us. Aden, bewildered and hurt. He wants to trust his older sister, but Reuben has a powerful influence on Aden now. Mother is grieving, her nose is red and her eyes swollen from crying. Papa is angry and silent. The walls of our once cheery home now drip sorrow, Rosella."

They sat looking at each other. Outside a dog barked at a buggy rolling by. A rooster crowed from behind the house. Rosella leaned forward. The rocker creaked. Steam hissed from a teakettle in the kitchen.

"I believe you're innocent, Susanna. I've known you since grade school. I've never known you to tell an untruth. I'll stand by you, Susanna, no matter what happens. And I'll help you all I can when the baby comes. I want to be there..."

The words only brought more tears to Susanna's cheeks. A trace of a smile crept to her lips. "What are my choices? Alternatives, Rosella?"

"Have you seen Reuben Maust lately? Does he come around?" Rosella seemed hesitant to bring up his name.

"Only the day Papa and I drove over to confront him."

"What did he say? How did he take it, Susanna?"

"He was angry. Even ugly and tried to blame me, or make Papa believe that I was somehow responsible."

"What would you do, Susanna, if Reuben Maust came to see you again? I believe, knowing him, that he doesn't want to give up on you so easily."

"You mean, come to see me, call on me?" Susanna's eyes opened wide.

"Be prepared, Susanna. Now that he thinks he's cleared his name at the Edenvale Church."

"Then, if Reuben comes back to me, then..." Susanna leaned back in her chair.

"What if Reuben proposes to you? You know how Reuben Maust is, he can slide quickly from anger to charm and warmth."

"I know, Rosella. I know from experience. He is charming and hard working, we have to remember his good qualities, too. I feel sorry for him. Of course, many of the girls are taken with his good looks. I've always wanted to marry a man who would put his family first, love them." Susanna stared at Rosella's green eyes.

"And, Susanna, everyone can change. That is, if they want to and allow God to lead them. Perhaps Reuben would be more dedicated in his Christian life, being a father, being responsible before a child. Your baby will be Reuben's, too, Susanna."

Susanna realized that she had focused so much on her own shame that she'd almost forgotten about Reuben. "Rosella, are you suggesting that there is an alternative to bearing a child alone, to being an outcast, my family embarrassed?"

"Well, I didn't exactly put it that way. But you need to be prepared if Reuben Maust drives up some evening. I believe he'll show up on your doorstep, Susanna. Soon, too. In spite of what he said in anger to your father, I believe he, in his own way, cares for you and doesn't want you to slip out of his hands."

"Then, I could, we might--?"

"Well, Susanna, it's something to think about, isn't it? More mint tea, Susanna?"

CHANGE YOUR NAME TO HESTER

7

“I won't stay home, Mother. I refuse to hide. I've done nothing wrong. Besides, you need help with the baskets and setting up your tables at Rosefield market." Susanna filled the last half-bushel with the wax beans and surveyed the pecks of cucumbers, new potatoes, red beets, and late radishes, washed, shining with color. Heavenly aroma from freshly baked pies circled their heads.

"If you insist, Susanna. It's just that you work so hard, bending over in that garden picking beans, then insisting on baking the pies. You know that you need to remember...." Anna, crows' feet at the corners of her strawflower-blue eyes, focused upon Susanna's flushed face.

"Since I don't go to the young people's gatherings anymore, or even the singings and I've made it clear that I won't be returning to Willow Bend Church again, I simply must get out once in a while. These walls are closing in on me.” At the mention of the church, Susanna felt her mouth go dry, her jaw twitch and her tongue twist. Loss. Excruciating loss, my church. Place of my baptism. Where I heard the stories of the Lord. Where I recited "Our Father which art in heaven..." the hymns, I'll have to sing them in my heart--"Love Divine, all love excelling...."

Daily she learned to bury her grief.

***

They set up their tables beneath a large hackberry tree at the west end of town beyond the blacksmith shop in the little open area reserved for the Saturday farmer's market. A warm July sun shot streams of light through the hackberry branches. The dirt street through town was splotched with shadows from tall oak, locust trees, and the overhead clouds. Murmuring of folks strolling the street and walk rose in the air along with horses' hooves clopping, drawing buggies, surreys, and wagons into town. The emerald green of grass and trees, the old brick and gray stone buildings to the east, the market tables sagging with produce from gardens, cheeses from cellars and spring houses, dazzling clusters of yellow, red, and orange gladioli, assorted sparkle of tall snapdragons, and bold-colored early zinnias for sale made the atmosphere pulse.

"See, Mother, I told you it'd be good for me to be here." Susanna brushed back wisps of hair beneath a plain blue kerchief, smoothed her cobbler's apron, drew up a folding chair under their display of near-perfect vegetables and baked goods.

"Townsfolk in good humor today, Susanna. Yes. I like it here, too. A change from out on the farm. Did you unpack the pies, Susanna, the apple, and the gooseberry?"

"Yes, Mother, but I have to keep them covered with tea towels. The flies from the livery, you know."

Just then Sadie Swick and her mother, Clara, backed their spring wagon up to the empty space next to Susanna's display. "That's it, Chester, now hold Dobbin while Sadie and I unload," Clara Swick called to her sixteen-year-old son. Sadie jumped out of the spring wagon and leaned in to lift out a basket of new red potatoes. Then her eyes fell on Susanna Steiner and her mother. "Mother," she hissed. "We don't want to display our market things, here, do we?"

Clara looked toward the left, glimpsing Susanna and her mother. Her eyes narrowed and her nose wrinkled.

"It'll have to do, Sadie. Under the shade of the tree. All the other good spots are already taken. Have to get here early to grab that spot under the hackberry the Steiners always pick."

Susanna, turning to the Swicks, overheard the remarks and realized that Clara and Sadie didn't have the gall to choose another spot, the embarrassment would simply be too great.

"Can we help you unload those baskets, Clara?" asked Anna, rising, her white apron catching in a sudden breeze that rattled the leaves of the giant tree above. Susanna pushed back her folding chair and started to rise.

"No, thank you, Anna. Sit by your--uh--Susanna. Sadie and I are able to lift our goods by ourselves." Clara shifted her eyes away. Her back clothed in drab gray with gathered skirt below, she grunted as she lifted her basket of green beans. She lumbered to the table and dropped them. "Sadie, hand me the pies. Don't want you sinking a knee or elbow in one before we get them sold." Neither Sadie nor Clara looked their way again as they drew up crates. After they'd spread their potatoes, they settled themselves, legs beneath the sawhorses and boards.

So this is how it is. Susanna's face slid into resolve, reflecting little more than the bottom of a new pie pan. She decided not to concentrate on rejections and hurt. She turned to smile at a young farmer's wife, toting a toddler on her hip.

"Such nice new potatoes. My Henry so dearly loves creamed new potatoes with fresh peas. How're you selling them today?" She smiled and shifted the squirming baby boy who dropped the spool in his chubby hand and reached for the bright red radishes.

"We're selling them at ten cents a peck. You're Lizzie Schuler, aren't you?" Anna's hand turned a few of the shiny red potatoes.

"Lizzie Schuler. You have a good memory, Mrs. Steiner. This your daughter, Susanna, isn't it? We met once when all the young folks from our district had a singing. Henry and I live over near Mt. Blue."

"Why, yes, I am. And this is Susanna right here helping me. She baked the pies, too." Anna smiled, obviously feeling the relief of a friendly voice after Sadie and Clara Swick's cold and awkward settling in. Lizzie bought a peck of new potatoes and two bundles of radishes, though she didn't need the radishes, but the baby howled when she tried to retrieve them from his hand.

"You still singing at the gatherings, Susanna? I remember your nice alto voice."

"Well, no, Lizzie, that is, I've not been going to the gatherings and singings lately." Susanna groped for words, but her heart leaped at the genuine friendliness in Lizzie's voice.

"You aren't married, are you? That what you did, Susanna? Up and married? Who was it? As I recall, it was a charmer named Reuben somebody-or-other. Whitest teeth I ever saw against that dark complexion. Kind of a man who shaves and yet the whiskers are there underneath. Makes their chins look almost blue, doesn't it?" She smiled again, revealing a gap in her front row of teeth.

A part of Susanna froze. How shall I respond? She felt a shiver at the mention of Reuben's name by another, a woman, too, and a voice drenched in friendliness. "No, Lizzie. No, I--I'm not married." Her heart palpitated and she felt weak. She saw her mother turn to her, eyes filled with concern.

"Susanna's still single, Lizzie," Anna said, trying to smile.

"Never know, Anna Steiner. Never know when a young blade'll sweep her off her feet. Susanna's got looks. Shucks, I sure thought she'd be hitched before me." At that, Lizzie wrapped an arm around her sack of potatoes, balanced the baby in the other arm and sallied off to complete her shopping and overcome her own loneliness by visiting here and there.

***

By early afternoon, Susanna counted the remaining baskets of vegetables and pies. "Mother, one peck of potatoes and only two pecks of green beans left. Everything else sold, except one gooseberry pie." Susanna tried to maintain an uplifted spirit, but a part of her felt chilled by the obvious shunning of more than a dozen of the folks of Willow Bend Church. A few nodded their heads and spoke, then lowered their eyes. The Wismers and the Derstines, who always bought Anna's cheese, hurried right on by and on across the street to Barbara Hunsberger's table. Everyone knew Hunsberger's cheese didn't have the flavor or the texture Anna's did.

"Soon be able to go home, won't we, Susanna? Yes, we've had a good morning here. People relish your baking, Susanna. While you were giving change to Abner Wismer, Lottie Shank whispered to me, "That Susanna makes a perfect pie crust. Has to use fresh lard every time."

Susanna knew that her mother was struggling like she was, trying to smile and ignore the obvious snubbing. She had gotten through the hours by thinking of the verses from the Beatitudes, "Blessed are ye when men...say all manner of evil against you falsely...."

But before they closed down completely, Beulah Beyler and her mother, Maggie, sidled up. Beulah reached out and dug a thumbnail into a new red potato, checking the freshness, her face stern as the side of an unpainted barn with no window or door. Her mother cleared her throat and clutched at her fringed shawl.

"Why, Susanna, surprised to see you out in public like this, you in a family way." Beulah's thin lips drew into a straight line.

"Come on, Beulah, Elmer's waiting over by the blacksmith shop." Maggie tugged at her sleeve.

Susanna could see that Mrs. Byler didn't want to tarry with sinners. Her cold eyes focused above Susanna's head.

"Hello, Maggie," Susanna said, forcing the woman to lower her eyes and meet hers.

Maggie cleared her throat, sounding as though she was brushing rust from the neck of an old bottle. "You've been excommunicated, Susanna. We don't practice the ban and shun like the Amish, but...."

The silence hung. "Maggie, Beulah," Anna Steiner said, face twisted in pain. "Think of what you are saying. We've been old friends and neighbors from way back. Have you ever taken time to hear Susanna's account of what happened?"

"Well, Anna Steiner. I thought you'd stand up for a wayward daughter. I might, too, if it happened to be..." she caught herself. "Come on, Beulah, we oughtn't to tarry in front of someone who refuses to confess her--"

"Maggie Byler, how can you say that in front of us? Have you taken time to listen to Susanna?"

"Why do you think we have the clear and undisputed words of deacons and preachers and of our blessed Bishop Weaver, Anna? You advocating stepping aside from authority? The authority of the church? Come on, Beulah." Her hand reached for Beulah's arm, but not before Beulah glared into Susanna's face as she rasped, "Sadie Swick said your name ought to be changed to *Hester*, Susanna." Then she swished around and trailed after her mother.

Anna wept openly as Susanna turned toward her. "Don't let it affect you that way, Mother. They just don't know, and they are not ready to listen. In time, give them time."

"What was it, the name Beulah called you, Susanna?"

"She called me Hester, Mother."

"Hester? Why on earth Hester?"

"Mother, Hester was the fallen women in Nathaniel Hawthorne's *The Scarlet Letter*. She was an adulteress, forced to wear an embroidered "A" on the front of all her garments. The church leaders forced her to wear it."

"Dear Lord, help us to forgive...help us to forgive," Anna said, as she grasped her last peck of potatoes and rose to start loading, then head for the security of home. But they had overlooked the tall young man with sandy hair striding toward their table as if in a hurry. Hands in his pants pockets split his black coat backwards revealing a broad chest beneath his blue broadcloth shirt.

"Wait a minute. Can't shut down until I've checked the pie. Been looking all morning for a gooseberry pie. Granny Hoover came for a visit and insisted I bring her one from market." He grinned.

"Just in time." Susanna smiled back as she rose to pull the cloth from the aromatic pie with the glistening sugar on top. "Baked it myself, just this morning."

"Well, now. Guess my search is ended." He laughed heartily. A hand searched in a front pocket for his coin purse. "How much is it?"

"Pies are a quarter. Uh, aren't you a Leatherman?" Susanna lifted her eyes to his face sheltered by a broad-brimmed straw hat. At the inquiry, he lifted the brim of the hat and nodded.

"That I am. Leatherman for sure. Milton Leatherman. I believe I know you, Miss...you're a Steiner from over south of Rosefield. Aden's sister. You go to the old church, Willow Bend."

"Aden's my brother. This is my mother, Anna. My name is Susanna. So, you're from the new Lynn Valley Church, I gather?" Susanna found a paper bag and slipped the pie inside and folded back the top of the sack. At his mention of "You go to Willow Bend Church" Susanna felt a heavy sadness weigh on her heart as the grief and loss surfaced. She tried not to let it seep to her face.

"I guess your folks, or grandparents, came from Willow Bend Church, then, didn't they? Mother, did you know the family?"

"Now that you mention it, I do. I was always fond of your grandmother, Caterina Hoover, your mother's mother. Give her regards from Anna Steiner. Tell her I'd like to see her."

"Thank you, Mrs. Steiner. That I will. Now, as for this pie, you say," he looked straight into Susanna's dark eyes, "you say you made it?"

Susanna realized that she was blushing. He had leaned forward and his smile was genuine. "Yes, I did, Mr. Leatherman. Stoked up the kitchen range and popped it into the oven early this morning. I hope it has enough sugar in it. Gooseberries, you know, are so sour."

"Tarty, Susanna, I do love tarty pies. Gooseberry, cherry, rhubarb. Well, I'll be on my way. You're here every Saturday during summer, aren't you? Then I'll just make this my pie stop." Milton tipped his hat at Susanna and turned, his long legs leading him toward the livery.

"Why, what good manners that young man had, Susanna. Yes--even if he is from that liberal church that broke off from ours over east, he certainly thinks of others, buying that pie for his grandmother. And if I do say so, Susanna, he comes from a fine family, the Leathermans. Yes, yes indeed."

But something else had suddenly crept into Susanna's mind-- Rosella's words of just a day ago. "What are you prepared to do if Reuben Maust calls on you and wants to...?"

THE MOURNING OF A DOVE

8

Susanna heard her father's voice out on the porch. Hurrying to hang up the pots and pans above the sink and empty the dishwater, she hadn't heard a knock at the door.

Words drifted in through the screen door. "I think, Mr. Reuben Maust, that after our last conversation it might be best for you to get back in your buggy and go home."

Reuben Maust. He came. Like Rosella said. "Be prepared." Suddenly Susanna's legs trembled. Her heart knocked like the handle of the pitcher pump on its iron housing. "Lord, what shall I do?" she whispered to herself. Then it hit her. What have I to fear? God knows my innocence. It's Reuben who should be writhing in guilt and pain.

She dried her hands on the kitchen roller towel and took long strides to the door.

"Papa, wait. I'll talk with Reuben." She opened the screen door and stepped out on the porch.

"You sure, Susanna? Want me to sit out here with you?" Hurt dripped from Joseph's voice.

"No, Papa. You may go back inside. Hello, Reuben." Susanna was surprised that her tongue hadn't tangled and that her legs had regained some strength, and her heart had settled back into a reasonable knock.

"Evening, Susanna. Been some time since I've seen you. My, you look radiant this evening. Have I ever seen that rose dress before? Brings out the color in your cheeks. I've got some things on my mind, Susanna, want to share with you. Could we sit down?"

Susanna, still clutching the edge of the screen door, stared at him for a long moment. Her eyes surveyed his face and a lock of wavy hair that had fallen toward his gleaming, dark eyes. She could see that he had shaved again this evening, but the blue shadow remained on his chin. Spicy smell of bay rum lotion he'd slapped on afterward drifted to her nose. Reuben, Reuben, how charming you can be, a part of her whispered.

"We can sit on the wooden lawn chairs." She pointed to the white painted wooden chairs by the railing overgrown with a silver lace vine. Susanna seated herself to Reuben's right. She could see the evening sun, red and sliding behind a purple bank on the horizon. A locust shrilled and frogs croaked from the pond beyond the barn.

Her heart started to pound again as it had in the kitchen. When she realized she might get a splinter from clutching the wooden chair arm, she made her fingers let go and clasped them together in her lap.

"Well, yes, Reuben. Been some time. What was it you wanted to say?" At least her tongue hadn't failed her.

"Susanna," he leaned forward, his bronze hands clasped before him, arms, sheathed in a freshly ironed white shirt, resting on his knees. "My, how I've missed you. I've been lonely for you." He grinned broadly, dark eyes softened by the last rays of the sun.

A thrush somewhere in a maple tree bid the sun good night. A gentle breeze rattled the leaves on the lace vine. Susanna studied his face, feeling her own face lose some of its tension. Where to begin? What have we to say to each other?

"The Edenvale Church didn't set you back, Reuben. Forgave you. Is that so?" Susanna realized that by these words she was putting him on the spot. But, to her, it was necessary.

"Why, that's right, Susanna. Yes. Forgiveness as the Lord commands. And Susanna, I ask your forgiveness. Even though you wanted to go on the walk that night, and you laughed and fell right into my arms when you tripped on a grapevine. I tell you, Susanna, sweet as you look tonight, and every night, fall in a man's arms, it's nigh on to impossible for him to let go." He lowered his eyes and pushed back a lock of hair with his hand.

"I've been thrown out of my church, Reuben. Excommunicated. I shall never go back. I tried to tell them all, Bishop Weaver and the deacons, that I was innocent, but they wouldn't believe me. You're talking to someone who is regarded in these parts as a 'fallen woman.'" She struggled, but could not keep the sadness shadowing her spirit from reflecting in her eyes.

"Not to me, sweetheart, not to me, Susanna. When I think of what you told me, about carrying our child," his soulful eyes drifted back to her face, "why, it's plain right I should be here on this porch with you, Susanna."

At the mention of "our child," Susanna felt a twinge go through her body. Just past three months now and if I didn't have on this gathered skirt, he could see....

"It's our child, Reuben." She couldn't hide the sadness in her voice, but she was determined not to cry.

"In my mind you've always been my sweetheart, Susanna. Look at me. I'm strong. Good carpenter. Mother wants to move into Rosefield with her sister, Emmy Bender, now she's a widow. That'd leave the stone house to me. You always liked it, Susanna, we could...."

"I can raise this child here, Reuben, here with Papa and Mama where it would receive Christian instruction. Even though I'm outside the church, that's still very important to me." Susanna could hear the grandfather clock inside strike eight.

Reuben brushed his hands upwards past his cheeks. His fingers combed back his hair. "That's right, Susanna. No doubt about that. You could raise a child here. Better, isn't it, to live with its father *and* mother?" He looked at Susanna, stretched out his long legs and polished boots. "Better with its papa and mama, both, Susanna."

"Yes, better, Reuben, but...how could I...?" Her innards twisted. How could she? Was she slipping further down a slippery slope? Her eyes cut up to his handsome face. There was a tinge of sorrow in his voice. Then, too, the Lord did command that we forgive....

"I haven't heard you say it, Susanna." He waited, lips parted as if he were ready to lift up a portion of scripture during the devotional at the gatherings.

"Say what?"

"That you forgive me. We were both involved, yes. But, I admit, I'm stronger, I should of--you know." He reached forth to clasp her hand.

"Not that, Reuben." She drew back her hand. "I have to take this slowly. I'll admit a child needs both parents and a rightful home. Yes. It would be much better. But, Reuben, I, I can't...."

"Don't say that word. Susanna, spirited as you are, you can do more than you know. I can tell you still have feelings for me. It shows in your eyes, no matter how you try to hide it. Look at me, Susanna."

She lifted her eyes to his face, sitting in silence as a tree frog started to chirp in a distant tree. Orange light shone from the dining room window as Anna lit the lamps.

Susanna continued scanning his face. Silence hung. He reached across to her lap. This time she allowed him to lift her hand. "Maybe in time, Reuben. It is Christ's command. By his power, I can do it. But, beyond that, Reuben--I'm still torn up inside."

"Beyond that is happiness, Susanna. A home. In six months a child in a real house, our house. Say it. You forgive me and want to marry me." He seemed to know that in the evening shadows with his face contrasting against his white shirt that he looked like youthful David kneeling before the Ark of the Covenant.

Again, she realized she was sitting in silence. She could faintly hear the mourning of a dove in the distant field. "It's that I'm, I'm..." she hesitated, fear reached up from inside to her throat. Then she thought, is the mourning of the dove a warning?

"It's me. You're afraid of me, aren't you, Susanna?" He laughed, a warm, rumbling laugh, and squeezed her hand.

"Yes. You said it, Reuben. After that night, I'm afraid of you. I don't trust...."

"Don't say that word. I can see how you would be afraid of me, strong as I was that night. I can be different, Susanna. Tender. I love you. I am different. I received the kiss of peace from the church brethren. Touched my heart." He reached for both of her hands. "Marry me, Susanna. I promise you that I'll never touch you in any hurtful way. Ever." His eyes pled.

"I wish I could believe you, Reuben." Susanna drew her hands from his palms, noting that he did not resist.

"What more can I do, Susanna? I'd do anything for you. Remodel the kitchen? Add a porch? Build a cradle for the baby? Going to be a little boy, isn't it, Susanna? Can't wait--me a papa."

Susanna thought that if she hadn't been so sunken back in the heavy lawn chair that she would have fallen out of it. His words. How he was able to wring her heart. Mercy. Lord Jesus. "Reuben, oh, Reuben. I--I can't tell you now. Can't give you an answer now. Give me five or six days. I want to pray more about it and talk to...."

"Take your time. Wouldn't want you to feel rushed at all, Susanna. You do know I love you. I gave my promise about how I'll treat you. Just think, in six months we both can look upon our child. I think I'll get down that cherry wood in the barnloft and start building a cradle."

She realized Reuben was a wringer of hearts and master of words. But he did promise, didn't he?

Susanna heard a goodly portion of herself say, "Reuben, go now. I'll pray. In a week, I'll let you know whether or not I'm able to marry you."

ALWAYS A SERPENT

9

Are these my very own black-stockinged legs holding up my body draped in this plain navy dress?

Susanna's brown braids encircling her head barely showed through her prayer covering with its cascading ribbons on each side of her chin. She looked straight at Peter Loux, bishop of the Blessing congregation, and wondered if he heard her swallow.

Reuben stood with her, arching his black-clothed shoulders. His wavy hair, parted on the side and combed back, rested easily on his head which rose six inches above hers. He turned his tanned face to her and smiled.

The bishop cleared his throat signaling, "Time to begin."

"Beloved friends...."

They stood in the living room of the bishop's modest home in Blessing, and the "dear friends" included his stout, plainly garbed wife, Katie, sitting on a straight chair, already wiping her eyes with a handkerchief. The other two "friends" were Rosella Meyers, Susanna's second cousin, who loved Susanna and gave her the promise each Christmas, "When you marry, Susanna, I want to stand up with you."

Heinrich Gross stood by Reuben, his buddy since eighth grade school days. Heinrich rocked on the balls of his feet until he caught himself. He held one calloused hand behind him, then clutched it with the other one and wiggled a bandaged finger, cut by a rip saw.

This is marriage. Concentrate, Susanna, concentrate. But everything seems out of place. Nothing familiar, the paunchy bishop, the room, his wife, and she scarcely knew Heinrich Gross. Mama and Papa, sitting back home on the porch swing. Faces frozen like masks set somewhere between confusion and hope. Aden, convinced that she'd seduced Reuben, his idol. She thought it a wonder, too, that Reuben had been able to lead this Blessing bishop to agree to marry them, under the circumstances. But looking at the bishop's round face and hearing his voice, she concluded that he must have pity on young people whom other preachers call "those difficult cases."

"If any one present should know of any just cause why these persons should not be joined in holy matrimony, let him now declare it." Bishop Loux leaned forward, peered over the top of his wire-framed spectacles, shifted his feet, and waited.

It seemed an eternity to Susanna. Was it the clock in the other room, or was it her heart? Protest? Any reason why they should? And she, only agreeing to marry Reuben seven days after he sat with her that night on the porch. Seven barren days. It seemed that God had abandoned her. Her soul, a drought in Egypt. Though she'd knelt by her bed and struggled to pray, her brain balked and her heart grew listless.

When she told Anna and Joseph about Reuben's proposal- "To make an honest woman out of me"- she detected flickers of relief in their eyes. Caution in their words, but nevertheless, relief. They were like their cow, Clementine, who circled all day and couldn't decide whether to graze from the rich spring grass in the pasture, or the alfalfa patch on the east side of the road. She didn't blame them, though. Her throat dry, she tried to swallow.

"Then, Susanna, the child will have a father. You a home." And Mother had tried to smile.

"Well, Susanna, you have to decide. Yes, Reuben will make a good living for you and the..." but it had been hard for Papa to say "child" when she was still single.

Someone spoke something in a nasal tone. Susanna looked at the little round-faced Bishop, his Minister's Manual now trembling in his stubby fingers. "Do you believe that matrimony is an ordinance instituted of God, and confirmed and sanctioned by Jesus Christ?"

When the bishop's lips stopped moving, Reuben rocked on his feet, lifted his blue chin and said, "I do."

The bishop then turned to Susanna and repeated the words which hit her brain like wads of wet cotton, "ordinance--instituted of God--confirmed and sanctioned." Where had those austere words come from? Had she ever heard them before? Susanna's head swirled like a trumpet vine branch caught in a sudden wind. She knew her pale lips were moving when she heard herself say, "I do."

No ring. They were of the "plain people." No flowers, as they were not permitted. But Reuben promised her a new set of bone china, the set in Hunsberry's window in Staunton with the rosebuds and pale green leaves against the ecru background. What were those other promises Reuben made just over a week ago? Susanna? "I'll never treat you in a hurtful way. Never."

Evidently the bishop had nodded to Reuben, because he turned, clasped her hands, leaned down and kissed her on the lips. Gently. Yes, a modest kiss. Couldn't prolong it here in the strange bishop's living room anyway. Reuben intuited the right response. Susanna's heart started knocking as if it were seeking some door for its own need without asking her permission. Now what? Now where?

Her ears began to ring when Bishop Loux raised his bearded chin and announced, "Go forth as husband and wife, live in peace, fear God and keep his commandments. Amen."

Noble exhortations. Blessed words. Like the Beatitudes from the mouth of sweet Jesus. Like Adam and Eve. Go forth. Did Eve tiptoe around in the dew, startled and full of uncertainty as she, Susanna, now was? Eve hadn't met the serpent yet, had she? There is always a serpent. Why, each summer out along the garden fence...once on the limb of her own apple tree. The falls and the woods along the Sweetbriar....

And Adam? He didn't just stand around and faint over Eve's beauty, did he? No, he rippled his muscles. Probably smacked her mouth with a juicy kiss. Maybe even hoisted Eve up in his naked arms and loped for a copse of willows.

When Reuben grabbed her hand, she felt the heat pulsing through it. Adam's heat from all the way back to the Garden. That's the way it was and that's the way it is. God's will.

Someone kissed her cheek and hugged her. Cousin Rosella? Yes. Of course, Cousin Rosella. And, at last, Susanna could laugh. A loud, bouncing laugh rolled out of her gasping mouth. Then she hollered, "Rosella, Rosella. I'm a married woman. Rosella, Rosella, Rosella..." Then she realized that someone ought to stop her from saying the same name over and over again. And why did she feel so hot? And her nerves, like a cat touched by lightning. Why, if they were dancing people, she would have kicked off her black buttoned shoes and lifted her heels. What matter if they see a portion of a petticoat? It's only a modest, blue petticoat, and quite plain bloomers underneath.

"And keep his commandments." Had God even told Adam and Eve about all of them yet? Serious business. Maybe it was a trap from the beginning. His commandments. Reuben and I, do we know them? Well, on that score, St. Paul helped the womenfolk a lot, didn't he? Instructing them to keep silent in the churches and if they had any questions, wait until they got home and then ask their husbands. Pliable and submissive women ought to be, as Bishop Weaver exhorted from his sturdy pulpit. Five or six ordained ministers sitting on the bench behind the bishop, punctuating his words with stern eyes as they stared down at the "weaker vessels."

Susanna was amazed to find herself seated in the buggy with such a dashing man, his white shirt showing off his bronze skin, climbing right up on the seat, clucking his tongue that way. And Duke, the horse, glancing back to see if she was all right. He nodded and lifted those perfectly formed legs, and the movement, the wheels turning in the dust of the road and not a dog barking, especially not the bay of a mangy hound. Susanna rocked and her loud, out-of-control laughter drifted back to the quartet of waving onlookers, who, no doubt, were overjoyed at such a happy bride.

As Reuben guided Duke, his hooves clop-clopping on the hard red bricks toward the William Penn Hotel, he turned, reached out with his arm to draw his bride near. "Fine service, wasn't it, Susanna?"

"Why, uh--yes, Reuben," or should she say, "My husband?"

She circled her fingers around his black woolen coat sleeve as she suddenly felt chilled. "Yes, Reuben. Bishop Loux got us through the service. Short. It was quite brief." She wondered if her words covered the empty quarry inside her heart, a quarry of unfulfilled visions when she day-dreamed, sitting on the floor in her room, arm and head resting on her hope chest. Daydreamed of the thrilling occasion her wedding would someday be. Mama, Papa, Aden, Bishop Weaver, and the ministers. The church sisters, some wiping tears, others smiling up at her. Tables spread. A dinner. Sausages and ham. Fresh baked rolls, pickles and cheeses.

"There it is, Mrs. Reuben Maust, our honeymoon hotel, ahead. Room on the third floor. Three dollars for the room. Manager said it was the best on the floor. They even have a bell hop to carry our suitcases and a lackey to deliver old Duke and the buggy to the livery."

"Yes, yes, Reuben. I hope it isn't too expensive for you, that is, for us. Why, I've never stayed in a hotel before, Reuben." Susanna realized that her voice was high-pitched and wobbly. She tightened her back muscles while resolving to "act normal." She had given her pledge before God and witnesses, "love and cherish him...kindness and forbearance toward...."

Duke stopped. Silence. A lackey in a navy coat with brass buttons over white pants reached out for the reins.

"Mr. and Mrs. Maust, I presume?" He blew his whistle and a fuzzy-faced bellboy hurried through the wide brass framed doors and his white-gloved hands reached for their luggage.

UNLESS WE CAN FORGIVE

10

Nine-thirty already and Reuben had insisted that they should still eat breakfast. Susanna swept her eyes over the wine wallpapered hotel dining room with its white wainscoting and crystal chandeliers. She raised her shoulders, looked down at her rose, long-sleeved arm, then reached for the china coffee cup.

"See, sweetheart, I told you you'd like it." Reuben lifted a morsel of golden scrambled eggs on the heavy silver fork toward his lips. His eyes reflected his delight with her. He'd said it at least a half-dozen times, "Darling, you look fetching in that rose dress. I can't believe you made it. My wife made it."

Last night, after she had slipped into her best nightgown, he had sauntered in from the bathroom, tall in his white nightdress, sat on the edge of the high bed, turned and lifted the cover and slid in alongside her, calm, smiling. Nervous though she was, she had trembled but little, and Reuben had shown no trepidations. None at all. When he had reached out a hot, pulsing hand to draw her closer, she remembered hearing his heart thump steadily, like the mill wheel at Rosefield picking up speed. He reached out his hair-covered arm, an arm like Esau's in the Bible, and turned out the wall gas lamp. The room had been almost completely dark, except for the light from the gas streetlight reflecting through the bottom of the lowered window shade. She had sensed, though, that he was smiling, and his voice had been like poured molasses over warm pancakes as it'd been that night.

She felt guilty for allowing that thought to slip in. He'd been tender. Tender but fierce, if she could say that somehow the two went together, balancing each other in a throbbing, mysterious manner.

Actually while he had been shaving an hour ago, his bass voice had rumbled from the bathroom as he sang, "'No one loves Susanna like I do', said the saucy little bird On Susanna's Hat." She admitted something to herself. He loves me. And he abounds in charm. She surprised herself at how she had edged into the sea of varied nuptial beginnings. Only, she was a Mennonite girl, an excommunicated one and she had no hat. Just the bonnet.

"It is charming here, Reuben. You made a good choice for our honeymoon weekend." She smiled, and recognized it wasn't a forced smile at all. Her fork was steady as she dipped it under the crisp fried potatoes. Maybe I was more than partially responsible that night. I did stumble on the grapevine and I did fall into his arms. I guess I should have known that a man can't....

"Susanna, darling, I want to tell you my plans for the house, now that Mother's moved in with Aunt Emma in Rosefield."

The house. With the hasty wedding, out of community, out of place as it was, she hadn't had time to focus on the house. Too much. An avalanche of newness dumping on her. And inside, a child growing..."Yes, Reuben, I'd like that, talking about the house." She took a sip of the rich black coffee while looking into his face, chiseled planes cleanly shaven, faint drift of bay rum in the air. Masculine. Reuben was masculine. She couldn't overlook how three women had turned to give him more than a cursory glance. Though she never thought she required a handsome husband, she could not deny that was what she had landed. Well, maybe she hadn't landed him, he landed her.

"Yes, Susanna. You know the little kitchen behind the dining room is too small. Mother liked a small kitchen, but my bride needs more room. I'm tearing out the west wall, raising the ceiling, and setting in windows so that you can look out and see Mt. Blue and the fields."

"It sounds lovely, Reuben. Can we afford it right now?"

"With me doing the work, dear, and Uncle Simon's discount at the lumber mill, I can manage it. Start on it this very week." His voice exuded confidence. He placed his cup in its saucer and nodded, smiling pleasantly at an older couple who also smiled and surveyed them both approvingly before they selected a nearby table.

Susanna felt her cheeks blush and reached for her water glass. Could everyone tell she was a bride? She looked at Reuben, acknowledging that marriage did befit Reuben. That she would have to admit.

***

Two months later Susanna sat in her new kitchen pouring hot tea for Cousin Rosella's surprise morning visit after having dropped her father off at Eli Kropf's farm to inspect yearling calves he wished to sell.

"It's lovely, Susanna. Warm and sunshiny. When you work at the cupboard making pies you can glance out at the cedars and mountains beyond. I'd be thrilled with a kitchen like this."

"Well, I hoped to whip up an apple pie yet this morning, I'm quick at it. I'm pleased you stopped by, Rosella." Susanna rose to get more hot water for the teapot. Warmth crept through her. Her eyes brightened and a smile traced over her lips. Hard though it had been, she'd vowed not to give in to despair over the many recent cold shoulders and rejections.

"Marriage makes you bloom, Susanna. Really, the way you and Reuben started, and, now, this...."

"It surprises me, too, Rosella. I'm discovering I can love Reuben. Since our marriage service he has worked hard remodeling this kitchen while taking on that new job building cabinets for Andrew Shelly. And he has been thoughtful of me, I must say. Only yesterday, he, knowing how much I love flowers, dug a new bed for me, even outlining it with stones. A new tulip bed, Reuben said."

"Before you know it, Susanna, you'll have a show place."

"You'll have a nice home, too, Rosella. You, too. Someday you'll marry...."

"No, Susanna. What do the English people say, 'it's not in the cards?'" No, God knows my place is with Mama and Papa, and Grandmother Meyers." Her deep blue eyes searched the hills beyond the window.

"How about Albert Kulp? Albert used to bring you to singings. I thought you said he had a heavenly voice?"

"He does. He is song director at Edenvale Church. But I guess I'll say, Albert doesn't sing my song." She chuckled and took another sip of tea.

"It's five months, now, Rosella. Four more to go. Reuben's making a cherry wood cradle out in his shop. I go out and rub my hands over the wood every morning."

"Not every child has a father who can do that. Going to be a boy, or a girl, Susanna?"

"Of course Reuben wants a boy. I feel it is a boy. I'll know in another week when the movements turn into kicks." Susanna laughed. She glanced into the dry sink at the freshly plucked chicken she'd killed and scalded just after sunrise and realized that soon she needed to cut it up, roll the pieces in flour and pop them in the iron skillet for Reuben's lunch. She stood.

"Then you'll really be a family. Three of you. Where will you go to church, Susanna?" Rosella dared ask.

"It's hard for me to face that, Rosella. So much pain, my name read from the pulpit in the congregation of my infancy and youth. I still grieve." She wanted to tell Rosella about the shunning whenever she met former chums at Rosefield. The older women were the worst. Looking the other way when she approached. Holding their children's hands tightly and dragging them past. She decided not to stir the pain by mentioning it.

Though Rosella had given Susanna and Reuben a Dresden china serving bowl, sporting large yellow roses and green leaves for a wedding gift, she was aware that for Susanna, there'd been no community or church bridal shower. "This will have to change, Susanna. No bridal shower for you in the community of your birth. It breaks my heart."

"I've accepted it. You mustn't grieve over it, Rosella. I'll always be a tainted woman in the eyes of many of this area. I know the Lord understands my heart." Susanna hadn't wanted to cry, but tears crept to her eyes.

Rosella rose, walked over to the cupboard by Susanna, put her arm around her and kissed her on the cheek. "Our churches are male dominated, aren't they, Susanna? But I guess our preachers all say it's in the Bible. St. Paul, to be exact."

"The Bible teaches that we ought not to make judgments falsely. We ought to listen to someone in a crisis and not make hasty pronouncements. I think I know why the Psalmist wrote so many psalms about forgiving enemies."

"It's true, Susanna. Unless we can forgive, the bitterness burns holes in our spirits." Rosella turned and looked out the window. Papa said for me to pick him up at eleven. I need to go, I wouldn't want to keep him waiting over at Kropfs. He wants to be home by noon and now we probably won't make it."

"Did you see the afghan Mother crocheted? I know she was saving it for a Christmas gift, but she gave it to me for a wedding present, instead. I received some fine gifts, including the lovely Dresden bowl you gave us. Step into the living room and I'll show you what Aden and Aunt Mary gave me."

Susanna walked over to the walnut secretary that had been left behind by Bertha, Reuben's mother. Opening the glass doors, she reached for the lead crystal vase her Aunt Elizabeth had given her. "See how it sparkles in the light, Rosella. Aunt Elizabeth worried so over whether or not I'd like it."

Next Susanna opened her Great-Grandmother Rebecca Steiner's chest brought long ago from Germany. Reaching in she lifted out and unfolded the afghan of rose and purple squares against the crocheted black background and draped it across the back of the horsehair couch so the light from the opposite window would illuminate the color.

"It is beautiful. I wish I could crochet, Susanna. You must teach me sometime, but I'm so dumb...." Rosella laughed as Susanna then reached in the bottom drawer of the secretary and pulled out a folded ecru linen tablecloth. "Father's sister, Aunt Katherine Hooley, gave us this. I'm afraid to use it for fear of spilling beet juice or something even worse on it."

They ran their fingers over the soft fabric, admiring the texture and quality.

"Fine linen like this isn't easy to come by, Susanna, and I'd say she spent a pretty penny for it, wouldn't you?"

"Aunt Katherine never goes cheap. You should see her table, Rosella, when she spreads it with her Lennox china against her cloth, just like this one."

"She must love you, Rosella. Love you a lot."

"She loves me, yes, in spite of what..." but Susanna stopped and turned, clasping Rosella's arm. "I so appreciate you dropping in, Rosella. But I need to get that chicken cut up and pop the pieces into the skillet. You must come again soon. I can't tell you how much your visit has encouraged me."

They both heard buggy wheels crunching gravel in the lane leading to the barn. It's Reuben driving in. Wonder if he forgot a chisel or saw? Unusual for him to drive in at mid-morning. Susanna, staring through the window, watched as Reuben leaped out of the buggy and twisted the halter strap around the oak sapling. He looks worried, she said to herself.

The porch door banged against the house wall as if he'd swung it too hastily. A heavy boot tread echoed from the pine floor and the kitchen door flew open more abruptly than even the porch door. Reuben's hair had fallen down over his forehead covering his frown. His blazing eyes betrayed the heat in his heart as they fixed upon startled Rosella standing in the middle of the kitchen floor trying to tie her bonnet.

"What are you doing here?" his taut voice, husky and harsh. Reuben's eyes were hard bullets aimed at Rosella. Then he turned a face with down-twisted lips toward Susanna who was holding her belly.

CHURCH, SUSANNA, THAT'S A LAUGH

11

Susanna thrust two split sticks of wood into the kitchen range, poked them with the stove lid handle, then settled the cast iron lid over its hole in the range top. She picked up a butcher knife and stepped over to the dry sink to cut the chicken into pieces. "Reuben, you spoke to Rosella so harshly, you..."

Reuben stood, legs apart, hands on his hips. His eyes swept over the kitchen then back to Susanna. "Company in the middle of a working morning, Susanna?" His voice sounded raw in his throat. "What are you, one of those girls who sleep till noon and expect others to do the work? That chicken over there..."

Susanna grabbed the pan containing the chicken and moved it to the cupboard cutting board. She bent, sawed with the knife to sever a thigh from the leg. "You know, Reuben, that I got up early this morning. Wrung this chicken's neck at sunrise." Her heart knocked at her breast. She could see her apron front pulse. She bent her head over her work, furiously trying to sever the pieces.

"Sitting there. Meat sitting there--probably let the sun come through the window on it. Mother always cut up the pieces soon's she singed the chicken and put it in cold well water." A pulse throbbed at his neck. His dark face tightened, lines marked his forehead. He drew back a table chair, straddled it with his arms over the back, facing Susanna, a boot-toe tapping the floor.

"Reuben, I had the chicken in cold water, right here in this blue granite pan. You can see--" The knife slipped. The gash bled and throbbed. She said nothing. Stepping over to the cupboard, she opened a drawer and pulled out a white rag and tore off a strip. She fumbled as she hurriedly wound it around the bleeding finger. "Reuben, see, I feel rushed. We can talk later. Let me..." Why was he home now? Did something happen to make him so angry?

"The range isn't even hot enough to fry a fritter, let alone that chicken. Fella would appreciate a cup of coffee when he drops in. Fire's not even hot enough to brew coffee."

Why is he needling me so? "Reuben, what is it? Did something happen that upset you so?"

"Upset? Upset? Me, trying to get your expensive remodeled kitchen paid off by busting my back setting those cupboards in Andrew Shelly's decrepit house. Uncle Simon pawned off old lumber on me nobody else wanted. Board split, and the finishing nails he sold me at an inflated price are too large, they leave big holes...."

Susanna sawed with her knife, separating the wishbone from the breast. She was nearly finished and tried to ignore her throbbing finger. Her stomach rolled from the raw chicken smell and anxiety. She grabbed a pan and hurried over to the flour bin, then back to her chicken pieces.

"Look at you. Wasting time that way. Scatttering flour on the floor. All those steps. Susanna, you aren't organized. Why, my mother had her kitchen organized--"

"I'm the woman of the house here, Reuben, not your mother." She dragged the iron skillet to the hottest part of the range top then reached for the lard can and spooned in a hearty chunk. "Maybe your mother, Reuben, was over-organized, too particular in her ways. This is my house now and I have my ways."

The chair crashed back on the floor as Reuben leaped to his feet, grabbed her high on her arm, holding her so tightly he raised her shoulder. His fingers a vise.

"Reuben. What are you doing? You're hurting me. Let go." She turned to face him. His eyes had turned to hard bullets again as he shoved his face against hers, noses touching. "Don't you get smart with me, Susanna. I'll not have you run down my mother."

"Reuben. Let go of my arm." Grease spattered from the hot skillet and burned her other arm. "Reuben, the grease, the fire. Let me go." He let go, but she knew there would be an ugly bruise.

"When I rode off to work, that what a fella expect? Lazy women gabbing, running down my very own mother?" His eyes scorched.

"I'm sorry, Reuben. I meant no disrespect. It was just that I thought this was my kitchen now, and I am trying to get a nice dinner for you, Reuben. Something's wrong. What is it? Why are you so harsh with me?" She fought tears, but reached for a chicken thigh, rolled it in the flour, spilled some, then dropped it into the hot skillet.

"Wrong? Wrong? Me rescuing you from being a forlorn nobody, your belly rolling out like that, all covered with flour, and you lying around visiting in the kitchen on a work morning? Mother's cabbages out in the garden waiting to be shredded into kraut. And that Rosella Meyers is nothing but a snoopy old maid meddling in your affairs. What did you tell her? You talked about me, didn't you? He moved back and forth at her side as she dropped in the chicken pieces and sprinkled them with pepper and salt.

"Reuben, no. We were talking about church, and wedding presents and...."

"Church? Church? That's a laugh, Susanna. A real belly-shaking laugh. Trying to get you to go to Edenvale with me for services. Did you tell the old left-over blessing you balked?"

"You know, Reuben, what they would require of me there. I am innocent of their charges. You know I cannot...."

Then his eyes flashed brighter as his head turned and he looked into the living room, secretary drawer open, cupboard doors above, ajar, afghan spread open on the couch.

"The room. Look at the room. Man sweating and getting sore muscles holding cabinets up to the ceiling and you and that long-necked spinster crawling around wasting time pawing your presents. Mother'd never leave a room scattered like that."

At that Susanna wasn't able to control the tears any longer. They streamed. She wiped her cheeks with the backs of her flour-caked hands. The grease popped. She smelled burning chicken. *Dear Lord, dear Lord, how I have offended him.* "I'll straighten it up in a moment, dear. Soon as I get the chicken browned." It was too late, it had burnt on the bottom side. She decided not to try to defend herself.

Fortunately, old Duke, tired of being tied to the sapling, neighed heartily. Reuben leaped out the door, obviously realizing he needed to water Duke and give him a couple of handfuls of oats.

***

In spite of her fear of being harshly accosted by Reuben again, she had to lie down at one o'clock. Pains shot down her legs. Her grease-burned arm throbbed and the other one where he had gripped her and lifted her, had a darkening bruise. She felt old. Weary and old and her back ached from her five-month-baby in her belly weighing her down. She couldn't sleep and she wanted Rosella or her mother more than ever. She couldn't forget Reuben, sitting with her at the table. His words. "Expect me to eat this chicken? Burnt on the outside, raw in the middle. Potatoes aren't done, either." He had shoved back his plate and scowled.

And she, the morning shattered along with her spirit, trying to brace up in her chair and get on with the meal, realized that the meal wasn't properly cooked, and he hadn't given her a chance.

When he finally leaped to his feet, he spoke with a throaty, low voice. "I won't eat this slop, Susanna. I'm hooking up Duke and riding back to Rosefield to the Red Bird Cafe. Wynona Bates there knows how to fry chicken, and one that hasn't been spoiling in the hot sun while she files her fingernails or folds some ugly, black rug slung over her couch."

Susanna, staring out the window, raised her hand, fingernails against her teeth. When Reuben galloped out of the barnyard, it was not in the buggy drawn by old Duke. Instead, he raced past the side windows on the sleek black back of her horse, Nell, the one Papa'd given her after the wedding. Nell leaped as his reins slapped her neck and his boot toes dug her flanks.

That evening, Susanna bathed herself and applied some Ungentine on the red burn on her arm. She splashed on a touch of lilac toilet water, took out her side combs and recombed her hair in front. Then she slipped on her blue dress with the covered buttons that he liked, one that she used to wear to Willow Bend Church on Sunday, although it looked like those days were gone forever.

She opened a quart jar of canned chunky beef, heated it and made a rich gravy. With fresh green beans and bacon, and the mashed potatoes, ready for a gob of butter when he came in, she believed he'd feel pleased. Aroma of her fresh baked rolls still filled the house. Reuben didn't come.

***

At eight o'clock she heard horse hooves scattering gravel on the lane. She rose from the sewing rocker and looked out toward the barn. Reuben, hat cocked to one side, a straw jauntily angling out of his mouth, unhooked a sweaty and obviously hard-ridden Nell. He jerked her toward the water trough.

"Evening, my lady," he said, rich voice molasses-like again. He strode across the linoleum, placed an arm around her waist, drew her toward him and kissed her on the cheek. "I was a little hard on you this morning, Susanna. Upset. Uncle Simon and that Shelly brother upset me. Their fault. But I'll reckon with them later. He kissed her on the other cheek, then moved his hands to both sides of her face.

Susanna tried to draw back. Her heart palpitated.

"Don't be afraid, Susanna. I'm so sorry for scaring you like I did this morning. Yes, the chicken was burnt, but I should've been more mature about it. I.... That's why I had to take your horse, Susanna, because of your behavior."

Hurt, anger, and sadness mingled in her heart. She clasped his hands on each side of her face and lowered them while looking him straight in the eyes.

"You have to tell me, Reuben. Tell me first when something bothers you. Then I'll try to understand. The way it was this morning, I was bewildered and...."

"My fault, darling. All my fault. Don't pull away from me. I need you. I especially need you tonight."

Susanna's hand automatically lowered to her belly. No. Not that. Not tonight. "Reuben, I'm quite tired. I fixed a dinner for you, roast beef, mashed potatoes--your favorite and all for you. Where were you? You never came." She tried to control the trembling in her left arm. Had she crowded him, asking him that? Would he be angry again?

"Couldn't work, Susanna. Couldn't work, especially build cabinets when Uncle Simon upset me like that. Rode on down to Sussex to visit a cabinet shop there and look at cabinet hardware. New things coming in. Brass handles, makes the cupboards look real sporty." He placed both arms around her waist, drawing her closer again.

"Please forgive me, Susanna, for frightening you. It won't happen again. You know how hard I work. I was just too overworked, that's all." He brushed her lips with his and she let him kiss her.

"Come on, my little pigeon, a bigger kiss than that for your prince." His fingers worked as he started to unbuttoned her dress. He breathed heavily, drawing her even closer.

"Let's go upstairs, my dear. Tired. You must be tired. Go to bed, both of us. Must never doubt my love for you, Susanna, spirited as little Nell."

***

After Reuben had left for Rosefield the next morning, Susanna returned to their bedroom to make sure it was straightened up. She smoothed the patchwork quilt which she used as a spread. She picked up his trousers from a chair, trousers he'd worn yesterday. She grabbed them by the hems and shook them, aligning the seams, reached for a hanger when two small pieces of pink paper fell to the carpet. What's this? She bent to pick them up. Startled, she read, "Admit one. Aaron County Fair." And there were two stubs.

FROM THE BITTER TO THE SWEET

12

Susanna strolled slowly on the hard-packed road that sloped toward the higher hills to the south where she could see the Overholt barn with its bright red and blue hex marks. September. How she loved September. Especially the contrast of the clumps of little white heath asters against the brilliant goldenrod.

As she walked she savored the spicy smells of fall and glanced up at the white-ribbed clouds drifting across a gentian blue sky. A lark sang from a tall sunflower and bounced up and down on the stalk. A balmy south wind caused her Mother Hubbard skirt to drift back against her extended belly and long legs. It was during walks like this that she found time to unhook her mind from canning, picking raspberries, or stomping kraut with a hammer handle into heavy three-gallon crocks. She could fit the pieces of her life together and see the developing pattern.

Going somewhere, Reuben and she. Rough places, yes, now and then. A matter of learning to know one another and respecting one another. She thought of the money Reuben had put in the bank from the cabinet job at Shellys in spite of his outbursts that day. Ida Shelly herself invited her to stop in on her way back from Rosefield two weeks back to see Reuben's craftsmanship.

"I never hoped to have it so nice." Ida Shelly had beamed over the rims of her glasses and ran her hands over the varnished kitchen cupboards. "Your Reuben not only built me fine cabinets, but he's easy to look at, too, Susanna." Then she grinned and put her hand on Susanna's arm.

Next she thought of how Reuben wanted to improve their house. "We'll have enough cash to paper all the upstairs rooms, Susanna, and in the spring I want to get started remodeling the front porch."

Well, it was true. Susanna had said that she liked the stone house, but after living there now for three months and beginning to get the "feel" of the old edifice, there definitely were some things besides the kitchen Reuben remodeled that would benefit from redesign, including the front porch.

The way the flaked painted door to the stairwell squeaked open and hung, brass knob on one side and cracked ceramic on the other. And the landing mid-way up the stairs, tilting slightly to the right, making her grab the rail as if the whole house was shifting when she turned to go up the remaining steps. Not to mention the ghostly howl of the wind at the north eaves and not even a very high wind outside, either.

In time. She had cautioned Reuben, reaching out and holding his warm hands. He liked that. She smiled, remembering it. In some ways he could be as charming as a little boy. One thing she was learning was how attached he was to his mother, Bertha. Susanna realized that she was glad Bertha and her sister, Emma, found life agreeable together. Sometimes those ventures didn't succeed. Live apart from someone for forty years, move back into their space, and--well, surprises, to say the least. The old woman hadn't complained much at all the day she came out for a visit.

The words of their conversation surfaced in her mind.

"I read in *The Intelligencer* newspaper that they have something new up there in the big cities."

"What is it, Mother Maust?"

She called her "Mother Maust," after seeking her permission. Susanna felt it was dignified and she liked it better than merely "Bertha," and "Mother" alone just didn't seem right. She remembered pouring her another cup of the black Pekoe tea Mother Maust relished.

"Moving pictures. They flash moving pictures somehow up on a screen. Though the preachers at Edenvale Church would never permit it, you know, Susanna, I'd like to see how those pictures move."

It'd surprised Susanna to see the way the old woman chuckled about it, as if she would like to step over the lines set down by the church. Maybe Reuben got his exploring nature from her, she thought. Testing the limits now and then. And she? Well, she still knew she was an outsider. Reuben had been patient about it. Susanna was glad for that.

But she had noticed something else about Reuben's mother. Sometimes she could joke and tease, but only slightly, then there was that drawing back like a land turtle's head when her foot approached. A timorousness, a shying away. And those long, silent periods when the old lady didn't talk at all. What had her marriage been like to Samuel Maust? He had the respect of the community, didn't he? He kept his hedgerows trimmed, his haystacks properly capped, the roof of the stone house always in repair and painted, and he let Mother Maust have those two big flower beds all along the lane with the peonies and irises.

Marching right into your mother-in-law's house and setting up houskeeping for Mother Bertha's only son had been more stressful than Susanna had realized. But it was better than the alternative. At home. Belly larger every day. Baby coming in December. Teenage brother underfoot, looking at the floor, cheeks red with embarrassment from the ribald talk among teenagers behind the barn about his sister. Pa and Ma trying not to show their shame and keep on loving her in spite of their own hurt.

She had made the right choice, hadn't she? She had prayed a lot about it. She realized that some of her former friends, who no longer spoke to her unless they met her face to face in the grocery store or on the walk, and even then, some who hurried past and turned their faces, were actually jealous of her. She couldn't think of the name of a single young woman her age who didn't think of Reuben as a "wonderful catch," and so handsome.

What was that Bible verse in the Old Testament? Something about from the bitter to the sweet. Could it be? Starting out her marriage with the bitterness of what had befallen her, that it was gradually being transformed into something sweet? Susanna vowed to look for traces of it here and there.

Suddenly the sun slipped behind a darker cloud and a large shadow swept across the countryside. A half-dozen crows cawed as if protesting, and flew haphazardly toward the wheat stubble on the hillside to the left. I'd better get back. She had reached the crest of the hill where she could look ahead and down into the copse of old oaks and willows along Sweetbrier Creek. The bridge. The gap where she had crawled through that night.

That night. A shiver raced across her back. She drew the gray shawl she had knitted during her rest breaks and evenings around her shoulders. Lord, you are helping me make the best of it. The best of it. From the bitter to the sweet.

Her eyes fell upon a dry stick that had broken off a limb from the ancient elm to the right. She picked it up and used it as a walking stick and turned, her feet leading her back home.

She could see the house ahead and wished she hadn't told Reuben that day that she liked it. What she meant was that it was the gray stone she liked, not the actual house. Now with the shadow from the clouds falling on it, it looked old and like a casket. The front of the house loomed narrow and disproportionate with its squatty slate hip roof, red brick chimney thrusting through in the middle and another one at the north end where the swallows nested. Susanna drew the gray shawl tighter as the wind suddenly whipped from the north and her skirts beat back against her swollen belly.

"If only they had put in more windows," she mumbled to herself. She stared at the gray house again, noting its off-centeredness with the three narrow windows on the front right and only one punctuating the entire left space where the spirea grew. Must have been some builder who decided to get up one morning and gather a crew and go out and build a house. A sturdy house, yes. But just what kind of blueprint did he use? Probably none. He had depended on his own vision, and as far as she was concerned, the vision failed him.

She glanced again where the shabby spirea bush by the north end flailed the mossy stone wall. And the middle chimney? What keeps it from snapping off in a high wind, soaring upward like that? Stark and sharp. It did not comfort her, or speak a welcome, this disproportionate old stone building she lived in, staring at her as the cloud darkened.

Was she rocking or rolling from side to side as pregnant women do? She grinned to herself. Yes, probably so. Her shoes crunched in sand by a clump of tall blue asters that leaned out invitingly. She bent down and picked a branch thinking how nice the blue would compliment her dark green vase on the library table.

The house. Yes, the house. How long will I live there? Twenty years? Thirty years? Fifty years? The thought of the time stretching ahead depressed her. Her mind stopped projecting.

Since "it" happened, time flowed differently, didn't it? Time didn't have that regular flow like water in the Sweetbriar. She didn't like to think of the Sweetbrier anymore either, nor hear the ripple of its water or even think of the falls. No. Once it had been her favorite walk. But the other day when Reuben had suggested a picnic along the bank by the pasture, she found an excuse. "It would tire me too much, Reuben, sitting on the grass all swollen like this. Besides, I've been wanting to try fixing fresh beefsteak for you. Heat the skillet red hot and sear the meat until it's tender. Rosella said she tried it and her father thought it was the best beef he had ever eaten." But then she had regretted bringing up Rosella's name, after that morning he stalked in, surprising her. He'd only smiled and said, "Do it, Susanna. I'll bring the steaks tomorrow from Baum's Meat Market and we'll get some Swiss cheese over at the Rosefield Creamery." Then his dark face had spread into that broad smile, reminding her of one of the Apostles in the Last Supper painting. But which one?

UNDER THESE CONDITIONS

13

“Mother, isn't this too stressful for you and Father, opening your doors, inviting all these people and putting on a spread like this?" Susanna turned from the kitchen range. She held a pot of white sauce for the potatoes her mother drained at the sink.

"I wanted my family together, Susanna. Family and friends again around my table, you know...." Anna's voice drifted, and steam from the potatoes swirled up around her white-covered head.

Togetherness, cordiality, family, the rhythms of family and community life as usual, that's what her Mother wanted--She wanted it, too. She found herself asking: “Lord, how shall it be wrought, things broken and shredded as they are?” She braced her spirit and resolved to do her part. She had spent an extra ten minutes in her bedroom this morning praying for grace and strength for the day while Reuben was out tending the sheep. "A moment at a time. A moment at a time," she'd told herself.

She could hear laughter and chatting as men's voices mingled in the living room. She caught a glimpse of brother Aden's face now and then. He sat on the mauve horsehair couch, leaning forward, chin braced by both fists. Sadness etched his face. Once he turned and focused his eyes on her as she smoothed the tablecloth. His eyes dropped when her own met his.

She had about concluded that Reuben couldn't stand the sight of her and her swollen belly. She prayed for grace. She looked at Aden again, attempting a smile, but he gave her no chance to meet his eyes again.

Susanna had refused her mother at first about such a fall gathering. But when she saw the love in her mother's eyes and knew that in her heart she anticipated good to come from her efforts, she'd given in, deciding that she could brave it. Maybe she only imagined so many were against her. Besides, Rosella being there made a big difference.

Then too, Susanna recognized that with the baby coming next month and winter setting in by then, it might even be late spring before they could all gather around her mother's table, notwithstanding the flu, fevers, children coming down with measles, whooping cough, and God only knew what else.

While Susanna stirred the white sauce into the boiled potatoes before she threw in some chopped parsley for color, Rosella sidled up to the cupboard, reached for the carving knife and fork. "I want to cut the ham, Aunt Anna." Her burgundy-clothed arm whisked back as she cut a slice of the smoked meat.

"Cut the slices thick. Those men, you know, Rosella, they want to taste ham when they fork it in." Anna smiled.

Reuben's voice drifted in from the living room. "Why, no, Aden. I used the twenty-two rifle when I went rabbit hunting during that little snow last week. Use the shot gun for quail," Reuben said, voice direct, as if oversure of his expertise in front of a novice.

"Isn't it good, Susanna, hearing Reuben and Aden getting along like old times?"

"Yes, it is, Rosella." Susanna realized she couldn't hide the reservation in her voice. Uncertainty cowered in her heart like a covey of quail at the approach of a hound. If only Aden's hostility would start melting. Maybe when he sees the baby....

Just then Reuben's sister, Rachel, stepped down the back steps by the pantry and marched resolutely into the kitchen. "This relish, Anna? Did you want me to open corn relish, or the green tomato?" She set both pints down on the edge of the cupboard, then reached up to feel if her covering was on straight. She straightened her shoulders in her navy plain dress over black stockings and shoes. Her black hair, parted in the middle and drawn skintight, and her equally dark eyes, gave her the solemn air of a convent novitiate.

Susanna tried to block out wondering why Mother had invited Rachel and Isaac; he, Bishop Weaver's son. But she knew Anna did it for Reuben's sake, a little balance, folks on his side of the family. Her eyes drifted to Rachel's face. "Yes, Rachel, Mother said earlier that she wanted to serve both relishes. Thank you. Here, I'll help you find dishes for both of them."

Susanna strode across the wide kitchen to the dining room, opened the curved glass door of the seven-foot-tall china cabinet with the carved eagle wings spread at the top. She could feel male eyes from the living room openly staring at her swollen body. Returning with the pressed glass bowls, she approached Rachel, struggling for words. What else could she say? Rachel's resentment seemed to drip as if she believed Susanna had set a trap for Reuben. "It was good that you and Isaac could come." The words crept out and she wasn't even sure that they were honest and well-meant. Nevertheless, they would plug some of the ragged holes of an even colder silence, encouraged by Rachel Weaver's unsympathetic eyes.

They sat, eleven of them, around the table, Aunt Katherine Hooley, and Aunt Elizabeth Steiner, Cousin Rosella, Reuben and she, his sister and husband, Rachel and Isaac Weaver, faces pious as Isaac's esteemed father's who had crushed Susanna's spirit by his plugged ears and unrelenting heart. Father and Mother, and directly across from Reuben sat Aden, immovable as the Sphinx.

The table groaned beneath the huge platter of smoked ham and the assorted bowls of steaming vegetables, breads and condiments. Pressed glass green tumblers contrasted against the white linen tablecloth and the blue-rimmed plates.

"Blessed Lord and our Redeemer, we thank you for bringing us together around this table." Susanna's father cleared his throat as if he realized he had to get across the widest part of the Sweetbrier during flood stage and hadn't exactly calculated beforehand. On and on he rambled. Nevertheless the essentials were there, thanks to God for the bounty and the family present.

Under the conditions, Susanna thought.

Dishes were passed up and down from hand to hand around the table. At first only the sound of cutlery, stoneware, and china, mixed with the easing and sloshing of food from bowl to plate, teased the ear.

"Well, now, everyone, eat up." Joseph dug at a slice of ham as his sad eyes glanced around the table, a lock of white hair lapping over his forehead.

"Baked tomatoes?" Reuben asked, fixing his eager eyes on Anna's face.

"Baked tomatoes, Reuben. My grandmother's recipe with buttered bread crumbs and grated cheese."

Susanna dipped the savory tomatoes on her plate, wishing that Reuben would honor her mother by saying "Mother Anna." So far he'd refused,insisting on calling her simply "Anna," or "the old lady."

"We had green tomato relish and sausage at the sewing circle September dinner," Rachel Weaver added. She looked directly at Susanna, her stare implying the unspoken words, "And, Susanna Maust, where were you? When are you going to fall on your knees, repent, and rejoin us to quilt for the sake of the poor?"

"I told Susanna, time for her to get back to sewing somewhere," Reuben said, his angular jaw worked on a morsel of ham. "A woman needs a church group."

Had to get back to sewing? Had to? What was Reuben saying? He who compromised me so? And me, trying to stay balanced like a circus tightrope walker. Reuben's words tipped a balance in her heart. A flutter traced through her stomach.

Aunt Katherine swallowed a mouthful of potatoes, then spoke up, "Well, now, Susanna's had enough change in her life for now. Marriage, setting up housekeeping. I know she's an immaculate housekeeper. And with the baby coming in another month, Reuben, perhaps you can allow her time for it all. Perhaps next summer?" Aunt Katherine attempted a nervous smile and dabbed her mouth with a napkin. Susanna knew she was trying to restore balance and remove focus from her painful excommunication.

Brother Aden lowered his own unhappy eyes, keeping them no higher than the rim of his plate, except when he glanced up at his idol, Reuben Maust. He chewed slowly, forgetting that his fork, clasped in his fist, pointed outward.

"Yes, Katherine, I'd say Susanna has had enough for one year." Anna turned to Reuben who sat like a sheik, half-grin on his dark face, light reflecting like diamonds in his coal black hair. "Reuben, how are things over at Edenvale Church?" Then Anna drew back in her chair as if recoiling from her words and realizing they only pushed Susanna deeper into the mire.

"Well, Christian of you to ask, Anna." Reuben spoke with force. "Susanna here won't bother to get dressed and go to services with me. Lonely going the five miles alone. Winter coming on, too." His face fell like Elija's must have when he spied a grove and idols where an altar to the Lord should have been.

"I, uh--I, uh, Reuben...." Susanna's tongue stuck to the roof of her mouth.

"Family ought to be united in the Lord. One Lord. One baptism. One church. You got any ideas to help me, Anna, or Joseph?" Reuben's eyes bore in on Joseph's face, "Any ideas on how to elbow a non-churched woman out of her kitchen come Sunday morning?"

Susanna dropped her fork. Tremors snaked up her body. Her thoughts whirled. Oh, Lord. Where? How? How could she get through this? Reuben. What was wrong with Reuben? Her hand rose to hold her throat.

"Church, church, church. You Willow Bend people always talk of church. Too much of anything can depress a person." Aunt Elizabeth shoved her glasses back with her thumb, turned her heavy-bosomed torso around toward Reuben, obviously trying to change the subject. "Reuben, your mother happy with her sister Emmy over in Rosefield?"

"Well, how would you feel, Elizabeth Hooley, someone moving in your own house--crowding you out, and you not even old enough for store teeth, either?" The edge in Reuben's voice was as sharp as the edge of his startched collar.

Joseph's eyes, with the dark half-circles beneath, widened as if in fright. He scanned Susanna's face, then he said, "Reuben, 'course you're teasing about Susanna, but things as they are, and have been lately, don't you think...?"

"Teasing? Teasing? I'm perfectly serious, Joseph Steiner. I'm in right relationship with my church. Susanna's the outcast right now and unwilling to do anything about it. I hate to use that word, but I refuse to beat around the bush. Mother would've never moved if it hadn't been for...."

Aden's face lifted. His eyes reflected, "Say it straight, Reuben. Tell it like it is."

"That's enough." Jospeh's knife clanked against the edge of his plate. "I can't allow you to talk about my daughter in such a manner, Reuben Maust. You are a guest here, and my son-in-law. For that, I must try to respect you. But when you speak ill of Susanna, it's my duty to...."

"Duty? You Steiners speak of duty?" Reuben's eyes quickened to the challenge. He drew back his shoulders.

Aden followed his idol's example and sat up straighter in his chair. His eyes gleamed encouragement: "Stand up for righteousness, Reuben."

"Don't speak to me of duty." Reuben shoved his fork toward Joseph. "Your duty, old man Steiner, was to raise righteous children. Seeing as one of them is fallen and balks before Brother Weaver and ministers at Edenvale Church, you, of all self-righteous people, have no right to preach to me of duty." The smirk on Reuben's face resembled that of a self-satisfied blacksmith giving a hot horseshoe a final hammer stroke.

"Reuben. I think you ought to apologize to Father." The words eked out from Susanna's throat. Suddenly a vise gripped her hand beneath the tablecloth. A large, calloused hand squeezed a near bone-breaking squeeze. "Reuben," she whispered, "Reuben, you're hurting me."

Rosella, viewing Susanna's constricted face and overhearing her whisper, rose from her chair and started to move around behind Susanna's chair. But by then, Anna Steiner shoved back her chair and staggered to the kitchen. Susanna knew she was crying. She managed to jerk her hand from the vise and stood up. She lifted the trembling, red hand to her cheek to try to stop her face from twitching. Stumbling through the door into the kitchen, Susanna fell into Anna's waiting arms. Rosella followed quickly, but not before staring back at Reuben in stunned silence.

The Seth Thomas clock ticked, measuring both time and pain. It seemed as if silence alone hung, a silence confused before its task of blending the brokenness in the air with any remnants of familial hope.

Joseph finally found his tongue. "I think we ought to count our blessings. Fall of the year. Bountiful harvest. Biggest corn crop folks ever harvested here in Sweetbrier country. Woods full of hickory nuts. Susanna, you going to bake another one of your nut cakes? Fruit cake for Christmas coming up?" Joseph called out to the kitchen, his face twisted like Peter's face must have contorted when he first noticed he was walking amidst churning water.

"Yes, Papa. Yes, I--I'll bake cakes." Susanna's voice wavered into the room. "I'll have to pick up some of the hickory nuts in the woods, Papa." *Oh, Papa, take me out of here. Let's ride away together, me on Nell, you on Prince.*

The pineapple layer cake crumbled when Anna tried to cut it and lay the slices on saucers. Her hand caught the edge of a china saucer. It hit the hard floor and shattered. Susanna dug at the cherry pie with a spatula, but the pieces tore, leaving ragged globs. "Let me take over with the dessert, Anna and Susanna," Rosella said, voice thick with her own tears.

Then to her astonishment, Susanna heard chairs scraping back from the table and a voice--Reuben's. "Come on, Aden, let's march out to the shed, get your rifle and head for the woods. We'll leave the dessert for the women. Bible says they're the weaker vessels anyway."

The door slammed.

THE DARKNESS AND THE FOG

14

Reuben Maust forked the dung-laden straw from behind the milking stalls. His ears rang and his blood pulsed through his body, muscles charged as if touched by lightning. His burning eyes punctuated his flushed face. A dung-covered boot flew out, sending Patch, the crazy-quilt cat, flying against the wall.

He swore. *High falutin' Steiners inheriting their land. Backs braced like Cape Cod New Englanders around the table. Withered, long-faced old aunts. Well, they're not better than me. Had to. Had to hold my own and show authority. Susanna's my wife. Belongs to me. She ought to listen more. I do love her.*

He stalked through the barn door with a heavy forkload and heaved it upon the manure heap.

I wouldn't have slapped her out by the buggy when we were ready to go if she hadn't challenged me about picking up the burlap bag of rabbits. Only three in it anyway. Gave the rest to Aden.

Only thing, hate it that her brother had to lift his head and see me slap her. Aden's smart. He knows a man is the head of the household. He won't learn it, though, with that old man of his bleating pious words and nodding like a preacher. Take Aden into the Berliner Stein at Mt. Blue, buy 'em one of those drinks in a dark brown bottle. Even take him to the carnival if I can get him away from his old man. I can patch it up with Aden. Introduce him to a real woman, a town girl like Roxanne Spitz. Something besides a Mennonite cow smelling of milk. A girl with rouge on her cheeks and one who doesn't mind if the wind heists her skirt a mite.

He staggered at the implosion in his brain of the dream last night. He hated the dream, always awakening from it bewildered, and wanting to cry.

Fog enshrouding the barn. The bobbing light of a lantern. He was only ten and in his childhood bed, iron, against that cold stone wall. Then the voices. Mother's voice--Father's voice. Then silence. Was it only a screech owl in the night, or was Mother crying out in the barn?

His white feet slid out of the covers while his heart knocked. He wondered, "Will Father hear my heart, knocking like it is?" *I can't. I can't.*

Something pulled him into the fog. He peered through the top of the opened barn window, searching for the lantern. No. Not Father. Not Father's arm behind the stall, harness reins in his hand. They swung. He heard the thud of leather against flesh. Or was it only against the wide boards of the cow stall?

A whimper? Only the cat, wasn't it? But why was his heart nearly stopping? Why couldn't he breathe? Creeping closer, he attempted to slide his head around the rough partition for a better view, but the fog enshrouded him and he awakened. The dream unfinished. The business in the barn incomplete. He reached down to slide his hand over his young body and began to console himself.

***

Reuben shook his head. Sweat beads dropped from his forehead as he tried to block out the memory of the one time he actually groped down the stairs and out to the barn on a July night, braving the darkness and the fog. But he couldn't remember. *Did I imagine it? Was it only a dream? Did I see Father--was it Mother's scream?*

Shame hung over his heart like the spider webs above his head in the milk barn at the memory of how, after the dream, he always awakened and realized he'd wet his bed.

A blast of cold north wind blew the barn door shut with a bang. Gray clouds slid over the pale-cheese sun. Snow by evening. Finish this cow barn and get back into the house with Susanna. How Susanna lumbers, belly rolling out like that. Why hadn't he noticed how grotesque pregnant women were? Well, he could hold himself back. She had let him claim his full rights until last week after that dinner. Pour out that baby in December. Soon he could announce his rightful claims. His property. It was the law, wasn't it? Otherwise the church would have to allow concubines like those Old Testament goats enjoyed, wouldn't they?

Reuben steadied himself and wiped the sweat from his brow with his coat sleeve. He resolved to brace himself in spite of the trembling at the lower part of his soul. Fear? How could a man have fear? Of what? Of whom? Not Susanna. Not of her. But if not, why did I slap her and command her to obey me? He shook his head and a lock of hair fell beneath his wool cap.

***

When Susanna heard him open the back kitchen door, she rose heavily from the rocker and laid her embroidery work on the edge of the table. Her arm automatically swept up to brush back a wisp of hair and check her covering. Her heart began to palpitate. His dinner. Yes, was all on the stove. She could hear him scraping mud and manure from his boots. The door swung open.

"Reuben, your dinner is simmering--"

"Come here, my darling." He marched across and enveloped her in his arms, swelling belly and all. He bent down, giving her little choice as he kissed her hard on the lips, then brushed his sandpaper cheeks against hers. Cow dung smells enveloped her.

"Reuben, not now. I need to--"

"Relax, my little pet. Relax."

Susanna tried to check her trembling and hold back the rising fear.

"You don't have to be afraid of me, Susanna. I only had to hit you because you disobeyed." The word slid out like the hiss of a puff adder as the bands of his muscular arms tightened around her. He pushed her back a step, dark eyes burning into hers. "I love you, Susanna. How can you ever doubt it?"

"I was so, so, humilia..." her voice trembled.

"Don't say it, Susanna. We'll learn how to get along together, you and me. Never, never anyone else but you. You know I can't live without you, Susanna."

Maybe I should apologize again for being disobedient. Susanna felt herself wilting. She hadn't thought of it as disobedience when she'd said, "No, Reuben, I'm not going to pick up your bag of dead rabbits." But the hard slap had jolted her flesh and soul. Because she was in front of her father's house and the guests all on the porch watching, she had forced herself to hold back the tears.

Confusion clouded Susannah's mind like the steam encircling the spout of the teakettle. *Maybe I do have a smart tongue as Reuben says. I guess I'm stupid. Just plain stupid. That's why it took me so long to understand fractions in school.*

"My dear, look at me." He hooked a dark thumb under her chin and tilted her head until her eyes met his.

There was light in his eyes. Could she believe him? Why did he have to be so handsome? She dared utter one more sentence. "Reuben, it was in front of my family." Tears pushed at her eyes, but she managed to hold them back.

"You'll have to learn, my sweet, that your parents aren't gods. They make mistakes and they are human just like the rest of us. Those old maid aunts of yours, rearing back, trying to humor me--I saw through it. Blue bloods. That's what they are. Blue bloods. You'll learn to see through it. You can't help it, Susanna, you haven't had anyone to ever poke holes in pomposity before. It's part of growing up, Susanna. Part of growing up."

Before they sat down at the table to eat, Reuben remembered to march out to the root cellar and bring in a bottle of elderberry wine his mother had made last summer. Uncorking it, he poured himself a hearty glass full, and a portion for Susanna.

"I--I can't, Reuben. The child, remember?" She tried to smile. "But the wine will be good for you after your hard work out in the barn." Her smile was genuine. Why, when his hair curled like that did he have to look like an innocent boy opening a Christmas present?

"Your dad is going to let Aden carpenter with me over in Rosefield at the Detwiler Butchery. Remodel the place before spring."

She pondered. How could Aden handle it? Witnessing him slapping her? When would she get to talk to Aden alone? Susanna remembered the flash of fear in Aden's eyes when Reuben shoved her into the buggy and drove off in a rage. Would Papa really let him work with Reuben? Tonight she had resolved to bring it up. Now, tired as Reuben was, relaxed by the wine, maybe the anger had subsided and he would mellow. "Reuben, I want to discuss the baby's coming with you."

"Of course, darling. Baby at the door, got to let him out." He chuckled and emptied the glass.

"I've been thinking about asking midwife Lizzie Wismer to come over when the pains start." She lowered her eyes, feeling shame at mentioning such visceral and earthy matters as giving birth.

"Old warthog Lizzie? You want old Lizzie Wismer? Susanna, I hate to tell you this, but that old creepy Wismer woman doesn't know anything at all. Wouldn't know how to get the seeds out of poppy pods. Don't you remember when Clara Mae Overpeck's baby got crosswise and wouldn't come out? Bert hurried over and dragged old Lizzie out to his place. She yanked off the baby's arm. By the time she got that fat boy turned around, he suffocated. Then, after she dragged him out, old Lizzie stomping around yelling for more cloths and hot water, let Clara Mae lie there and bleed to death."

Susanna laid her fork down, still loaded with green beans. Her stomach churned. Before she could excuse herself he said: "My mother, Susanna, I've already asked my mother to do for you when that baby starts knocking at the door."

Suddenly it seemed to Susanna as if the old house groaned and shifted and the very walls themselves crept in closer around her.

A COLD WIND DROWNED THEIR WORDS

15

February--the north wind howled, drifting the snow in ghostly forms along Dogwood Road, and the pike toward Blessing. Susanna sat in her rocker before the roaring fire in the giant cast iron stove with the chrome footrest and top ornament. Savory odors from the bean soup and ham bone in the Dutch oven on the kitchen range drifted under her nose.

Susanna's eyes lowered to the face of the baby nursing at her breast. Timothy. He would be like Timothy in the New Testament, one who loved the Lord. He was a handsome baby, six pounds at birth. Popped out after only nine hours of labor. I'll bring him up in righteousness and goodness. A smile traced her lips. Focused upon the child, her ears closed out the wind slapping a loose shutter on the east side of the hulking old stone house.

Susanna surprised herself the day they quarreled over the name. "I want to name our child Timothy, Reuben, if it's a boy." She had looked him square in his eyes, feet firm on the linoleum. At first he was startled.

"Timothy? Like hay, Susanna, Timothy hay out in the field? Sounds bending and weak, doesn't it? I would prefer a meaty name like Barnabas, or Noah. Substantial. No wishy-washy tinny little name. Timothy? Don't think I can allow it. Sounds like a mouse scampering up a plank in the corncrib, Susanna, not a proper name for my son."

"His name is going to be Timothy, Reuben." She didn't flinch in spite of her heart knocking at her ribs. She'd been surprised that he had backed down, but after the episode with the sack of rabbits when he lost control and slapped her, she realized, but not often enough perhaps, that Reuben Maust did feel hangdog and uncertain at times, in spite of his angular jaw, iron muscles, and unyielding tromp across floor-boards or hard-packed roads.

Surprise and relief had swept over her when he turned and headed out to the barn without another word. Even when he glanced back at her only once, his face hadn't reflected "You ignorant milk maid," as it sometimes did.

Susanna desired to be alone with the feedings. Her time. Her and the child's time. Reuben seemed to admire the child and brag about his lusty appetite and hungry howl every three or four hours. When he drew up a chair and parked himself before Susanna and the baby while she nursed, a part of her drew back. She felt the push to hide the infant and her breast with a blanket, but Reuben insisted on having his full view. But now, with Reuben tending his sheep in the barn, lambing time approaching, this ten o'clock feeding was her favorite. Timothy's and hers.

Susanna hoped it wouldn't snow any more today, roads drifted--bitter cold. Mother. If only I could see Mother and Father. And Aden? When last had she seen him? She couldn't remember. So far he hadn't come down at all to look at his little nephew. And Father and Mother only once. Well, yes, there was that second time....

A fleeting thought swept through her brain. *Why don't I remember more clearly? Am I smoothing things over to hide my own blundering*? The memories leaked through her defenses which she did not even name.

The pains had started a day after Christmas. Six o'clock in the evening--ripping, piercing. "I believe it's time, Reuben. You'll have to go now and fetch..." and how she had hated saying it, "your mother, Mother Bertha."

Have to thank her, the old woman, though she'd given birth to only two herself. Fortunately, she had at least one virtue, cleanliness, and Susanna gave her credit for that. She was glad, too, that Mother Bertha finally shoved Reuben out of the bedroom, she with her legs wide apart on the rubber sheet, belly poking up like Mt. Blue, biting down on an old shoe tongue Mother Bertha stuck between her teeth.

She would never forget, though, while stretched out and waiting for the onslaught of another cramp, how the old woman braced herself, feet apart, hands on her hips at the foot of the bed as she glared down at her in such a compromised position.

"One thing, Susanna, I gotta tell you and I won't mention it again. Never. Without my son, Reuben, marrying you, this would be a sorry hour. A sorry hour indeed for a Christian girl stretched out birthing a bastard. In this community, too."

Pains seared like fire, but Bertha Maust's words sliced like a sharpened butcher knife ripping at her heart. "My son did his duty and rescued you from that life, you, drifting around long-faced in this community with a bastard child."

Another pain ripped and Susanna, though she had vowed not to cry out, let forth a howl that outmatched the wail of the wind at the stark eaves of the front of the house she had begun to loathe.

Thank God for the pains. They stopped her tongue. Forced her to busy herself in the task at hand like a badger burrowing a hole before a pack of hounds.

She remembered that the old woman looked scared as she tromped back and forth from the bedroom to the kitchen range for her hot cloths and the boiling water. At least she knew how to keep things clean.

"This is woman business, Reuben Maust," Mother Bertha had said. "You get yourself to the kitchen, or even better, out to the barn."

Susanna was surprised that Reuben obeyed her without a challenge. And when Bertha finally let him back into the bedroom, he slid in like a ten-year-old boy ashamed he'd stolen cookies. She remembered feeling sorry for him. He had walked right over and kissed her on the forehead, pulled the blanket back and stared at the red-faced child.

"Well, I declare." That's all he said, eyes popping in his head, mouth hanging open. "Well, I declare."

"Your son, Reuben. Our son." Weary as she was, she had tried to smile at him. She remembered suddenly feeling thankful for what Reuben provided, a big house, warm in bitter winter. His mother's help without any catastrophe, even though she did feel compromised. If only it could have been her mother. And that was another thing. Maybe in the future she and Mother could talk about it, Anna Steiner being closed out like that at the birth of her daughter's child, her only grandchild so far.

The child had finished nursing. She covered her breast and lifted the infant to her shoulder to pat and burp him, caught in the warmth and love between them.

She stood and rocked Timothy in her arms while glancing out the dining room window and the snow-packed road toward home. In her mind she saw the Steiner home, set back amidst those old maples and cedars. A Christmas picture today. Longing and loneliness flooded her soul, and the wind, picking up again outside, moaned loneliness. Then she remembered the second time Anna and Joseph Steiner ventured down.

***

"What are they doing here, your folks?" asked Reuben as she half-turned from the kitchen range where she stirred a pot of raisins for a pie.

"They only want to see Timothy again, Reuben. That first time, he was just two weeks old. He's changed a lot in six weeks. Besides, we weren't together at all during Christmas." She pushed the pot off the hot part of the stove and turned to look directly at him. Her months of marriage had taught her that it was best to stand straight and look directly at Reuben and speak in a calm voice.

She realized Reuben felt threatened by her parents. He may have been afraid of them because of the scene she had caused that day, but neither of them had mentioned a word about it. And for that, Susanna was glad. No use stirring smoldering embers.

She saw them at the door, her mother, draped in a black shawl beneath her black bonnet, mittened hand over her face to protect it from the cold blast. She heard her father's knock. She could see Reuben stall, his brow crease as his eyes seemed to say, "Let them cool off out there a while. What's the hurry about opening the door?"

Finally, though, without her saying anything more except silently praying to God and to herself, "Give me strength and help Reuben...."

Just when it was becoming obvious and approaching embarrassment, Reuben stalked to the door and jerked it open.

"Hello, Reuben, we just thought...." Jacob's teeth chattered in the frigid air.

Father's voice, he sounds frail. Susanna turned toward the door, her pulse quickening.

"We just want to see baby Timothy." Her mother's voice wavered. "I know he can't eat them, but I brought him a few sugar cookies I baked just this morning." She attempted a smile. "Maybe, Reuben, you can help him out?" Her mother, wise in her ways, waited no longer at Reuben's hesitation, caught the screen door with the toe of her shoe and leaned in. Reuben, surprisingly, backed away as Anna and Jacob both edged into the dining room.

"So glad you drove down, Father, Mother." Susanna smiled, careful not to sound too exuberant in front of Reuben. Nevertheless, the words must have conveyed too much feeling. "Let me have your wraps, wouldn't want you to get overheated, that stove blasts the heat."

"No need to take off your coats. We can't have Timothy exposed to God knows whatever you might carry on them, or on your breath, measles, mumps--Susanna, what's that coughing thing babies die from?" Reuben stared coldly at her.

"Whooping cough, Reuben. There's been no whooping cough in the community this year. No need to--"

"Don't give me directions, Susanna, you're getting too big and too old to not listen."

So this is how it's going to be. She remembered wiping her hands with her apron, but they were already clean and dry.

"We only intend to stay a few minutes, Reuben, wish a new father well. Anything I can help you with out in the barn with the sheep, Reuben? Be glad to." Her father's pained face rose to the task his tongue and heart commanded for her sake.

"You never had any sheep, Jacob Steiner. What would you know? You can see Timothy for a minute. I meant what I said about exposing him to God-knows-what."

Susanna could tell that Reuban's mood was sliding into more uncertainty, and unknown threats lurked at the edge of his mind.

"That's right, Reuben. I'm glad you think of Timothy." Susanna's pained eyes sought her mother's. Her mother reached for her hands, but Susanna withdrew them, hoping she would understand.

"Everyone have a chair, here." She pulled a heavy oak chair from the round table. "Sit down, Mother, Father."

She hated it, that she'd had to look over at Reuben as if to seek permission to go into their bedroom and get baby Timothy. She felt herself wilting and knew that traces of anxiety were now showing in her eyes.

"Let his grandpap hold him," Reuben announced, throwing back his shoulders, forced smile on his face.

Susanna placed the baby into Jacob's willing arms. Jacob, still in his heavy coat, rocked the baby as he looked tenderly down at him. She could see tears in his eyes. Made her think of old Simeon in the Bible when he blessed the baby Jesus.

Just when Jacob looked over to Anna and started to move the child to her waiting arms, Reuben marched over.

"That'll do, Jacob Steiner. No wonder what old women carry on their clothes, dragging around in the community, church, the chicken house, the post office, and the store at

Rosefield. I'll take my son, now." Reuben reached and grabbed the child who had awakened and had given his grandfather a serene stare. At Reuben's rough clasping, the child whimpered and started to cry.

"I told you. Now look what you've done." Reuben's blazing eyes focused on Anna, her face a moon vying with a cloud. Then it broke as she failed to hold back her tears.

"Susanna, see how they are? Can't have them here until the child gets bigger. Upsetting him. Look at her blubber. That what you want in front of your son?" The infant howled and Susanna knew that she should not reach out to take him. Not then.

They stumbled out, heads bent, their words muffled. "Come and see us, Susanna, when you can. You come, Reu..." and the cold wind drowned out their words.

FOR WANT OF A NAIL

16

Susanna, gray scarf tied around her head and wearing her garden smock, set her pail of milk on the bench on the back porch. She'd strain it after breakfast. She had arisen early while Reuben was still sleeping soundly in their upstairs bedroom.

Her favorite spot by the kitchen table overlooked her tulip bed and the garden beyond where blackbirds and larks gathered on the dew-laden fence for morning songs. She smiled, grateful for Reuben and his generosity. The tulips he planted last fall, now a lovely burgundy, red, and pale pink. He promised me, didn't he? The nodding tulips softened the contours of the old house, the gray stone a perfect backdrop for the colors.

The soft morning light lifted her spirit and illumined the greenness springing forth in the hedge and garden rows. Late April sporting apple trees with pink-tipped swelling buds. Open by the middle of the week. The white dogwood contrasted against the red bud. Even myself, she felt her abdomen, new life. Pregnant again, and Timothy, so filled with affection. Her heart radiated warmth at the thought of another child, though she would have preferred a space of at least another year.

Susanna stoked the fire in the kitchen range, filled the coffee pot with water, ground a measure of coffee beans and added the ground coffee to the water. While the coffee boiled, she sat by the table and opened her Bible.

Ephesians. Ephesians fed her soul, chapter l. She could read it over and over again. Her mind embedded itself in bread for the soul as given by St. Paul. "Blessed be the God and Father of our Lord Jesus Christ, who hath blessed us with all spiritual blessings in heavenly places in Christ; According as he hath chosen us in him...."

She savored the last words. "Chosen in him...." Her life, together with Reuben and Timothy flowed along like a river, headed--well, who could predict exactly ten years ahead, twenty, or even more? And the waters, like the Niagara up in New York state, flowed over crags and sharp rocks. Today she blocked out the rapids and waterfalls of life--the falls of the Sweetbrier, small and dried up in August, enough for her.

A lamb bleated and a rooster crowed. She lowered her eyes to read more uplifting verses. Finished, she shut her Bible and moved her lips in prayer. She thanked God for her home. She asked for strength when the obstacles loomed. She prayed for young Timothy that she might be a worthy mother to him, and for Reuben, that God would bless his heart. "Take away the burden that seems to press against him so."

She felt a tremor of guilt deep within. Church. She would need to make some decision about a church. Yet how can she go to Edenvale after--and she had vowed she would never go back to Willow Bend? God would understand that...wouldn't he? *Lord, help me get it evened out with Reuben some way.*

Reuben seemed on as even a keel as one of those canal boats on the Delaware. She did not allow herself to think of the calmness ending, a calmness she had enjoyed the entire month. "Lord, I yield myself into your hands for guidance. Help me guard my tongue and learn to forgive."

The rich aroma of the brewed coffee reached her nostrils. She heard Reuben stirring upstairs as he prepared to shave. Eggs. He liked scrambled eggs and corn mush scrapple. She rose and pulled a cast iron skillet from her oven and reached for the lard.

How merry Reuben had been lately. She hadn't gotten over being surprised that he suggested they leave little Timothy with her parents one night two weeks ago. She smiled thinking of it even now. He'd thrown the lap robe around their legs, touched Duke's rear with the buggy whip and off they rolled to Clearfork School for the community ciphering match.

What fun, dividing into two teams, while the teacher, Jacob Fretz, read off the arithmetic problems. Since she had dropped out of the young people's gatherings, she had forgotten such fun existed. At first, she worried because she and Reuben ended up on opposite teams. What would she do if it happened that she had to go up to the blackboard and compete against Reuben? She remembered thinking of an excuse. Break her chalk, drop it on the floor, act ignorant, but she hadn't needed an excuse. Fortune smiled and she ended up ciphering against Mary Shaddinger with Reuben back on the bench laughing and encouraging her on. And poor Mary, slow in long division which Mary herself had chosen.

Susanna grinned, remembering how she had outwitted and outperformed five on the opposite team with her quick hand and brain in long division. In the merriment of it all, she startled herself, realizing that she had thrown her head back and was laughing. And she even forgot to worry about little Timothy at Anna and Joseph's and to be too nervous about how Reuben might quickly change moods. Worries had drained away like spilt water in dry sand.

The way, too, the money had rolled in lately. Reuben, finishing the implement shed for Aaron Beck. Two hundred dollars. "Empty the basket of money on the floor, my dove, and we'll both roll in it, then we'll stuff it in the bank," Reuben had said with a wide grin, proud of himself. "Maybe you and I can hop on the train and head for a week-end in Philadelphia, come summer."

No. Not she. She'd be too far along then. Besides, they needed to save the money. The farm still belonged to Bertha Maust. When she died, the estate would be divided between

Reuben and his sister, Rachel Weaver. No. For now, put away as much money as they could. She had thanked him generously, just the same, and remembered to give him the new shaving mug she'd bought at Miller's Store in Rosefield. The one with the pheasants on it. She remembered teasing him, "You know, Reuben, a country girl like me doesn't know how to walk down a Philadelphia street. Besides, my clothes are country clothes. I'd have to put away my bonnet and buy a hat, and you know how much they cost."

"You're prettier than any Philadelphia woman, my bride." He had embraced her and she had felt the old fear diminish and the love spring up. A part of her, however, registered, "One day, when it is possible, I want to review Reuben's childhood with his mother." But the other part of her had reservations--doubts as to whether or not it would be possible. When on earth would she have such an opportunity? If such a chance presented itself, would the old woman even talk?

Those wild dreams that awakened Reuben in the middle of the night concerned her. Seemed like one at least every month. How he would bolt straight up as if he didn't know where he was. Once he had to change his nightshirt because it was sweat-drenched. No matter how much she had inquired and offered help, Reuben would not disclose his dreams to her.

Reuben, dark skin showing off in the blue denim shirt she'd ironed for him yesterday, seated himself at the end of the table. Susanna filled his cup with the strong, black coffee. He waited until she drew up a chair, then bowed his head and murmured a prayer of thanks for the food.

They ate. "This scrapple is well browned, Susanna. That brings out the flavor." He forked another portion from the platter.

"Well, thank you, Reuben. I'm getting better at it. At home, Mother never fixed scrapple, though it certainly is the Pennsylvania Dutch breakfast dish, isn't it?" She smiled, her cheeks flushed as she was closer to the kitchen range and the heat radiated around her.

"Believe I'll ride Duke over to Mt. Blue and check out a lead I have for a remodeling job on an old pre-Revolutionary War house, Susanna. Could earn some good money if it is salvageable. Anything you need?"

Susanna searched her mind. "Can't think of a thing, Reuben. Thank you anyway."

"You may want to check before I ride out. The dry goods store there might have a sale."

"I'm behind on my sewing now, Reuben. Better not buy any more goods. Besides," her face split into a smile and she blushed, "I'm in the family way, and I'll be wearing those fabulous Mother Hubbards you like so well." She laughed.

"Keep it up, Susanna, we'll have enough boys for a ball team. Yep, I always wished I'd had a brother." His voice trailed and Susanna noticed an edge of sadness at the mention of "brother."

Breakfast over, Reuben brushed Susanna's cheek with a kiss, grabbed his fresh-laundered denim coat, smashed his black hat on his equally black curls. "Headed for the barn, Susanna. See you and Timothy early afternoon. Bring back good news, I hope." The door closed as he strolled with a jaunty swagger toward the barn.

Susanna spooned a few small bites of oatmeal with milk and a dash of sugar into Timothy's mouth, he, wide-eyed and fist-waving in excitement. She smiled at the way the child wiggled his arms and squinted up his face in protest when particles of food lingered around his mouth. She laughed. He's going to be as neat as his father.

By ten o'clock the sun had dried the early dew. She lifted Timothy into his cradle for a morning nap, then snatched her blue sunbonnet, slipped on a sweater and headed out to the back porch. Grabbing a hoe, she strode to the rows of chartreuse-green lettuce by the row of Concord grape vines with their twisting new growth. While she raked around the lush green plants, her mind wandered. Rosella. She wondered how Rosella was after her grandmother's death? Big funeral. Church men had to descend upon the Meyers place with teams of mules and horses dragging scoops, their drivers bundled into their heaviest coats, earflaps down on their caps, and scarves catching in the bitter wind.

Had to dig through the deep drifts all the way up the lane to allow the horse-drawn hearse to make it up and down the lane to the church. Susanna decided that she must get over to see Rosella when the roads were better. *Surely Reuben will allow it.*

The garden work fostered a hearty appetite. She nursed Timothy, then warmed up some left-over fried potatoes and a savory slice of smoked ham. She dipped a scoop of green beans from a stewing pan onto her plate. While she ate she thought of opening a jar of cherries and making Reuben a pie for supper, but decided she could do it later in the afternoon. Dig out those Mother Hubbard dresses and see if sshe could restitch the hem of one of them and find some buttons to dress up the second one.

But as soon as she pushed the material under the sewing machine needle it snapped off. Susanna dug in the drawer. Needles. Where are they? Her frustration grew. *How can I be so absent-minded as to let myself run out of sewing machine needles?* Then she remembered that she needed some of that new rickrack and a roll of bias tape. And her canister of sugar had no more than three cups left in it. Larks sang outside her window and the balmy wind and April sunshine called her.

Only a few miles over to Miller's Store. Ride over there with Timothy, enjoy the drive. Be back in plenty of time to bake a pie for Reuben. She realized she was smiling. The winter had been long and frigid, and at times she had felt like putting her hands on the walls of the old house to push them outward, especially when the days were gloomy-gray and the cold rain fell.

Why not wrap Timothy in his blanket, tie his knitted cap under his chin, put him into his basket and harness up Nell, who, no doubt, was restless herself for a trot into town?

Why not? Reuben gone all day to Mt. Blue, or maybe over to Blessing. Anyway, the warm wind called her and the nodding lilacs encouraged her as if to say, "Dare it, Susanna. You and Nell dare it. Ride on into Rosefield. Better than sulfur and molasses tonic."

Nell seemed united with Sussana's heart as she lifted her tail, snorted, and clip-clopped friskily down the road toward Rosefield. Even when Susanna saw the slate roof of her old home loom up over the spring-plowed east hill, she was able to ride right on by without any serious heart pangs dictating a stop.

Even the old fears lay low at the sight of Sweetbrier Creek and the iron rails of the bridge, the greening hickory, oak, and ash woods to the east. She caught glimpses of purple and white dogtooth violets along the road. Soon, she thought, the woods will be splashed lavender-blue with the sweet william.

Timothy, bundled tightly in his basket perched on the leather seat beside her, cooed and gurgled, relishing the rocking movements of the buggy ride.

Nell and I. I and Nell. When May comes, Nell and I must go riding together. Then she realized she had forgotten that she was pregnant. She couldn't help smiling, for today her heart felt like spring itself. Then Nell limped, stopped, and lifted her left hind hoof.

Back by the bridge, Susanna remembered hearing a clatter and splash and blackbirds scattering, but with her heart exuberant, and preoccupied with the drive into town, she had paid little attention. A clod. A rock dislodged and dropping into the Sweetbrier. But just ahead of her in the traces, Nell halted and looked back at her with her limpid eyes as if seeking further directions.

Susanna gathered her skirts, stepped down on the foot pedal and then onto the soft roadbed where the yet unopened primroses shuddered in a breeze. Then she saw. Nell had lost a shoe. Now what? She knew the hill ahead was stony and threatening to an unshod horse. Can't have her frisking along too many miles without a shoe.

What would Papa do? Climbing back into the buggy, her mind made up, she called to Nell, "Get up, Nell, we're heading for Silas Stauffer's blacksmith shop for a new shoe." Yes. Responsible thing. "For want of a nail the shoe was lost, for want of a shoe..." *don't want any harm coming to Nell's shapely foot by any unforgiving rock, do we?*

They rocked along up the hill, Susanna allowing Nell a placid walk. In the hazy distance she could see the large white house over northeast on the old Slotter farm. An imposing red barn stood out against the deepening blue sky. She pondered the strange happenings there, how that Plum Township teacher, Miss Della Delaney, had managed to purchase the Slotter place. Rumor had it Miss Delaney had cleaned it up and made it into a home for wayward and homeless boys. Christian thing to do. Folks said Miss Della dressed well. Never caught her in town without a smart hat on her well-coiffured hair as she marched down the sidewalk in a dressy suit or tailored coat. Like to meet Miss Della, someday.

Susanna decided it was best to buy her sewing supplies and the sack of sugar first. She hurried out of Miller's Store, Timothy gurgling in her arms, while Johnny Gross, a teen-age helper, carried the twenty-five-pound sack of sugar. "That's fine, Johnny, drop the sugar in the back of the buggy. Nell threw a shoe on the road by the bridge. I must drive her over to the blacksmith shop for a new shoe." A tinge of worry crept into her mind. Will this make me too late? What would Reuben do?

Ahead she saw blacksmith Silas bending over, already shoeing someone else's shiny, black horse. As she pulled Nell up to the hitching post and descended from the buggy, she heard the ping of an iron hammer as Silas pounded the shoe on the anvil. Bitter smells of burning coke and iron from the forge hit her nose. "Good afternoon, Silas. Got another one right here. Nell threw a shoe back by the Sweetbrier bridge."

Silas, finished with his hammering on the red hot shoe, lifted his shaggy head crowned by a leather cap. "Hello, Susanna Maust. Well, now. Don't want to keep you waiting but I have to finish this job for Mr. Leatherman here. This black Morgan of his is short on patience." He gave a throaty, low chuckle.

Susanna glanced at the tall man leaning against the frame of the shop door, one booted foot braced against the doorframe, hands in his back pockets, coattail bulging backwards.

"Mrs. Maust, Susanna Maust, pleasure seeing you again," he grinned.

"Why, Mr. Leatherman, a surprise, our horses challenging us on the same afternoon."

"Well, Silas is about finished with Bruce's shoe. Actually, he likes it here. Doesn't want me to ride him back and hook him up to a plow." Milton Leatherman's eyes glanced up and down Susanna as the wind caught her skirt and she reached up to draw her bonnet forward. She glanced back to see if Timothy was content in his basket on the seat.

"You having any gooseberries come June, Susanna? I have to tell you, my Grandmother Hoover said your pie was the best gooseberry pie she'd ever eaten. Would like some gooseberry jam, too, if you decide you can spare any."

"Well, I believe I can do that." Susanna didn't know yet whether or not Reuben would allow her to take her baking and spring produce up to the market on Saturdays. No, she hadn't discussed it yet with Reuben.

Silas, astraddle Bruce's front foot, nails sticking out of his mouth, began fitting the shoe onto the horse's hoof.

"You've got a young one asleep there in the buggy?" Milton glanced over at the buggy and the basket with the sleeping baby.

"Yes, I guess, Mr. Leatherman, you haven't met our son. Born in December. Almost a Christmas baby. We named him Timothy." Susanna hoped the child continued napping: it was his feeding time and that could pose some problems.

"You folks still going out to Edenvale Church, Susanna? You and Reuben, that's where he attends, isn't it?"

"Well, uh...." How should she answer? Did Milton Leatherman know? She, considered the "fallen woman" of the community. Or, if he knew, was he only trying to be polite? When she lifted her eyes to his, she could see that he was sincerely interested and being neighborly.

"Mr. Leatherman, that's something Reuben and I have to work out yet. In time." She forced herself to smile through the pain the question aroused. Nevertheless, she didn't blame him.

"Finished, Milton," Silas said as he wiped his hands on the big rag he dragged from his hip pocket. "That'll be two bits. You can bring your horse right up, Susanna. If you need help, I can step out there."

"Thanks, Silas, I'll get Nell unhitched in a jiffy."

As she bent to unhook the traces from the singletree, she glanced up. Someone surely galloping down this way in a desperate hurry. She led Nell toward the smithy. Silas strode out to reach for Nell's bridle with his stout hairy arm. Susanna glanced at the approaching horse and rider. Do I know that rider? Reuben? Not Reuben, he's over in Mt. Blue or....

Gravel flew as a sweaty and frothing Duke galloped up in front of the shop. "Whoa. Whoa." Reuben, hat brim dipping over his forehead, glared with black onyx eyes beneath his bushy eyebrows. "Susanna? Can't believe it's you, Susanna Maust. Who gave you permission to sally into town?" He raised one eyebrow in a questioning slant.

Susanna's hand reached for her breast. Her heart pounded. *O Lord, this will anger him.* She tried to hide the fear in her eyes, realizing if fear showed on her face, it'd only incite him more. "Reuben, I needed sugar, and my sewing machine needle broke." She stepped toward him, noting that he was sweaty, along with his frothy horse. He had obviously been riding at high speed for several miles. "I thought you were over in Mt. Blue, Reuben. I needed some supplies, that's all." Susanna had the sensation of a spider crawling up her back.

Reuben leered at her. "I was out of sugar and my sewing machine needle broke," his voice a mocking falsetto. Hands like vises gripped both of her arms. Nostrils flaring, lips curling, he glared into her face. His breath, hard and hot. "Who you sneaking off to visit, Susanna? Who? Keeping your grocery list a secret so you can ride into town behind my back? Even worse, a lone woman at a blacksmith shop. Wait until your mother hears about that." His scorching eyes focused on Milton Leatherman whose face tightened.

"Mr. Maust, Susanna's horse just threw a shoe on the way to Miller's Store. That's all. Proper thing for her to--"

"You keep out of this, Milton Leatherman." Reuben's voice trembled and a vein throbbed at his temple. "Your family leaving the Willow Bend Church and setting up your own God-knows-what church down the road. Don't you lean in and mess with my affairs."

Susanna, anxiety increased by Timothy, who had now awakened and was crying in the buggy, saw the tilt of things and dared to speak. "Reuben, I thought you would want me to take care of Nell. What would you have done had Duke thrown a shoe?" Then she realized that if he was as angry as he was now before her, he would have continued riding Duke, maybe even whipped him toward a faster pace. *O Lord Jesus, help me. "Reuben, please let go. You're hurting me," her eyes pled as they focused deep into his. What is that I smell on his breath?*

Reuben stepped back a foot but still gripped her in both hot, muscular hands. "I'm beginning to get a drift of what's going on here, Susanna. You and Mr. Leatherman having a little meeting behind my back? Been meeting him in the woods, too? That it? That it, Susanna?" He shook her. Her bonneted head flew back and forth.

By now Silas Stauffer and Milton Leatherman stepped toward Reuben. Smithy Stauffer dared to speak. "Better let your wife go, Mr. Maust. She's done no wrong. Only dropped by to have me put a shoe on Nell."

"Stay out of this, Silas. Who are you to intervene in another man's affairs with his wife? You and that time you stumbled up in front of church to make that confession before communion...don't you Mr. Maust me."

At Timothy's loud wail, Reuben let go of Susanna. By now her bonnet had become untied and rested back on disheveled hair.

"Reuben, the baby," Susanna whispered, the breath catching in her throat. She gathered her skirts in her trembling hands and attempted to head toward the buggy. *I mustn't let him confuse me so that I don't think.* Reuben grabbed her again. Her neck ached and throbbed.

"Don't you run away from me, Susanna. Folks all know what kind of a woman you are, and a yowling pup in the buggy to prove it. A whelp. That what you doing? Sneaking up behind my back with smooth Mr. Milton Leatherman so that you can whelp again come Christmas? Or, how about sneaking around with a real stout blacksmith? That ought to be a treat. Hard muscles of a smitty with stinking underarms embracing you behind my...."

Driven with fury, Reuben failed to notice the two strong men approaching him, Milton on his left, Silas on his right. Their iron fingers closed around his arms.

"Mr. Maust, I'm afraid you're distraught. Better step back here in the shade. Calm down. Let me get the horse."

"Let go, you stinking Silas. Let go of me. You have no right to interfere in my and Susanna's affairs."

"Mr. Maust. Silas is right. You're upset. Don't know what threw you so. I could see you were already torn up when you rode in here to the shop. What is it? Maybe Silas and I can help?" Milton attempted to turn Reuben so he could look him in the face.

"Let me loose, you backsliders. I saw you, Leatherman, leering at Susanna. You, Stauffer, I wouldn't trust my grandmother in your presence."

The two powerful men dragged a protesting Reuben back into the blacksmith shop and parked him solidly on a bench. Still gripping him, they seated themselves beside him.

"Mrs. Maust, why don't you let one of us just hitch Duke there to your buggy, you and the baby get started home. The baby's upset and needs attention. Silas and I'll see to it that Reuben gets home when he feels better." Milton

Leatherman's body jerked and bounced as the restrained Reuben fought for freedom.

"I'll bring this up to the church bishops. You'll see. Holding me down. Ordering another man's wife around. Susanna, don't pay any attention to them. I'm commanding you, get over here and help me. Grab that crowbar...."

Susanna, her neck bruised and throbbing from the rough shaking, reached for Duke's bridle. "There, Duke, only going to slip you into Nell's harness and head for home." Her hands trembled. Chains clanked.

While Stauffer held Reuben in his iron-band arms, Milton Leatherman leaped forward to remove Nell's harness and transfer it to Duke, then hook him to the buggy.

"Go get Constable Crowley." Reuben roared. "I command you, Susanna, have him arrest these men for holding me down like this."

Silas, tightening his hold on the still writhing Reuben, spoke up, "That's right, Reuben. We'll all send for the constable. Sure he'd like to review the goings on here and how you're acting. Good idea."

Reuben fumed and bounced on the bench. Susanna saw that he ignored any contradiction.

"You passing yourselves off as church brethren and sending for a constable to break up a home? Wait until I tell Bishop Heatwole about this."

Milton Leatherman raced back to the shop bench to help Silas hold Reuben until the storm passed.

LAUGHINGSTOCK OF PLUM TOWNSHIP

17

Aden Steiner dug his heels into Mose's flanks as he galloped over the last hill. Ahead loomed the L-shaped stone house with the slate hip roof and red chimneys where the smoke curled up in the morning light. Susanna--how could she do it? Have to talk to Susanna, humiliating her family like that. Disobedient to scripture and to her husband. Under instruction for baptism. Studied it last week in Bishop Weaver's living room, Ephesians, "Wives, submit yourselves unto your own husbands, as unto the Lord. For the husband is the head of the wife." Clear as day. Aden's cheeks flushed and his toes curled in his shoes. Their family put down, mocked, laughed and snickered about because of Susanna having to get married. Now this Rosefield thing. Before church brethren, too. Disobedient to Reuben. No wonder he got angry.

Through the window Aden could see Susanna holding Timothy. She tilted her head and looked out toward the gate as he tied Mose to the post and tromped up the flagstone walk where the purple irises lifted their dew-laden heads.

The door opened. "Aden, oh, you pay me a visit? Come in, Aden. I'll fix breakfast for you." She smiled and shifted Timothy to the other arm.

Aden, breath catching in his throat, stepped over the threshold and into the warm kitchen. "Already had breakfast, Susanna." So this is where she lives. Reuben, fixing this spanking new kitchen for her. He glanced over the cupboards and back to Susanna's face. Then he noticed the bruise around Susanna's eye, extending across her left cheek. She must have fallen against something. Susanna, always stumbling along, forgetting to look where she's going.

"Aden, I'm delighted you came. Reuben left for work already, but if you like, I can make some hot cocoa for us." Timothy gurgled and sucked on the back of his hand.

"So that's the--the boy." Aden stared at the chubby child who reached a hand out toward him. *Susanna, why is she holding her neck so stiff like it hurts when she turns her head?*

"Your Uncle Aden, sweetheart." Susanna stepped closer to Aden who had drawn up a straight chair and seated himself.

"Don't know nothing about babies, Susanna." He dug his hands in his pocket. *If I don't stick them out she won't shove the--the--into my lap.*

Susanna stepped back, her face draining of color. She clasped her breast with a dishwater red hand.

She's getting the message. Aden cleared his throat. "Better sit down, Susanna, I got something to say to you."

Susanna drew up another kitchen chair and adjusted Timothy on her lap. "I miss you so much, Aden. No matter what, I'm still glad you came to see me and Timothy. You look upset, and I think it's right that you talk to me about it."

Aden was aware that she was attempting a smile. "We're the laughingstock of Plum Township, Susanna." There, he'd gotten it out. A beginning. His chest heaved. Why did his blood seem to boil and his voice quiver?

"Yes, Aden, my dear brother. Yes. People often mock and rebuke those they don't understand." Her eyes mellowed and focused on his face.

"Why did you have to do it, Susanna? First, the--the--well, Timothy, there. You know."

"Aden, I tried to explain that, you wouldn't--"

"Forced to marry. You out of the church. Now galloping up to town when your husband's back is turned. He doing so much for you. Look at this house, what Reuben did for you. Taking you in, making a home for you."

"Aden, maybe you won't be able to understand everything now, or much about Reuben's and my relationship. I told you I had to make a decision. I decided to marry Reuben because I was going to bear his child. Reuben has good qualities. I'm trying to make the best of our marriage."

"Best? Best? Sneaking off behind his back and causing a scene down at Silas Stauffer's blacksmith shop. Doing your best? Susanna, that's a laugh." He lifted his head and exhaled.

"Maybe when you're older, Aden, you'll understand. I wasn't disobedient to Reuben. I was sewing and my needle broke. I needed a few things. Only a few miles into Rosefield. Nice day. I knew I'd get back in time to do more sewing and cook Reuben's supper."

"I heard that there was another man, Susanna. You making eyes at another man. One who goes to that other church, the liberal one where the women don't even wear coverings. You ought to know how that is, too, in our family."

"Are you talking about Milton Leatherman, Aden? Milton?" Susanna's hand lifted to her chin. She sat back, shifting the baby on her lap. "Milton Leatherman is a fine man, Reuben. His Grandmother Caterina Hoover is an old friend of Mother's."

"You telling me you are warming up to him, Susanna?"

"Aden, I can't let you make statements like that. False statements. There was no secret meeting. I was not 'warming up' to anyone. Nell threw a shoe. I was taking care of my horse." She sighed and looked out the window where the light danced off the edges of the maple leaves.

"I want to hear Reuben's side of it in person, Susanna. Reuben does a lot for me. Teaches me skills I need to know to make a living in the future. Reuben has never lied to me. Mother heard it from Clara Swick over at sewing that you and Milton gab a lot together at the market and that you bake for him."

"Clara doesn't like me, Aden. She thinks I'm a great sinner. I forgive her, anyway. I baked three gooseberry pies for Milton Leatherman's grandmother, and, Aden, that was before I even married Reuben."

Aden realized that he was making no bigger dent on his wayward sister that a tossed flint rock would make on Mt. Blue. His eyes shifted to her bruised face. "And that, Susanna, that bruise around your eye and cheek. You still bumping into things?" He could see her draw back. Her eyes widened, her face paled. *She's uneasy. Look how she shifts on the chair. Hit something there, didn't I?*

"Aden, I love you. When you are a little older, you'll be able to see things you don't see now. I know you don't believe me. But it is true. You must pray for Reuben and me, and little Timothy, too. I wish you could let yourself get close to him."

"Don't shove the baby at me, Susanna." He gritted his teeth, eyes smoldering.

***

"Anna, Aden's not in the barn. Have you searched his room?" Joseph Steiner leaned into the kitchen as Anna scooped up the fried mush with a spatula.

Anna turned to face him. "No, Joseph. But I know he isn't in his room. I heard him get up early. I thought he was doing his chores so that he could get an early start with Reuben on that carpentry job down at Mt. Blue."

"Well, he must have left already. Mose is gone and Aden's saddle too. He sure keeps his commitment to Reuben Maust. Good thing that is. Commitment a good thing. Necessary to learn a trade."

"Well, it's unusual, Aden riding off like that without his breakfast."

After their prayers and after Joseph had read a portion from the Sermon on the Mount, they ate, largely in silence as the clock ticked and the wind picked up outside.

Breakfast over, Anna stared at Joseph. "We ought to talk about it, Joseph."

"I know, Anna. I know. So sorrowful. Everyone talking about it--our Susanna. How? We raised her in the Lord." Joseph realized he couldn't hide the pain in his eyes.

"I couldn't believe it. Sunday, sister Weaver whispering to me, 'Susanna still having problems, Anna?'"

"It was a sad thing for her to do. She ought not to have said it to you, Anna. She could be wrong. We could all be wrong on lots of things." Joseph swallowed, but the lump still hung in his throat.

"Was it disobedience to her husband, Joseph?" Anna's eyes pled as they searched her husband's lined face with the shock of white hair falling down.

"Well, as I got it, Susanna didn't have Reuben's permission to ride in to town. Yes, she probably needed something. Nice day. Take the baby for a ride. I understand all of that. If only Nell hadn't thrown the shoe."

"What do you know about Milton Leatherman, Reuben? Isn't he a member of Lynn Valley Church, the *new* church?" Her voice halted as she said "the new church."

"He is. And Anna, time to drop old grudges between churches. We can't hold that against Milton Leatherman. That church split happened almost fifty years ago. We mustn't let old animosities about that cloud our thinking about Milton Leatherman, or Susanna, or anyone, Anna."

"His grandmother Caterina and I spent many happy hours together at sewings, long ago. No one made finer stitches than Caterina Hoover." Anna cleared her throat.

"I'll have to ride down this evening when Reuben gets back from Mt. Blue. I plan to go over it with him. Get it straight."

"Do you think you'll get a direct answer from Reuben, Joseph? Sister Weaver told me that Reuben was red-faced with anger at Susanna. I don't know about the rest. Did they have to hold him down?" Tears crept to her eyes.

"Well, Bishop Weaver told me that, too, after services."

"Do you think Reuben would have struck Susanna, Joseph?"

"Struck her? As I got it, no, he didn't strike her. But he bawled her out for disobeying him. And, I guess, looking at it from his side, she did go in to town without him knowing about it. Had he ridden home, he wouldn't have known where his wife was." Joseph couldn't hide the sorrow in his voice.

"Maybe we don't see things as they really are with our Susanna. Reuben is giving her a good home. Togetherness, such a good thing. Timothy..." Anna bent over and started to weep in her handkerchief.

"I thought too, Anna, better than Susanna, you know--drifting around--homeless with a baby. 'Course she could of stayed here, but it always would have been so...."

"Yes, I thought marriage was best, Joseph. Maybe it's just a matter of adjustment. Folks have to get used to each other. Reuben didn't actually court Susanna. She didn't know him that well."

"And, Anna, we didn't really socialize much with Reuben's parents, they going to Edenvale Church like that."

"Bertha Maust seemed like a good woman to me. Though I sometimes thought about it, she frequently seemed sad. And, you know, they didn't get beyond their fences very often."

"Well, there was that time when Reuben's father took his mother up to Blessing to the hospital. Broken arm or something. As I remember it she fell down the cellar steps." Joseph cleared his throat and focused his eyes on Anna's face.

"And when Reuben was little, he was the cutest little boy." She smiled at the memory.

"Worst thing, that blacksmith shop episode got in the paper. That's on account of the constable being involved, I guess. For shame. And we Mennonite folk, too." Joseph shook his craggy head.

***

They had eaten their supper in an awkward silence, Reuben and Susanna. *Why does she have to sit with her head out at an angle like that? All I did was shake her a little. Deserved it, didn't she? She's got to learn. The eye? Well, maybe I shouldn't have*. He heard a firm knock at the back door. "Now who? Susanna, you expecting anyone?" He glared at her.

"No, Reuben, but I'll go to the door." She started to rise.

"Stay put. No telling who it is. I'll go." He rose and stepped back to the kitchen door and opened it quickly.

"Why, uh--uh--, Joseph. Susanna, it's your father. Well, since you're here, Mr. Steiner, might as well step on in, but I'll tell you now, we're tired and we intend to go to bed."

"I won't keep you up long, Reuben." He glanced around Reuben's shoulder at Susanna who seemed to be hunching over, hand on her neck. One eye looked swollen, but maybe it was only the dim table light.

Reuben clasped the hard oak door. "Well, then, state your purpose, Joseph. We've got a baby to put to bed."

"Step outside so we can talk out under the tree, or in the barn, Reuben." Joseph's eyes were stern, his voice firm. His eyes fixed on Reuben's face.

"Well, if that's what you want. Can't imagine what you want. Talk just as easy around Susanna's table. You're her Pa, suit yourself if you don't want the company of your only daughter."

"There's a little light yet, Reuben. Maybe we ought to step out to the barn." Joseph was surprised that Reuben didn't resist, in fact, he shifted his shoulders and grinned like an eighth grader who had just pulled a fast one on his teacher.

***

"We can visit here in the doorway leading to the hay mow, Joseph. Get to the point though." Reuben picked up a wheat straw and stuck the end in the corner of his mouth.

"Reuben, I'm going to tell it straight. Right before you. Folks in the community are all talking about the happenings at Silas Stauffer's blacksmith shop last week. They say you came riding in there noisy as a dog before a copperhead."

Reuben slid the straw out of his mouth and put one arm out to lean on a heavy vertical beam. "That's all? That's what it is?" He laughed, a hearty ricocheting laugh that startled the pigeons. They fluttered and rose to a higher beam inside the barn.

"I'm a busy man, Mr. Joseph Steiner. Busy man breaking his back for your daughter and newborn. Been all the way to Mt. Blue checking out a new carpenter job. Just hurrying home to my wife and son. Only thing, got to Rosefield, dropped in the store there, and Ernest Miller blabbed it out before God and everybody that Susanna was in town and on her way to the smithy."

"Nell threw a shoe at the Sweetbrier bridge, Susanna said."

"Mr. Steiner. You are sticking your nose in private affairs. Thought you would be a better father-in-law than that. But based on the way Susanna acted, disobeying her husband, flaunting herself like she did, somebody had to do some correcting. That's my responsibility, head of the household. Susanna had no business hooking up Nell and riding into town. None whatsoever." Reuben lowered his arm and moved closer to Joseph.

"Bishop Weaver said that someone went after the constable. That right, Reuben? What for?" Joseph didn't move back and his eyes fixed on Reuben's face. He noticed Reuben's cheek twitch. Was it fear creeping into his eyes?

"Yes, Constable Crowley loped down, stupid gun in a holster on his hip. Sporting that silver badge. You would have thought he was a General resurrected from George Washington's army of the Potomac." Reuben spat in the dust.

"Who went after the constable, Reuben? Why?"

"You won't believe it, Joseph Steiner. That stinking smithy Stauffer, he's got arms like railroad rails and when they're bent around you, you can't breathe. That sissy Leatherman went for the constable. I have his number. Making eyes at Susanna. She standing there simpering at him. Belongs to that God-knows-what church down the road from yours."

Joseph realized Reuben was trying to sidetrack him by mentioning the church, siderail him onto old arguments of long ago.

"I heard that it was necessary to restrain you, Reuben, that you argued with Susanna before others. That you grabbed her and shook her. Is that the truth?" Joseph's eyes burned into Reuben's as he waited for an answer.

Reuben turned. He kicked up straw and dust with a boot toe. He slapped his palm downward on the rail of the horse's stall. "Lies. Lies. Got in the paper, too. They write up things like that to sell newspapers. You ought to be old enough to know that, Joseph Steiner."

"I need to tell you, Reuben, you don't get angry with my Susanna again and shake her or slap her either. That's what witnesses say you did." Joseph thought it better to leave Milton Leatherman out of it for the present.

"Susanna's had enough, giving birth, marrying you, setting up a home. Enough. She's bound to get tired. Upset, herself, at times. Reuben, where's your Christian forbearance?"

"Don't talk about Christian this and that to me, Joseph Steiner. Who are you to bring that up? You want a bastard grandson and fallen daughter wandering around from one old maid aunt's house to another? You want that?" Spittle flew from Reuben's lips.

"I want Susanna to have a happy home. You, too, Reuben. I feel shame for you and what happened in Rosefield last week. Susanna's got to be feeling pretty low about it, too."

"I told you, lies, all lies. Her old man refusing to believe it? Well, that's tough luck. I can tell you straight in your face that I did shake her a little just to get her attention, she silly and acting up in front of those men. But, Joseph Steiner, I did not hit your daughter. What kind of a man do you think I am?"

"Tell you what, Reuben. It's getting dark. Now we've talked about this out here, I'm going on back and ask Susanna about it. You can come on in too if you want to." Joseph turned and headed toward the orange light reflected from the kitchen window.

Reuben Maust kicked more hay. He swore at the sheep. "Get on up there, old man Steiner, to your heifer I saved from ruin. She ain't going to tell you nothing. That I know."

***

Susanna sat in the kitchen rocker, her face waxy and pale, eyes searching his face, the left one encircled with a purple bruise that ran across her cheekbone. Her head still leaned to one side.

"Papa, don't--you startled me."

"Susanna, don't be afraid. Reuben's all right, he'll be coming in a little while. I have to ask you something. Susanna, did Reuben strike you? He said he shook you because he thought you were disobedient to him for riding into town without his permission." His pained eyes searched Susanna's face. A hand trembled and crept to her lips.

She looked like a wounded pup searching for an opening in the yard fence. "Why, uh--uh, Papa. Why, yes, Reuben was angry up at Rosefield. He grabbed me. Yes. But, Papa," her eyes shifted to Reuben who'd slipped silently through the kitchen door. "No, Papa, Reuben didn't strike me. Reuben, tell Papa how clumsy I am and how I tottered, going down the cellar steps and banged my cheek against that beam that sticks out."

THAT'S NOT SARSAPARILLA, IS IT?

18

"You mean you wanna open four bottles of beer here at the counter? Gonna drink all of them yourself?" The bald bartender with the fringe of curly yellow hair glared at Reuben.

"Well, uh--no, keep the caps on. Gotta take them to a picnic. How much?" Reuben hoped he looked as "he-man" as the Mt. Blue regulars who kept eyeing him, which made him nervous. He would have preferred to sit on a bar stool and savor the cold, bitter beer and listen to the ribald talk.

What if someone recognizes me, or even worse, calls me a flat-headed Dutchman? Don't believe I look like one. He straightened his back, his hat cocked on his head, the planes of his face and mouth drawn straight, eyebrows raised in a slight frown, which he hoped added a tough touch to his face.

"I said four bits, mister," the bartender rasped. Reuben slung the two quarters on the table, grabbed the bottles and headed for the door.

Have to show Aden the world. Won't grow into a man in that Sweetbrier community without someone showing him how other folks live. Look at Susanna, overprotected by her old pa and ma sticking their noses into everything. Why, she's so shy now, she hesitates to leave the house.

The beer bottles clanked in his coat pocket as he dug his heels into Duke's sides and galloped to the Duck Creek Park where Aden waited in a picnic area. Too bad the kid is still underage. Roxanne, she could show him a real good time, bring in another girl more his age, and the regulars at the tavern would surely demonstrate what "he-men" were like.

Reuben drew Duke up to the shaded area by a pond where Aden sat on a picnic table bench tossing stones into the water. The boy looked sad. This would cheer him up. His hand reached for the cold brown bottle. "Thirsty, Aden? Thought you'd like a taste of a 'he-man' drink." His white teeth flashed as his lips curled in a hearty grin.

"Well, yes, I am, Reuben. Thirsty, yes. But, but--that's not sarsaparilla, is it?"

"Shucks, no, boy, no indeed. This drink here will grow hair on your chest." Dismounting, Reuben tied Duke loosely to a sapling, strutted over to the table, knocked off the cap of a bottle on the table's edge. He hoped he looked like an old pro. Foam spumed over his hand. Handing it to the bewildered boy, he reached for another for himself.

"Drink up, Aden. Little of this'll lift your spirits. No wonder you get down, living where you do. Everything is 'No, you can't do that.' Gotta experiment in the world. In another year I want you to meet Roxanne, she'll grease your buggy wheels for sure. Town girls who have a little color on their faces and know how to laugh."

"Who is Roxanne?" Aden's gray-green eyes searched his face admiringly.

"A town girl. A divorced one. But she's pretty and she likes people to take her to the carnival." He shoved Aden's shoulder, edging him on. "Drink up, Aden."

Aden took a slug from the bottle, squinted his eyes and swallowed hard. "Whew, Reuben, pretty tough stuff, isn't it, this beer?" He coughed and wiped the froth from his mouth with his hand. "It tastes, well--it tastes sort of like something from the barn." He grinned sheepishly.

"You'll get used to the taste. Surprised how it'll lift your spirits, Aden. Something bothering you. You needed this outing today. Come to think of it, Roxanne just might know someone your age. But for now, let's down these bottles." Reuben gulped, hoping he demonstrated tough masculinity.

"What would Bishop Weaver say if he found out?" Aden asked. Reuben's eyes tinged with guilt.

"Thought you'd bring that up, Aden. Listen, those old birds hound their wives to stow away elderberry wine, dandelion wine, wine from berries they scrape together. Why, didn't you know that old midwife, Lizzie Wismer, stumbles around half tipsy most of the time from her own beer? Brews it in her basement." Reuben swallowed hard and swiped the back of his hairy hand across his mouth, noting that Aden eyed his hand enviously.

"Well, yes, folks make wine, but that's for times when they're sick, or old."

"You kidding yourself, boy?"

"Well, the Bible says, 'Wine is a mocker, strong drink is raging.'"

"Old birds who wrote those words had dozens of wives, stepped over boundaries everywhere. Sure, they loved the Lord. Wrote poems and such. You really ought to read all of the life of David. You heard of Bathsheba, haven't you?" Reuben cocked his bottle at an angle, stretched a leg and stared at Aden, who had removed his hat and wiped sweat from his brow with his handkerchief.

"Well, I guess one ought to know how others live, but...I don't think Susanna would like to know about this, Reuben." He took another gulp as Reuben stared at him.

Reuben noticed Aden's cheeks beginning to flush and saw his shoulders relax. He uncrossed his legs, held the bottle recklessly and grinned over at him. *Loosening up. Kid's loosening up*. He took a long drag from his bottle.

"Susanna, why, shucks, Reuben. We men can't take our directions from women. Ain't biblical. They don't know anything at all, except having babies." He tossed the empty brown bottle into the pond, watched it bob, tip, fill with water, and sink.

"Susanna knows more than that, Reuben." He blushed and shuffled his feet, obviously uneasy at the "having babies" remark.

"Gotta learn it, Aden. Everything about women. No, they aren't those pure white celestial virgins you've been taught to believe. Take Eve in the Bible. She seduced Adam." He dragged out the word *seduced*, quite aware that it sounded slick and sinful. Edge in, little by little.

"Well, I never quite looked at it that way, Reuben."

"Women like same things as he-men like, Aden. Surprised you didn't know that already." He scanned Aden's flushed face, watching him empty the first bottle.

"They--they, women do?"

"Here, you old pro, you," he shoved Aden on the shoulder. Aden chuckled. Then Reuben conked the cap off the other bottle. "Don't it feel good, boy, loosening up like this? Feel it running through your body, can't you?" He slapped a hot hand on Aden's thigh.

"Whew." Aden wiped his forehead again, stretched out his legs and grinned. "Think you're right, Reuben. Fella needs something to relax him now and then. Guess I been uptight lately, things like they were with Susanna."

"That's enough to make a preacher uptight, Aden. But Susanna's going to be all right. Another baby. Yep. This time good and married. Not so many problems." He could tell the subject still made the adolescent restless. And his cheeks, was it embarrassment?

"Reuben, maybe it's not a good thing for us to be talking about Susanna and you and--and...."

"Sex? Sexual things?" Reuben threw back his blue chin and howled. "Why, boy, you wouldn't be here if it wasn't for sex. How old are you anyway?" He knew, but why not elbow him toward feeling ignorant and inexperienced?

"Well, I do know about all of that. At least some of it. You know, boys talk behind the barn. Now and then, things, uh--they happen."

"Yep, sure do, Aden. Sure do." He howled again at what he considered a witty remark. "Things happen."

"You going to take that remodeling job at Rosefield bank?" Aden obviously wanted to change the subject.

"Thinking of it, boy. Only do it if you can help me. You getting to be a fine carpenter yourself, Aden. Fine carpenter." He reached out and felt Aden's right biceps. "You and me. You and me, Aden. We do make a team."

"We do, Reuben. We do." Aden looked at him, eyes glowing with new energy and admiration. He grinned.

"Want to meet Roxanne sometime, Aden?"

Silence hung for a moment. Wind tossed limbs of the old walnut tree.

"Meet Roxanne? Meet Roxanne, you mean--you mean today?" Aden's eyes brightened and opened wide.

"Well, don't want to make you do something you don't want to do. 'Course, I thought I'd have her say 'hello' to my best friend while I was in town. But, if you don't want to."

"You say she knows girls my age? Town girls?" Aden swallowed and held a wrist with his opposite hand to keep it from trembling.

"Drinks we had move right through the blood, don't they, Aden? Gets a boy to thinking. Gets a boy to thinking."

"But you're married, Reuben. Married to Susanna. It's not right, is it? Talking about town women, that, that Roxanne?"

"No harm in meeting people, Aden. Where is it written in the Bible one can't meet people? Jesus met all kinds of people. Liked the sinners best of all." He waited as he noticed the boy ponder his words, lift his head and grin lopsidedly.

"You always put things so I can understand them, Reuben." Aden's eyes widened, filled with trust and adoration.

"Well, then, Aden, we do need to get riding for home. Why not ride past Roxanne's place? If she's on the porch in one of her pretty dresses, won't hurt anything at all to just stop and say 'howdy do,' now, will it?"

"Guess not, Reuben. You always know best."

Reuben slapped Aden's back. "Straddle your horse, her house on the street we'll be galloping along on our way back. No extra time at all." He noticed how Aden wobbled and how he had difficulty getting his foot up in a stirrup.

The crooked grin on Aden's face made him laugh.

THE WILLOWS FLAILED IN THE WIND

19

Susanna staggered down Old Meetinghouse Road toward Rosefield. A cold August rain drizzled down, and now and then a chill wind swept sheets of foggy rain soaking her muslin sunbonnet and her dress. She'd grabbed a thin garden jacket she wore early mornings. She hunched her shoulders and her feet found purchase in the slick mud.

Will anybody see my face and notice? Maybe my eye won't swell shut this time. A bruise? She lifted a hand and swiped it across her left cheek and eye. No blood. When she'd fallen, she hadn't hit the edge of the table and made a cut like two months ago.

"When will I learn? Stupid. I'm stupid." The words caught in the wind which swept the tops of the hedges along the road. Her heart pounded when her ears picked up the roar of Sweetbrier Creek ahead. Have to walk across that bridge. Won't look to the right where it happened. Look at the planks--one step at a time.

A part of her knew it was crazy waddling down the road in a cold rain when she was eight months pregnant--no plan.

Something within her ordered her to "get out." *Didn't Jesus tell his disciples, "Take no thought for the morrow," how he cares for the birds of the air, the lilies of the fields? Foolhardy of me to race off so. But like being a prisoner in that house where the stone walls inch in on me. I know I would have suffocated had I stayed in that dank coffin.*

Her breath came short and hard as she struggled and her heavy wet skirt bagged around her legs, her belly outlined, full, ripe. Reuben, leaving in a rage, God knew when he would return. Time to run with Timothy all the way down the lane and up the road to Mother's house. She remembered pounding the door--her mother's face. White, lined, mouth falling open. And surprisingly, Susanna recalled, she'd felt no fatigue at all. None at all.

"Take him, Mother. I'll get him when I can." She'd shoved the screaming child into grandmother's arms and turned. No questions. Get away. If Reuben gallops in here and finds me--God help me. And it'll be even worse for Father and Mother.

The willows at the bridge flailed in the wind. Thunder cracked. A streak of lightning zigzagged across the sky. How had it begun? She remembered saying, "Reuben, don't go. You stay over there at Mt. Blue too late evenings and when you get home your supper's...."

She remembered falling to the floor, but she didn't recall the actual blow. Her mind had been on her brother, Aden, and how her parents were worried about him coming in so late at nights after work. And the way Aden secreted himself in his room and refused to allow them any questions. Aden, convinced they were against the idol of his life, Reuben Maust.

The bridge. Get across the bridge. Only one glimpse of the boiling water rolling over the rocks at the right. A howl of the wind over and under the bridge brought echoes of the Sweetbrier from two years ago.

A whippoorwill called that night. What was it? "Whip poor Willa, whip poor Willa." Yes, that's it. Her heart palpitated. Something in her then whispered, "It's not Willa, it's Susanna." She threw back her head and gasped. *O God, give me breath.* She puffed as she made herself plant a mud-laden foot on a bridge plank. One, two, three. She loped and tromped. Why does the bridge have to be so long? A limb from an old dead poplar cracked and fell with a thud ahead and bounced off the rusty iron railing, then unbalanced, toppled into the boiling waters below.

Lord God. Keep away from the railings.

She knew she should find a place to rest. But what if Reuben rode into Rosefield, horsed around in the general store, or even rode down to the blacksmith shop to needle Silas Stauffer? Reuben would do it--he had no trouble finding reasons to justify himself. But if he finds me there--she tried not to think of it.

Why didn't someone point out to me how unfit and ignorant I was before I married? No wonder Reuben gets mad at me. He's right. His supper, a disaster last night. Pie dough baked hard as a sheet of iron and burnt all around the edges.

But Timothy had a stomach ache and she had to hold him and rock him, and then she noticed Reuben, or someone, must have left the back barnlot gate open and Reuben's sheep were galloping off down the side pasture lane. When they came to the creek, she knew they could dip down, trot under the bridge and heave themselves up onto the pike.

When she got back, her dress shredded from the blackberry briars, the pie was ruined. And the roast? Don't even think of it. *Maybe I should throw out the pot. Heave it over the garden fence*.

Why am I so dumb? Susanna ignored the ache in her legs and the increasing pain up her side.

Is that sloshing behind me? Or is it only the wind and rain? She glanced around, droplets dripping off her nose. A rider, or is it a horse and buggy? Dear God. No. Her throat constricted. She stopped in the muddy ruts, chest heaving for breath. *If it's Reuben, I'll--I'll never get out of the....* She thought of the rot and mustiness of the corncrib where he'd locked her for a whole afternoon. But, it wasn't Reuben, was it? A woman?

Buggy wheels churned the water and mud. A horse clomped its feet across the wide bridge boards. The buggy wheels rattled the bridge, the sound softened by the water-soaked planks. Yes, a woman. Big scarf tied over a wide hat.

Susanna waddled and staggered over to the side of the road. Now what'll I do? Think I'm ready for the crazy house down in Lancaster, lone woman running out in the mud and rain like this.

"Whoa, Beaut. Whoa." The buggy stopped.

Susanna turned, her dark eyes wide in worry. A graceful woman leaned toward her from the buggy seat. A smart black suit outlined her slender form. The wide-brimmed hat, held down by the black scarf tied under her fair-skinned chin. "Miss, Miss--I don't know your name, but may I offer you some help? A ride?"

God above, you heard my prayers. "A, uh--a--a ride?" She staggered and nearly fell sideways.

"I'm Della Delaney, on my way from Mt. Blue through Rosefield and on out on Farm School Road to my school." Her voice, well-modulated, cultured.

"Della? Della Delaney?" Susanna's weary mind circled like crows looking for a landing spot. "You the schoolteacher who helps those homeless boys? Yes, well, I'm pleased to meet you." Susanna made an effort to drag herself closer to the buggy.

"Please do climb in the buggy, Miss, Miss--, you ought not to be on the road in a rain like this." Miss Della looked down at the drenched cloth clinging to Susanna's swollen belly. "And in your condition, too."

"I'm Susanna Maust, Mrs. Reuben Maust, I--, I'm on my way to..." but just where was her destination? She hadn't clarified it yet.

"Here, Mrs. Maust, let me help you." A black-gloved hand reached down to help struggling Susanna as she stepped up on the foot-pedal and heaved herself toward the seat.

"What on earth brings you out on the road on a day like this? Some emergency?" Susanna drew back. Her mouth hung open as the lady focused on Susanna's eye, swollen nearly shut.

"You're injured, Mrs. Maust. You need help. In your condition, too."

"No. No. No help. Just the ride into town, that's all. There's a hotel there. Yes, hotel." Lucy wiped water from her drawn face. "And you may call me Susanna. I've got relatives in Rosefield." There she'd said it. Not a lie at all. Reuben's mother and aunt. Yes. In-law relatives. But she knew she wouldn't darken their door today.

"Well, you're a Mennonite woman, aren't you, well, of course, not in your Sunday bonnet today, but--"

"Yes. Long history in our family. Church important to us. Family lines go back, way back." Was it a lie? *I'm not a member of any church? Dear Jesus, dear Jesus, am* I *still a Mennonite?* Chills shook her frame. She coughed, her cold fist at her mouth.

"Your people have been very generous, Susanna. The Moyers, the Kulps, the Clemmers. Helped me clean up the Slotter place, make it a real home for my boys."

Susanna knew Miss Della was trying not to stare at her and be polite with the conversation. "Our people do give generously, but other Christians do too." She tried to smile, but a pain shot down her face from the swollen eye.

"Did you fall down, or stumble against the bridge back there?" Miss Lucy's brow wrinkled.

"No, no. Didn't stumble. Why, I--." How to answer that? Does Susanna Maust lie? Well, yes, that other time when Papa confronted Reuben. Yes, she was a a liar, too. She begged, *Dear God, forgive me*. "Why, I am a clumsy woman, Miss Delaney. Clumsy. You wouldn't begin to understand how I stumble around in my home. It was out in the barn this morning, Clementine, our Guernsey was most uncooperative, most uncooperative, you wouldn't believe how she kicks."

The buggy rocked, the wheels slung mud. Della Delaney's fine Morgan steadied himself in the increasingly difficult mud as he headed into Rosefield.

"You say you have relatives here? Would you prefer to let me drop you off at their door or at the hotel?"

Susanna tried to hide the uncertainty in her face and eyes. She pulled her soggy bonnet over her left eye. "Why, uh--Miss Delaney. Yes. Here at Ernest Miller's store.

"Whoa, Beaut," Miss Delaney said, drawing back on the reins. "If I can ever be of any further help, Mrs. Maust, you may let me know. And please, if you find time after the baby comes, do drive over to my school and visit my boys."

Susanna leaped out, surprising herself as she staggered toward the walk. Llewellyn and Leah Gayman at the Miller's store door turned, their mouths flying open as their shocked eyes surveyed Susanna.

MADAM CARMITA AND THE THREE BLOSSOM

20

Look at their faces? Susanna stared at Llewellyn and Leah Gayman's drawn faces. *I can't go in that store, sorry state I'm in, it would create a scandal*. Help me, Lord.

Like a coyote chased by hunters to the corners of a field, she turned, her feverish eyes searching a half-block down and across the street. The Three Blossom Hotel. Yes. Lobby in the hotel. Maybe a merciful attendant there would help her get out of her wet clothes. Dry herself while she collected her brains.

Her shoes sank in the rich mud of the street as she heaved herself across; her skirt, now torn by the wind, dragged behind.

Should I knock at the door? Hotel like this is different, not like the William Penn in Blessing where Reuben took me for our--our.... Her trembling hand hesitated, then turned the brass knob on one of the double doors. It eased open.

Three women faced her. One sat behind a varnished Queen Anne desk writing in a ledger. Two others lounged lazily on a purple couch, one filing her red-painted fingernails, while the other munched from a cluster of luscious-looking grapes.

The portly woman at the desk lifted her large head, reddish hair piled high with silver combs at both sides. Three strands of large pearls circled her neck. Her skin was fine textured, though heavily rouged. And her bosom. ...

Susanna dropped her eyes, noticing a rich wool carpet with pink and purple roses under her feet. Her eyes focused on an ivory-painted newell post sporting a naked Cupid, one foot dancing in the air. The carpeted stairs led to another floor. *Wh--wh--where am I*? Her cold hand searched for her mouth. She struggled to open her swollen eye.

"Why, honey, did the rain drop you right in the street in front of my place?" The big-bosomed madam with rouged cheeks leaned forward and smiled. Her wine-colored dress dipped low. She wore some kind of garment underneath that made her large, creamy breasts plunge almost out of the low neckline.

"Why, uh, I must have made a mistake, Miss, Mrs.--. I thought that this was the hotel." Susanna half-turned toward the door.

"Don't think you made any mistake, Miss. This is a kind of hotel, honey. Nope. No mistake at all, considering the way you look."

"I'll swan, Carmita," one of the girls on the couch said, "some smart Alec man and his big hairy hand sent us another one."

Susanna stared at the younger woman with the yellow hair and silky red dress who had spoken, her voice rich like maple syrup.

The taller woman set her saucer of grapes on a stand and brushed the back of her neck with her red-nailed hands. "You're right, Sabrina. The Lord himself, I'd say, sent us another one. Step on in, Miss--Miss--I didn't get your name." She swiped the back of her hand across her full red lips, removing droplets from the grapes. "You can call me Alvina, dearie."

"Why, uh, I'm, I'm Susanna. Susanna Maust. Mrs. Reuben Maust, I should say." Water ran from her torn Mother Hubbard down onto the magnificent carpet. Her eyes dropped to view the wet circle around her muddy shoes. Her sunbonnet sank in around her face, giving her a forlorn pioneer-woman-at-the-edge-of-the-wilderness look. "Oh, what have I done, I'm so sorry."

"Think nothing of it, dearie. Nothing at all. Chloe will clean it up in a minute when I ring for her. Alvina, Sabrina, hop up off that couch and take this little lady back to the bathroom. Not expecting Banker Hollis 'till after three o'clock, are you? Strip her out of those soaked clothes. Mercy, mercy. Dry her off, roll her in a warm blanket. And she's far along, too. Far along." Her big brown eyes glistened as she stared at Susanna's belly.

"Well," Alvina said, "won't be the first time a baby was born at The Three Blossom, though, of course it couldn't stay here." Her cheery voice drifted. She and Sabrina hurried to help Susanna shed her drenched coat and bonnet. "We'll get these off you, Susanna: Sabrina can hang them in a bathroom upstairs until they dry. We'll get you dried out in no time. No time at all."

Alvina's hand felt comforting and warm on Susanna's chilled skin. Her voice, why, it was just plain cheerful. A smile twisted upon Susanna's face. "This is, this is--not a regular hotel, is it?" She looked back at the huge woman at the desk. "I'd, I'd only like to rest awhile and get dried out a bit, Miss, Mrs...."

"Why, honey, didn't tell you my name. I'm Carmita, this is my place, these are my girls." Her arm, encircled by three jangling bracelets, swept out toward the working girls.

"She's Madam Carmita," Sabrina said. A rollicking laugh cascaded throughout the room. It seemed to Susanna that even the crystal chandelier started shaking above her head. *Dizzy. Hope I don't faint.*

"She's worn out. Look at her shoes, Alvina," Sabrina said, bending over in her green dress with the bustle and hourglass waist. "This little lady's running away from her man. But, we'll get to that later. Most definitely get to that. We always get to that, don't we, Carmita?" She cast her warm blue eyes over to the buxom madam. Sabrina's eyes filled with tears and her voice conveyed pain as if she knew from experience about black eyes, bruised backs, and arms and legs trembling from fatigue, even on pregnant women.

"Go get a half of a beefsteak from the icebox and cold compress that eye of hers, Alvina."

***

Reuben was glad the rain had stopped, though it challenged Duke as he pulled the buggy across the Sweetbrier bridge and up the hill towards Rosefield. He brushed a bit of dandelion fluff from his navy blue suit lapel, then lifted his hand to adjust his new homburg at a saucy angle on his head. Scared. Susanna just got scared. Only thing, other time she ran off was just to the ditch at the back of the pasture. *These women and their wiles, she just wants to tease me. I can play the game with her.*

He pondered their conversation a month ago about the farm. Susanna had thought it a good thing, his mother receiving payment from one-third of the farm produce when it was sold.

Well, he tried to make her see it. How it would be better for Mother. This arrangement not good enough for her. He recalled being firm about it. "Mother, you need to deed this farm over to me. I bust my back taking good care of it. Hard to develop my carpentry work and farm both."

Well, she had looked startled at that remark. Then he told Susanna how he'd stopped in Rosefield last week to go over it with Mother. "She's sixty-one, Susanna. Can't ever tell when a person that age will drop over dead. The probate court step in, take a big chunk of the estate. You wouldn't want that, would you, Susanna? Your children missing out on their rightful inheritance?"

Well, she'd drawn back, hadn't she, and started to protest. Shut her up by butting in. "Give Mother time. She warms up to ideas. She always comes through, especially when it involves her only son." Glad he'd clarified it. Angered him, though, when she'd said: "Maybe you should talk to a lawyer about it, Reuben, get it all sorted out so there are no problems."

She ought not get sassy and try to intrude with suggestions. Told her, "You ought to be grateful. You didn't have to put out any money, moving right on in as if you always belonged here." Old Pap Steiner didn't put out anything for his daughter. *Shoot. Have to do it over again, I'd marry Susanna, but under the conditions, should have demanded a thousand.*

He smiled as he looked down at his polished boots stretched in front of him on the buckboard. He realized the challenge it would be to keep them that way with all the mud. Funny, how both exuberant and relaxed he felt.

Course, after the full bath, haircut and shave at the Mt. Blue Barber Shop, he'd had time to browse through a McClure's Magazine, article on train travel, and have barber Heavener anoint him with that Brilliantine hair tonic. Susanna'll like the smell. He wished there would had been time for one more Bourbon at the tavern, but a part of him, at least, awakened to his family duties.

When he found the stone house cold and empty, Timothy gone, too, it'd taken only a minute to hitch Duke to the buggy and head over to old man Steiner's. Expected to find the boy there. Only thing, old lady Steiner surely was reluctant to hand him over. "Where is Susanna? You hiding her here, Anna?"

"No, Reuben. No, of course not."

Sure, the old lady looked scared out of her wits. Good for her, keep her blood circulating. Ought to have taught Susanna how to cook and how to obey her husband. The toddler, Timothy, knit cap on his head that matched his blue sweater, leaned into his side.

"Going after Mama, Timothy. Got her a new dress spread out on the bed back home. Spent ten dollars for it. When she sees it, she'll wish she wasn't one of the plain people so she could dance a jig in it." Timothy gurgled and started to suck his thumb.

He had concluded that smacking Susanna was for her own good. She understood it. The liquor had softened the edges of his inferiority feelings and the guilt about his behavior. Right now, time to turn on the charm. Susanna was gullible. He could bed her down, come evening. Reuben chuckled and gave Duke's rump a slap with the reins.

Surely she wouldn't be hiding out in that smelly blacksmith shop. Even worse, stinking Silas, licking his lips at her. Probably in Miller's Store. Couldn't get those women away from the dry goods. He felt in his pocket for his wallet. Claude Dickinson paid him well today. Susanna probably in there pawing purple goods. He concluded he would buy her five yards. *Naw, she wouldn't be in the drug store swilling a sarsaparilla.*

***

The hot cocoa warmed Susanna's body and soul. She held the fragile china cup with the violets on it in both hands. Alvina had insisted that she put on a warm, dry pair of bloomers as hers were still damp. She looked down at the sack by her feet which held her sunbonnet and coat. Sabrina seemed not to mind at all cleaning up her shoes. But how would she keep them that way, walking home?

"I'll pay you, Alvina, when I come in to town with the eggs next Thursday," Susanna said. "I just can't take these nice undergarments and not pay."

"Wouldn't hear of it. Anything we have a surplus of here is undergarments." Alvina's rollicking laugh echoed up the stair rails sporting the dancing cherub.

"Well, I just can't thank you ladies enough. Drying me out. Even my hair." Susanna lifted a hand to check her hairpins. "And for the hot soup and toast. You shouldn't have put yourself out so."

"When Rufus gets back from Blessing with my order shipped in from New York, Miss Susanna, I'm going to have him drive you right on out to your folks's house." Madam Carmita, hands on both wide hips, spoke with authority.

"No, I couldn't allow it. I've put you through enough. But I do need to get back to Timothy. Reuben, too. He'll be coming home from work, probably worn out and late. Maybe still time to stoke up a fire and make a hot potato soup."

"There you go, busting yourself for a man that knocks you around. You not going back with him alone, are you?" Sabrina's eyes widened.

Susanna's brain still whirled when she remembered the girls' words, "Mrs. Maust, your husband knocks you around, and don't lie about it."

"But I'm clumsy and I do stupid things. Reuben tells me so. I'm not as smart as he is. Sometimes, I can't say I really blame him for...."

The other part of her awakened slowly to the thought--were they correct? These women, of all people? Then she concluded they ought to know. How could she ever forget Alvina's account of her man grabbing the ax and chasing her out of the house and down the street. Then she remembered something.

She dug in the paper bag, pulled out her damp coat. Her fingers searched through the pocket. "Here." A smile spread across her weary face. "A silver dollar. I forgot that I put it there last week when I sold the eggs. I can hop down to the livery, hire a horse and buggy and ride out to my place by myself."

"You won't go alone, Missie," Carmita's thick voice boomed. "Not except over my dead body." A dog barked outside.

"There's a real good-looking man riding up in front of Miller's Store over there." Sabrina pulled back the purple velvet drapes and peeked out. "Whew, a real dandy. One of them fine homburg hats. Looks like a new suit, too. Got a little child by his side. It couldn't be your man, Reuben, could it?"

Though her knees still trembled, Susanna raised herself out of the chair and stepped over to the window. "Reuben? Yes. Yes, isn't he a good-looking man? Why, he must have bought a new suit. And Timothy, look at Timothy, he'll need me." She reached for the doorknob.

"Your bag, honey. Don't forget your bag. Hate to see you climb in that buggy. That man lay a hand on you, you report it to me come next week egg-selling time. I don't really think he would want a tangle with me." Madam Carmita glared, and her second chin trembled.

"I'll bake you a pie. Least I can do. Good bye, how can I ever thank you?" Susanna opened the door, stepped out on the porch just as Reuben bounced out of Miller's Store. When he saw her, he flashed a bright smile, reached up like President Theodore Roosevelt himself and tipped his homburg.

"Dear God, help me." She cleared her throat and stepped down the flagstones to wait his arrival.

Sabrina's voice drifted from the open door behind her.

"Why, Alvina, that Reuben Maust is the man Roxanne Spitz goes on about when she works here Thursday nights."

After Reuben drove Duke across the rut-filled street and stopped in front of the Three Blossom Hotel, he threw back his head and howled with laughter. "Well, now, Timothy, have to take this to the bishop. Looks like your mother got herself a job at the whorehouse."

IS THERE A CATCH SOMEWHERE?

21

"Susanna, that double wedding ring quilt's just plain beautiful. I had no idea you knew how to piece together something like that." Reuben smiled and stood close to her back as she bent over the quilt frame where she worked on the edge of a blue circle overlapping the pink and pale red ones.

Susanna smiled when she felt the warmth of his hand on her shoulder. She glanced over to the left on the grey-blue rag carpet where three-year-old Timothy and baby Aaron rolled red and purple balls of yarn back and forth. A yellow kitten, Fluffy, lay on its back, strands of bright blue yarn entangled in its feet. The double bedroom windows to the south allowed two broad shafts of light to cascade over the quilt, illuminating the area where Susanna worked.

"Well, Reuben, we women have to do something besides canning and sweeping and," she chuckled, "filling kerosene lamps and stoking up the kitchen range." *Dear God, thank you. Reuben's been steady as a stone fence post for a whole month now. How long will it last?*

She could have added to the list of things women do, "bearing children," as she was wearing her last year's Mother Hubbard again. Baby due in Feburary next year. After Christmas--1903 already. New century. New hopes. Why, the paper had an article about Congress authorizing a canal across a narrow strip of land in Panama which would connect the Atlantic and Pacific Oceans. And Reuben sitting before the fire, kerosene lamp at his shoulder, glued to the pages of a new book, *The Virginian*, he'd picked up at some store in Mt. Blue.

Have to see if Reuben'll let me buy one of those hand-crank washing machines. But I'll bring that up later.

Reuben pinched her shoulder lightly, then patted her. "Going over to Lynn Valley with Aden. Putting up new shelves in a drug store there. Wish every young carpenter learned as quickly as Aden. Have his own business some day. Or maybe he and I oughta form our own corporation." He chuckled warmly.

Susanna knew he wasn't serious about the corporation, but that his attachment to Aden and Aden's uncritical loyalty to him never seemed to waver. She swallowed as she felt a lump in her heart about her relationship with Aden. Some day, maybe when he fell in love, he'd warm towards her. She refused to allow herself to think of insults and old neglects from family members this fine June day with the mock orange filling the air with its sweetness. She tried to block out his voice that, at times, still echoed in her ears, "Susanna, is it true that you spent an afternoon in a, a--." He hadn't wanted to say "whorehouse," so his voice cracked and his cheeks turned bright red as he rasped, "that house of ill repute? How could you bring such shame on our family?"

She wanted to say, "Aden, Aden, you are blind to the corrupting influences of Reuben Maust. You excuse him in your idolatry of him, blind to his faults." She knew better. Instead she smiled and said, "Aden, stop by this evening after work, and I'll have fresh baked apple pie for you."

Feeling Reuben's hand still on her shoulder, Susanna started to mention the front porch, but she caught her tongue in time. Why say something he might interpret as criticism? The old porch, right portion torn off, boards and pieces of tin heaped at the edge by the spirea, a rusty tin roof hanging to one side. Though she'd tried to trim the wormy yellow climbing rose, it hung with dead branches, and the few remaining greening ones clutched the air for a trellis. He'd promised to have the porch remodeled two years ago. If she thought about it, streaks of anger and embarrassment shoved up around her heart. The old lichen-covered stones of the house were creepy enough without the sagging-eyelid porch. She didn't like it, either, that he'd turned some of the sheep into the yard to graze.

"No use either of us shoving that lawn mower, Susanna," he'd said, forcefully.

"Better let sleeping dogs lie," she'd said to herself. She learned to bite her tongue about the sheep eating her tulips and hyacinths.

Though she had shoved the tough-rolling lawn mower herself many times, she had to admit that it was a relief not to have to do it, especially when she was carrying Aaron in the hot summer. But the sheep droppings--and didn't they graze too closely? The children, though, loved romping with the sheep.

"Why don't you ever have your mother, or Rosella Meyers come over and help you on this quilt, Susanna? Seems to me like it'll take you till doomsday getting that thing done." He withdrew his hot hand and brushed his hair back.

Reuben Maust? Reuben Maust suggesting she have Mother and--and Rosella come over?

Her mouth closed, lips tightened together, her head lowered closer to the stitching. She'd learned it was better to wait before responding to Reuben. Was there a catch somewhere? What was the saying, "Someone hidden in the woodpile?"

When he remained silent, she looked up at his face, framed by the dark curly hair and the freshly ironed blue denim shirt. "I'll think about it, Reuben. Plenty of work on this quilt for six months. A good idea, though. If I see them..." But when? Maybe she would run into Rosella at Edenvale Church where she'd managed to muster the courage and swallow her gall to attend three times with Reuben. Wonderful if that new telephone company ever strung its lines out here in Sweetbrier country. But then, conservative members of the churches would probably start quarreling over that, saying it was too worldly and would split up homes. Maybe she could go to church with him this Sunday.

Her body stiffened at the thought of it. Would there still be cold looks, silences, deacons with dour faces? Would they corner her and say, "We'd be glad to see you and your husband united in a church, Susanna, but you know what is required, just a few words from you in front of the church. Longer you back away and harbor sin in your heart, more damage it'll do to your husband and children." Maybe, for the sake of the children, she should do it, clear the air for everyone. But that night in the woods wasn't.... Tears flooded her eyes.

She reviewed briefly how her mother didn't drive down for more than a nervous "howdy do" at the yard fence unless she was certain that Reuben was in a good mood or gone for several days.

"I'll be going, now, Susanna." Reuben gave her shoulder a squeeze. "Going to have your red dress on for me when I get home?" he teased.

"I'm glad you like me in it, Reuben, but not if I'm going to be cooking. Good bye."

She heard Reuben's steps as he descended the creaky old stairwell.

"Good bye, Daddy," called Timothy. He ran to the window to see his father mount Susanna's horse, Nell, given to her by her father when she married, and gallop away.

LIKE MORNING FOG ON THE SWEETBRIER

22

"A daughter this time, Susanna?" Rosella glanced over at Susanna while she stitched at a purple circle overlapping a pink and blue one. Anna, glasses perched on her nose, bent over at the left where she worked on the straight lines across the white center of a circle.

"We'll let the Lord decide that, Rosella. I was so thankful that Aaron was a healthy baby." A chill swept up Susanna's legs as she remembered going into labor soon after she got back that rainy day from Madam Carmita's Three Blossom Hotel when Reuben looked as dashing as what the English folks call "a movie star" in his new homburg and fine new serge suit. And the new dress, a deep red-violet. She had to wait until after Aaron was born to try it on. She'd worn it once to church, as it was long-sleeved and had a high neck, and with her hair piled high, giving her that cameo look.

"Reuben is in a good mood today, Susanna, isn't he?" Rosella said. "Carpentry work going well for him?"

"Reuben brings in a good living. People compliment him on his craft." What more could she say? *He gets nervous sometimes? Did you ever see him throw a hammer, or break a window pane? Have you been with him when he sulks and won't talk for two weeks and you don't have a clue as to what is bothering him*? She tightened her lips and tried to take the required small stitches, though her hand started to tremble.

Then a beam of warmth crept into her soul. Mother here. Rosella here. She'd dreamed about it, but it had happened only once or twice before that they came and spent several hours with her. What all had they heard about her and Reuben? She had a feeling they knew much more than they could ever tell her, unless something ripped open right in front of them.

At ten thirty Susanna rose from her chair. "Going to have any dinner, I've got to stoke up the range and get it on." She put her hands on her hips and braced her back in the blue Mother Hubbard. "Come, Timothy," she swept down and picked up Aaron, "Mother'll see if she can find you a cookie."

"Don't you need me to help? Can I peel some potatoes, or shell some peas?" Anna asked, lifting her snowy white head, her hands still for a moment.

How she is aging. I know my marriage and Aden's gloomy withdrawal causes Mother grief. Dear Lord. Susanna smiled. "Thank you, Mother. I made an apple pie early this morning. Just put on a pot and make some potato soup, throw in some chunks of our smoke-cured ham. The fresh baked rolls you brought, Mother, are enough. I churned yesterday."

Susanna descended the gloomy stairwell papered with ancient, grey wallpaper, now blistering from the walls. Reuben's words circled in her mind. "Waste money on new wallpaper for a hall nobody but us sees? Susanna, you'll bankrupt me yet."

***

Rosella and Anna quilted in silence. The wind moaned and old beams popped. A maple limb scratched at the north window. Rosella looked up and stared at the three circles on the ceiling by the chimney, the inner circle the darkest. She smelt the odor of rotting plaster.

***

"She's doing well, for now, our Susanna." Anna looked over at Rosella, but she couldn't seem to hide the tears in her eyes. She dug for a handkerchief and wiped her nose.

"For now, Aunt Anna. For now. God forbid. How did it get this way? Me even standing up with her at her wedding in Blessing. How could I have done it?" Rosella's face sagged at the thought.

"Don't be so hard on yourself, Rosella. I didn't strongly encourage Susanna to marry Rueben, but under the circumstances, both her father and I thought--"

"Reminds me of the two men on the road to Emmaus."

"How's that, Rosella?"

"Why, that's what the two of them said to each other, before the Lord joined them: 'We had hoped.' They had run away from Jesus's crucifixion and burial." The mantle clock downstairs clanged eleven o'clock.

"I was here once, Aunt Anna, when Susanna's forearm was black and blue and her right eye swollen shut. I asked her what had happened, but she only gave me a vague answer about stumbling out in the corncrib." Rosella stopped stitching and looked at her aunt who rested her needle on the pink curve of the circle and lifted her eyes to her.

"I--I, Rosella, it's so hard to talk about. Joseph and I discuss it sometimes, but then, we have to stop. He breaks down and grieves so. His shoulders are getting so round. I think he carries guilt about letting Susanna marry Reuben. Sometimes I think we should go to Bishop Weaver, but then, I, I don't know."

"Who would have known? Well, considering what happened in the woods that night, we all should have known. I feel guilt, too, Aunt Anna. Lots of it. And the way folks in the churches freeze Susanna out is a sin. A big black sin. I pray each night for her. I really don't see how she does it and now two little boys and expecting again..."

"Yes, Rosella. Pray. Pray about it. God can change hearts. I don't understand it, men treating their wives so."

Sounds of a poker stoking the range and a skillet banging on the stove lid echoed from below. Drifts of sweet smoked ham wafted in the air.

"Aunt Anna, did you know Reuben's mother very well?" Rosella halted her stitches.

"Well, yes and no. You know we didn't go to the same church, but then, only about five miles down the road from our farm. Yes. I can say I knew Bertha Maust rather well."

"How do you think Abraham Maust treated Bertha?"

The downstairs clock chimed a quarter after eleven.

"Well, to be truthful, Rosella, I have to admit I had my worries sometimes. I remember coming down here once when Reuben's sister, Rachel, had the measles. Course Bertha wouldn't let me inside the house as measles are catching, but, I, uh, I do remember she had a bruised jaw and her eye was nearly swollen shut."

Rosella started to stitch again. "Did you ask what happened?"

"As I remember, I did. 'Bertha Maust, what happened? You trip down the porch steps?' But she only took the fresh rolls and meatloaf I brought down and tried to shut the door on my foot."

"On your foot?"

"Well, she didn't want to hurt me, I'm sure of that. But I always thought she was hiding something."

"Abe Maust seemed a bit of a recluse, didn't he? They didn't go to church too often and seemed to keep to themselves."

"That they did. Many a community gathering, Wasser Hill School, church, lots of events when the Mausts stayed at home. I thought about it sometimes." Anna picked up her needle, leaned forward and began to make her fine stitches. "Seemed like Abe wanted Bertha to stay within the four walls of this house and inside the yard fence, as I remember it."

"I hate to say it, Aunt Anna, but do you think it's possible that old man beat up on poor Bertha Maust? You know how she was and still is, hesitant, forgetful. A part of her wanting affection and friendship, the other part searching over her shoulder to see if the lightning might strike?"

"Lizzie Wismer mentioned something to me once, Rosella. Please keep it from Susanna. She has enough to worry about. She mentioned that her husband, everyone called him *Old Lootie*, came down there after ten o'clock in the evening. Something about buying some sheep or a goat."

"Something unusual happen?" Rosella stopped stitching and rested her shoulders.

"Well, Lizzie said Old Lootie couldn't find anyone. But there was a lantern light in the barn. Said he stepped out there, thinking maybe a cow was calving." Anna stopped and cleared her throat. Her white head shook as if in the beginning stages of palsy.

"Do you remember what Lizzie said after that?"

"You know how Bishop Weaver warns about gossip and telling tales...." Anna hesitated.

"But when you consider Susanna, Aunt Anna, it just might be an important clue."

"Well, as I remember, and you must know that it was at least ten years ago, Lootie glanced through the crack in the barn door and saw Bertha Maust facing the wall of the cow stanchions and, as I remember it, he said old Abe Maust had the buggy whip in his hand."

"Dear Lord. From one generation to another." Rosella slid her needle into the material and stopped sewing.

"Soup is ready," Susanna called from the bottom of the stairwell. The savory odor of ham and potatoes ascended into the room.

Composing their faces, Rosella and Anna, hands bracing against the wall, descended the steep, gloomy stairs.

***

Susanna was already in bed in their upstairs room when she heard Nell neigh and Reuben gallop in the lane. She remembered hearing the clock downstairs strike ten. Weary from the day's work and from the anxiety of waiting, she threw back the sheet. "I'd better get up. Stoke up the fire and warm the fried potatoes. I can scramble some eggs for him. He likes a half-glass of eldeberry wine." She grabbed her summer robe, slid her feet into her felt house slippers and headed for the stairs.

She barely had the fire stoked and the skillet dragged over the heat when the door burst open and Reuben slouched in, hat looking as though it had rolled in a muddy ditch. His whiskers, charcoal, his jaws setting off his grinning teeth and his shiny black eyes.

"Well, would you look at that? Woman in her nightclothes, couldn't even wait up for her working man. Hair hanging down her back, belly sticking out for God and the whole world, waddling around in the kitchen. Enough to take away a man's appetite." He burped. She could smell the sour beer on his breath.

"Reuben, you must be very tired and hungry. Sit down, I'll have your plate ready in a minute." She reached for the fresh eggs.

Then she remembered. He hadn't even taken time to rub down Nell. Riding all the way from Lynn Valley or Mt. Hope, she would be hot and perspiring, needing water and feeding. If she could get him into bed before he exploded about something, she would run out and take care of Nell. Not even breathe it that Mother and Rosella were here.

Every time she tried to slip out the back kitchen door and head for the barn to attend to Nell, he stopped her.

"Get back here. Woman can't go out in the night dressed like that. Crazy or something?"

"Reuben, I just wanted to go out and say 'hello' to Nell. Take her an apple." Her hand clutched her robe tightly over her bodice.

He cursed. "Good-for-nothing mare. She spooks when she sees a tree limb waving in the wind, or even if she sees another horse coming down the pike."

Susanna knew that it was not Nell. Nell was obedient to her rider and well-trained. She was used to love and kindness, and she returned the kindness with all she had.

"She ought to be rubbed down, Reuben. You did ride her all the way out from Mt. Blue, didn't you?"

"Shut your mouth, woman. You're trying to embarrass your husband. I've told you before that you're getting too old and too big to be disobedient." He scooted back his kitchen chair and glowered.

"I meant no harm, Reuben," she said, trying not to tremble. She knew it was useless to use logic or reason. She would have to wait until he was asleep.

In bed, Reuben tossed and turned, grumbling and moaning from some old bad dream where he cried out and sat up drenched and trembling.

"Reuben." Susanna shook him. "Reuben, wake up. What is it?"

"Let me be, Susanna. Let me be." He lay back down.

By now she realized it was too late to rub down Nell. Her own weariness overshadowed her like morning fog on the Sweetbrier.

BETTER NOT SMACK HIM, CARMITA

23

Reuben was so proud of his little red-headed daughter, Emily, that he hitched the team to the spring wagon and rode over to Mt. Blue to Hunsberger's Furniture and bought a spanking new wicker perambulator. "Roll her down the lane on a fine May day, Susanna. No need for you to tote Emily when you go for a walk."

Reuben was glad Susanna hadn't resisted. In fact, she was obedient most of the time, as the Bible instructed, "Wives obey your husbands." Too bad she'd made him correct her when she tried to stop him from whipping Timothy. Boy sat right there at the table and spilled his milk. Weak, wishy-washy mother. Who was to teach the boy? Spare the rod and spoil the child. She thought the bruises on his bottom were from his hand. He knew the child got them from falling on his butt yesterday on the barn door sill.

Didn't hurt Susanna any, there in the corn crib. Ought not to have talked back to me. Kids taking their naps anyway. That was a sissy thing, too. Had to get her to stop putting Timothy down for an afternoon nap. Getting too big. He'd get that boy on the back of Duke one of these days, instead, and show his Ma what a man he was.

Triumph rippled in his heart like cottonwood leaves in the wind when he'd let Susanna out of the corn crib come four o'clock. Chickens squawking for their feed, weren't they? Emily, howling, needed her mother's breast and her diaper changed. Reuben sighed. She thinks I'm a rich man, harping to me about a washing machine, as if the two new wash boilers and scrubbing board aren't good enough. Claims she could crank the thing. We'll see.

***

Susanna hurried. She'd finished nursing Emily. Timothy helped her scatter corn for the chickens. Aaron toddled along clutching her skirt. Needing another bucket of shelled corn, she went to the granary. Looking over the fence in the barn yard, her eyes fastened on Nell. "Nell, what's wrong with you?" The horse stood half in the shade of the locust, head drooping. When Nell took a few steps, she limped badly, stopped, then turned and looked imploringly at Susanna.

Susanna dropped her bucket. "Nell, you're lame. What's wrong?" She unlatched the gate and slid through. "Timothy, hold Aaron's hand. Mother has to see about Nell."

At first Nell shied. Then recognizing her caring old friend, she tried to take a step toward Susanna. Susanna reached out with the palm of her hand. Nell nuzzled as if she were munching an apple.

"Let me take a look, little girl." Susanna patted her side as she walked back and bent over to lift her foot. Inspecting closely, she saw a triangular rock embedded in the soft part of her hoof where the hoof and flesh met.

"Nell. No wonder. We'll have to send for Veterinarian Miller. This'll become infected. Poor girl, Reuben rode you so..."

"You talking about me?" A vise gripped her arm. Her throat tightened.

"Reuben, you scared me. Let me go. The children..." She felt herself sinking in the soft earth of the barnyard. Sinking. Sinking. Then those strange birds along the creek by the blowing willows started that song: "Whip poor Willa. Whip poor Willa."

"I could have told you your horse is a weakling. Nothing much wrong with her hoof. Putting on." His face flushed red.

She could tell he was chagrined that she lifted Nell's foot and inspected it.

"Reuben, please look at her foot. It needs attention. If you don't care then I shall..."

"Shall what? Shall what, Susanna? Sally up to the front of my church and tell them the reason our family can't go there and worship in peace as a family? That it? Threatening me, Susanna? Why don't you stand up there and tell them you spent an afternoon in the whorehouse?"

Dear God. No. Not again. She shivered, wondering if she could even take a step. A flash of the new book she was reading, *Uncle Tom's Cabin*, raced through her mind. *Eliza, Eliza. I'm Eliza and I'm at the shore of the Ohio River. Ice all broken into floes. I must get across. My children.* Instead of the bloodhounds, Reuben's harsh breath echoed like a lost wind in the caverns of her ears as he dragged her away from the fence and kicked her through the gate with his boot.

"Get to the kitchen where you belong, woman. Anyone spend an afternoon in a whorehouse needn't tell me what to do. Nell's my property. Your property, my property."

Thank God the children were on this side of the fence. "Come, Timothy, come, Aaron. Mother wants to take you into the kitchen. You can help me peel the potatoes and make supper for Papa." Tears scalded her face as she stumbled up the walk while those weird birds kept on screaming about poor Willa.

***

Reuben must have left with Duke and the dappled grey hitched to the spring wagon while she was milking. Susanna had thought it was neighbor Levi Fretz rattling by, taking his cream up to Rosefield. Strange for Reuben to leave without his breakfast. But he did, now and then, relish those German sausages and fried potatoes at Wynona Bates's Cafe. What did he tell me he was going to do today? Build a corn crib for Elias Brunner?

Susanna set the bucket of milk on the back porch, then raced back to the barn. "Nell. Nell, poor Nell." The horse hung her head. Susanna grabbed a scoop and threw ground oats into her feeding trough. "Are you able to drink out at the stock tank?"

Nell lifted her sad eyes, her back shifted and humped as she attempted to put her weight down on her left hind leg. Immediately she picked it up again.

"I'll get you a bucket of water, Nell." Susanna grabbed a cedar pail and ran to the oval stock tank, then trotted back again, arm out, balancing herself as the wind caught her apron and flapped it around her waist. "I'll have to get back to the house. Emily needs feeding, the children want their oatmeal. There, Nell, drink."

Susanna watched Nell drink, then lift her head and turn sad eyes upon her.

"We need to take another look, Nell." Susanna stepped back, brushed her side tenderly, then took the hanging hoof in her hand. She could see the flesh swollen and red around the embedded stone. *Should I try to dig it out? Better get help, Nell, for this. I can't leave the children. What shall I do? I can't ride Nell in this condition.*

It was almost nine before the boys finished their oatmeal. She changed Emily, gave her a quick bath with lukewarm water and a soft cloth, slipped her into a long gown, then plopped into the rocker to let her nurse.

Next she placed Emily, her red curls framing her angelic face, into the new perambulator her father had splurged on her. Susanna raced back to the kitchen window.

I can't leave the children, and Nell needs attention. She will stop eating entirely if she gets sicker. Worry creased her brow as Susanna dried her chapped hands on the roller towel. Have to stop a neighbor going by.

Thursday. Levi Fretz took his produce to Rosefield on Thursday. Plastering herself before the kitchen window she waited a half-hour. Finally she heard the rumble of wheels.

There came Levi, tattered straw hat, beard flapping in the morning breeze, cream cans in the back of his spring wagon as he headed down the road toward town. Susanna raced out the door and around the house to the front yard, yanked open the rusted gate and leaped across the ditch. She flagged with her apron. "Levi, Levi, whoa."

Smiling, Levi drew back on his reins as his matched team halted. "Morning, Susanna. My, ain't it a fine morning. Corn popping up six inches a day."

"Yes, Levi, yes, it is a fine day. I need you to do something for me, for my horse, Nell. She has an injured foot. Could you please stop at Veterinarian Miller's and tell him to come out to my place as soon as possible?"

"Well, surely, Susanna. Surely. Something Reuben can't take care of, is it?"

Maybe could have, but neglected or refused, thought Susanna. "Thank you, Levi. Tell Dr. Miller I'll be here all day." That was a laugh. How on earth could she get away? Baby and two little boys. No horse to ride. The wind caught a wisp of hair from her bent head as she walked with leaden legs toward the stone house, two windows and the torn porch grinning at her like the face of a ghoul.

***

Reuben staggered as the wind caught a long pine two-by-four which he tried to settle over the bolts in the concrete foundation of the new corncrib. He swore and growled at Aden. "Get over here. You going on eighteen now, aren't you? When I was your age, I took on a job like this all alone."

"Sorry, Reuben, I was straightening the lumber, checking the sizes so that we wouldn't make a mistake." Aden cleared his throat.

"Grab ahold. Settle it down over that far bolt." The board settled, except at Aden's end. He stomped down with his foot but Reuben still had a finger slightly under his end of the two-by-four. Reuben danced in a circle, shaking his hand in the wind. "You idiot." Reuben's face twisted into a knot.

"Sorry, Reuben. I thought I was being careful." Aden's eyes reflected his own pain at having injured his idol. "Let me look at it, Reuben, is it cut?"

Reuben stared at the blood blister rising on the inside of his finger. He stuck it in his mouth and sucked on it.

"I can already see what kind of a day we're going to have." His cheeks flushed red. Maybe the boy needed a good dose of opposition and challenge to toughen him. Susanna surely did. Sometimes worry over whether or not he was too sissy, like that sheep-eyed Milton Leatherman who bought Susanna's sour pies. "Hand me that crowbar." He glared at Aden.

"Start with the studding at this end?" Aden waited for instruction, his eyes searching Reuben's face.

"You ought to know that, boy. How long you been working with me now? Two years? Have to ask where to begin? Next you'll be asking me if I have any wiping paper in my hip pocket."

Aden started to murmur, "No, Reuben, I'd not...." But his voice faded in the increasing wind. Sounds of hammer and saw echoed in the moist air. A billowy grey cloud overshadowed the sun. They worked, pounding nails in the increasing wind.

"You been going out with Sarah Ann Yothers? Ever think of taking her for a walk along Sweetbrier Creek in the moonlight, Aden? Believe Sarah Ann would like that. Girls don't mind at all when their boy friends take them into the woods." Reuben grinned, licking his lips, pleased at the hidden meanings which would goad the boy. Took after old man Steiner, that pious long face. Boy needed someone to gouge him enough to get the blood circulating.

"Why, uh, yes, Reuben. Sarah Ann and I are friends. We spend time together at--the--gatherings." Aden lifted another board awkwardly.

"Spend time together at the gatherings." Reuben sneered. "Well, boy. Girls demand more than just simpering around with them in the crowd at the gatherings. They want a man's hot hand around their waist and, like I said, some of them really don't even care whether or not the moon is shining. They'll take the walk into the woods with a red-blooded man, anytime." His laugh ascended like swallows flapping out of a chimney. His eyes shiny with the delights of goading Aden.

Aden straightened and rubbed the small of his back, hammer dangling from his hand. "Reuben, I, I can't see where you're going with talk like that. Sometimes I think you want me to do things a Christian shouldn't think of."

"'A Christian shouldn't think of.'" Reuben mocked again in a falsetto voice. "Put you in front of Roxanne's friend, Charlene, you stood there hopping from one foot to the other. Action is what girls like that are waiting for, Aden."

"Well, I took her for a ride on the Ferris wheel." Aden dropped his eyes, then fumbled for another board. Sweat broke out on his forehead.

"On the Ferris wheel." Curse words caught in the wind. "Baby Aden took the girl for a ride on the Ferris wheel. Bet you were clutching the guard rail in front of you instead of sliding your arm around her waist. Am I right?"

"Reuben, I, I--uh--I don't know why you are doing this to me today. I'm trying to do my best. You are digging into my private life, Reuben."

"What private life, Aden? What, for goodness sake? You'll probably end up being a schoolteacher like Henry Traguer. Buy the boy a beer and it doesn't even help him pump up his will and determination."

Thunder rumbled and the wind began to sweep debris from the barnyard into their eyes. Reuben felt droplets of rain on his face. "From the looks of things, boy, we'll have time, soon, to leave this pile of wood and head for The Three Blossom. You ever met any of the *ladies* there?"

"Uh, why, yes, Reuben. Think possibly we'll have to quit before noon if this rain gets worse. Why, no. No, I haven't met those ladies you mention."

The wind roared at the edge of the barn behind them. Reuben could feel pellets of hail on his hat and shoulders.

"Cover the lumber with the tarp, Aden. I'll help you weigh it down. We're going to ride right back to Rosefield, have a beefsteak for lunch. Something besides a sissy sarsaparilla to drink. Gonna visit over at Madam Carmita's place, young man ought to drink something that will grow hair on his chest." Reuben hooted, proud of himself, goaded even further by the shock registered on Aden's face.

***

Almost three already. Reuben slapped the reins and Duke and Dapple leaped. Let the young blade walk home. Shouldn't have stumbled out of the hotel like a sick puppy who'd just peed the rug, anyway. His stomach rumbled, turning sour from the beefsteak and beer. He placed a hand on his belly. "Curdling from that fat old Madam's rebukes," he muttered.

Who would have thought it? Old worn out bag like that passing herself off as a New York City evening girl.

Well, my dad always said, "Reuben, when you pick one, pick a big girl so's when you put your arm around her you can feel she's there." Reuben's head hung in half-shame and half-regret.

Well, that yellow-haired Alvina was quite taken with sissy Aden, running her ringed fingers through his hair, Aden, grinning, cheeks redder than a Georgia peach. And that luscious Sabrina in the purple dress that dropped clear down.... But when she found out who I was, she turned into a wild west panther. Clawed and scratched, her breath hot in my face. Her words still echoed. "Carmita, this is Roxanne's man but even worse, he's the one who knocks around that angel, Susanna Maust."

"Lord, have mercy upon us," Alvina's eyes widened, her red-nailed hand clasped her red pouty lips.

Madam Carmita's voice boomed. "Bring hell fire down on our roof if any of you girls touch this reeking goat."

Carmita shoved Sabrina back and heaved her heavy bosom under Reuben's chin. "You gotta be the most scurrilous bastard this side of New York City. Laying those hairy paws of yours on that sweet angel. Bruised, nearly choked to death. Run off her place. You, you...." She lifted her heavy arm and attempted a slap before Alvina reached up and grabbed her arm.

"Better not smack him, Carmita. Don't need the law in our place. Can't stir up things here, according to the constable. You wouldn't want to be put out of business."

"And how old are you, Mister Steiner?" Alvina had turned back to the golden boy, Aden, her smile broadening with encouragement.

"Why, uh, uh," his quivering legs betraying him. "Why, uh, Miss Alvina, I'm--I'm almost eighteen."

That'd done it. Why did he have to be so black and white? So yes and no? "Why, uh, Miss Alvina, I'm--I'm almost eighteen."

Why wouldn’t the boy lie a little? After all, hadn’t he put himself out like that just for Aden?

Reuben slapped the reins. "Giddyup, you fools." The horses leaped at the sting. They were in full run, and their driver's face grew blacker than the clouds boiling above them.

FOR BETTER OR FOR WORSE?

24

"Reuben disapproved of me calling the veterinarian, Miss Delaney." Susanna trembled like a chilled woods waif as she hunched in the oversized walnut rocker with the burgundy cushioned seat.

"Please call me Della, and I shall call you Susanna?" Della Delaney's low cultured voice and warm eyes already had a calming effect on Susanna who clutched Emily, wrapped in a small quilted blanket. Timothy, with his dad's bright dark eyes, peeked from behind her left side and little Aaron sagged on the floor like a bag of sand at her right elbow. She tried to stop her trembling, but she couldn't help a furtive glance out the left double window at the sound of wagon wheels on gravel.

"Don't be afraid, that's only Milton Leatherman: he volunteers to assist the boys here on the farm one day a week, Susanna. He and two of the boys are returning from town with some fencing I needed. Don't worry, you will be safe here."

Milton Leatherman? *That Milton Leatherman?* Susanna's brain tried to piece it together. How did I get here? How did I manage it? Her hand lifted to her black and blue forehead. "I was afraid for my life, Della. This time Reuben knocked me down the cellar steps." She lifted her pain-filled eyes as she choked back a sob. "Longest six miles I ever took by horse and buggy in my life."

"God forbid. I know such things happen. But, Susanna, I wouldn't have suspected it. Not among <u>your</u> people."

"I wouldn't have, either, Della, hadn't I experienced it myself."

"I knew you were running from your husband the minute you stepped into my buggy that day. Lone woman walking in the mud. You had all the signs of someone whose husband knocks her around. The bruised and swollen eye."

Knocked around? Bruised and swollen eye? What words! Susanna lifted her eyes. "I don't think Reuben is completly responsible when the rages overcome him. I think he drinks to try to control his anger, but that only makes him worse."

"I see it many times, Susanna. Angry men, needing help, take their frustrations out on their families. Some of my boys here at the farm have been violated by their fathers, and sometimes their mothers."

"Yes. Yes, I know Judge Rice sends you boys who need a home, who need love and--"

"You say you sent for a veterinarian?"

"Yes, my horse, Nell, had an injured foot. Reuben had ridden her too hard. He was angry and tired and ignored giving her a rub-down and attending to her foot." Susanna shifted the sleeping Emily to the other arm.

"Angry persons sometimes strike out at animals before they take it out on family members. I see the terrible effect it has on my boys." A sadness swept over her classic face, high cheek bones reflecting a touch of Indian blood, hair swept back in a French roll.

"Would you boys like to play in that room just beyond those doors? See the hobby horse and the toy farm and animals?" Della smiled.

Timothy's thumb lifted to his mouth. Aaron grinned and took a couple of steps toward Della, then they both meandered into the cheery play room.

"They're tired and hungry and I know they have been frightened." Susanna couldn't keep back the tears.

"Tillie will have soup and bread and milk for them in a few minutes. You may put the baby in a crib I have in the east bedroom. You're hungry too, Susanna, I know."

"Yes, but I don't even think of food. I couldn't believe it. Awakening on the cold floor of the cellar." She glanced at the back of her right arm at the long purple bruise which spread up underneath her gray dress sleeve. She knew there would be more bruises and welts when she removed her dress and undergarments.

"Important thing is that you decided to leave. Most women in your situation don't do it. Or," Della's sad eyes lowered, "they wait until it's too late. Fortunate that Reuben had left the house."

"Yes, Della, it was. Surprising to me, too. Of course I couldn't hook Nell to the buggy with her lame leg, and Reuben had ridden off on Duke, so I had to run to the end of the pasture and drag up old Dapple." She grinned as she thought of his slow plodding and his reluctant soul.

"Even so, you found the strength to do it. And the children, they didn't witness it, did they?"

"They've seen Reuben slap me, I regret to say. Not often. I do all I can to prevent that. I really can't say this time. But I believe both of the boys were upstairs at the time, since that's where I found them when I came to and crawled up the stairs." Susanna's shoulders sagged at the embarrassment of sharing such shameful events.

"You are not to blame, Susanna. Don't blame yourself."

"I, I--I must be responsible too, somehow. I try to do the things Reuben wants. It's just that I get nervous and I guess I'm not obedient enough. Reuben tells me that I'm stupid." Emily opened her eyes and smiled at Susanna.

"No, Susanna, not that. Don't even think it, a bright woman like you? Not that. It isn't your fault. Not at all." Della Delaney shook her head sideways, then glanced through the double doors at the white-aproned and white-capped cook, Tillie. She turned back toward Susanna. "We'll have a little snack in five minutes."

"I think I need to have Dr. Rush take a look at you, Susanna. You could have broken some ribs, rolling all the way down a flight of cellar steps."

"I don't think so. No. Not just yet, anyway. I know I have some bruises, including the knot on my forehead. Thank God, no broken arms or legs or I couldn't have rounded up Dapple, gathered up the children, and driven over here."

Then it hit Susanna. What have I done? Breaking up a home? Am I a woman who ran off from her husband? What will the community folks say about that? Shame swept over her heart like bats sweeping across the face of the moon. What about that marriage commitment I made, "For better or for worse?" Marriage, an institution ordained by God? *What of Reuben? Dear Reuben. What on earth will he do when he comes home and finds....* Cold fear clamped down on her heart.

***

"Dumb woman went to bed early again. Why didn't she leave a light on for me?" The house rose up, ghostly as a neglected undertaker's mansion in a weed lot. Reuben galloped in the lane on sweaty Duke, coattails billowing behind.

He slid off and struggled with the bridle and saddle, gave Duke a push toward the water tank by the windmill. His shouders sagged like a sapling glazed with heavy ice.

Did I go too far this time? But didn't Susanna talk back to me? I told her not to get the big mouth. Going on about Nell and that veterinarian Miller. He said we shouldn't ride her for a month. Shoot, what does that runt know about horses? Even worse, Susanna probably bending over, simpering up to him like she did to stinking Silas. How come she waited until I was gone to get that egghead out here? Just a slap, wasn't it? Can't help it she is so clumsy that she tumbled down the steps. That's not my fault.

His boots hit the back porch. He grabbed for the doorknob. *Always confusing after she makes me do somthing like that to know how to reconnect. Don't feel like humoring her tonight.* Reuben stumbled, wiped his stubbly chin and tromped into the dark kitchen. *Though I wouldn't want Susanna to know about Roxanne. That makes me mad, too. Riding all the way over to Mt. Blue and Roxanne "had company," whatever that means.*

Don't even smell any supper left on the back of the stove. A mother. Yes, she needs her rest, put three of them to bed. But, you'd think she could at least... The old house creaked as the wind picked up. His fumbling hand knocked a saucer off the table. He cursed. "Where is the lamp? Where are the matches? Susanna? You upstairs?"

On second thought, he regretted bellowing out her name. Be worse in front of three howling children if Susanna got disobedient again, or criticized him in front of them. Ought to know better.

Reuben managed to adjust to the silences, the creaks and groans of the dark old house, even if it had to be done while sleeping alone. When he awakened, he decided he'd shave after he stoked up a fire in the kitchen range and fried himself some eggs and a slice of ham. The fire wouldn't catch and take off. He'd have to go out to the smokehouse and cut off a chunk of ham. Do those roosters and those silly hens always make that much noise, mornings?

"Give up the ham," he muttered to himself. "How on earth does Susanna make coffee?" He filled the blue enamel pot with water from the pitcher pump and dumped in a half-cup of coffee beans. Then he realized he should have thrown them in the little drawer of that grinder and turned the crank. Let it boil, anyway. But, the fire. Fire always this slow? He kicked the leg of the cast iron range. He opened the fire box door and smoke billowed out into his face. Clementine and her three sisters bellowed from the barn. *Was there a suckling calf to feed by bucket? Sloppy. Have to dip your hand in the milk and let the fool thing suck on your fingers getting him started?*

Expected old Pap Steiner to bring Susanna down by the time sun up this far. Reuben squinted out the east window. Corn's gonna have to be cultivated soon. Hook Nell up to the cultivator along with Duke next week. Show Susanna how wrong she was.

Neglecting to shave, Reuben stuck his head under the pitcher pump and heaved the handle. Cold water drenched his head. He staggered toward the roller towel, eyes shut.

He swore. *If I can find Duke, ride on over to old man Steiner's. Give him a piece of my mind for sticking his grizzled old neck between a man and his wife. Bishop Weaver ought to know about it. Pompous fool ought to know not to intervene. Simpering old Anna, wringing her hands and bawling. Sure, they can keep the kids a few days. Good for them. Take Susanna down to Lancaster to one of those movie houses and dine in a fine hotel.*

As Reuben galloped down the lane, the half-raw eggs settling unsteadily in his stomach, he smiled to himself, anyway. *Naw, I won't bow and scrape. Things always better when a man clears the air with his wife. The last time, why Susanna didn't step out of line for three weeks. You'd think she'd learn.*

***

"Why, no, Reuben, Susanna and the children aren't here." Joseph stared at Reuben, face and chin the color of charcoal on account of his heavy, unshaven beard.

"You better tell it straight, Joseph Steiner. I'll ask you again, are Susanna and the kids here? Hiding them upstairs?"

By then Anna recognized Reuben's voice and hurried to the door. Her forehead creased as she wrung her hands in her apron. "No, Reuben, no. Why would we keep a thing like that from you?" She stepped out the door onto the wide porch boards.

Reuben turned, looked down at his boot toes, shifted back his hat with one hand. "See. See what kind of daughter you have?" His eyes flashed fire. "Disobedient. What kind of woman would run off with her children, not even tell her husband? You know what this'll mean in this community, Joseph Steiner. You and Anna shoving your soiled goods off on me. Look what you've done." He stalked down the porch steps and out the yard gate and heaved himself back into the saddle. "Giddayup, Duke." He dug ferociously with his boots into Duke's flanks. Duke sprinted down the gravel lane. Reuben turned and glowered, "You haven't heard the last of this, you pompous Steiners."

THE WORD SLICED THROUGH HER BREAST

25

"Two days? Susanna's not home yet? Out somewhere with the children? How can that be?" Aden turned and faced his weary parents.

"I didn't want to stir up Reuben any more than he is already. You don't poke a stick at a hornet's nest. But I had to ride down to see if Susanna came home." Joseph turned to look at Aden.

"Wonder he didn't run you off the place, Joseph," Anna dug in her apron for her handkerchief.

"No, I found Reuben strangely silent, walking around with his head down. I think he's feeling real sorrow. 'Course it'll take time before we know exactly what happened." Joseph looked at Aden while leaning on the door frame with one hand.

"I'm going to search for Susanna and the children. You'd think if she went to Rosella's or some of our people, she would have returned by now, or they would have ridden over to tell us something. I, I--"

"We thought that, too, Aden," Anna said.

Aden struggled. Then his tongue unlatched. "Papa, Mama, I found out Reuben Maust is not who folks think he is. He leads two lives and has gotten by with it. I'm ashamed to say I looked the other way while he took advantage of Susanna. How it all started out, the Sweetbrier Creek thing--how she got married."

"Aden, we are sorry to admit it, too. We've been discussing the same thing." Tears coursed down Anna's face.

"Papa, I'm going to search for Reuben. I have to tell him something. I haven't worked for him for a week. 'Slow time,' he said. After I find Reuben, I'm not coming back until I find Susanna. I know she left some tracks, close as people are in this community." He loped down the lane toward the barn to saddle Prince.

***

First Aden checked with Ernest Miller at Miller's Store. "Why, no." Ernest tugged at one of his sleeve-garters. "We haven't seen Susanna in the store for two weeks at least." Is there something I can do?

"Just if she comes in, tell her I'm looking for her." Aden turned and raced back to Prince. Leaping into the saddle he headed eastward down the rise toward the blacksmith shop. Aden didn't dismount. "Silas, has Susanna been by here? She left with the buggy. Children with her. Old Dapple pulling the buggy."

Silas dropped his hammer. "Well, no, Aden. I haven't seen any buggy go by drawn by a dapple grey. That kind of horse stands out, don't it?" He grinned and wiped sweat from his brow with his arm.

Aden turned Prince around and galloped across the street to the lumberyard and leaped from his saddle. He burst through the office door. "Simon, do you happen to know where Reuben Maust is working today, or this week?"

"Why, no, Aden," Simon Ledrach said, looking up from his accounts ledger. "Reuben finished the Fisher job two days ago. I did think he looked like something was bothering him, though."

"Did he say where he was taking his next job around here?" Aden's eyes focused intensely as he waited.

"As a matter of fact he did, yes, said he wanted to check out a job at Hershey's dairy. Mentioned something about putting on a new roof."

"You say Hershey's? East of Rosefield?"

"That's what he said as he left."

Aden slapped his reins and Prince galloped down the dusty road and through the hazy little valley by the creek toward the Hershey farm. "Another mile, Prince, keep it up. Gotta find the two-faced..." Shame crept over him, his cheeks flushed red at the thought of standing in Madam Carmita's plush parlor. That yellow-headed Alvina approaching him like that. Ladies did the right thing, pitching Reuben out. Me, too. What would Susanna think if she knew?

Prince sweated: nevertheless, he obeyed Aden's firm instructions. "Keep loping, Prince. We've got some work to do." The Hershey barn loomed ahead in front of a stand of black locust. "A half mile yet, Prince." Dust flew as Prince dug in, racing past the white-flowering elderberries.

Then Aden saw Reuben leaning a ladder against the east side of the red dairy barn as he looked up at the shingles. Aden dug his heels into Prince's ribs as they galloped down the hollyhock-lined lane toward the barn. "Whoa, Prince, whoa." Aden slid out of the saddle and ran toward Reuben.

"Finally caught up with you, Reuben Maust." Aden's heart pounded his ribs. His throat constricted and his mouth, desert dry. His eyes burned as he stared straight at Reuben.

"Well, look what the dogs dragged in," scoffed Reuben, one hand on a ladder rung. His face twisted as he attempted a feeble smile.

Aden could see Reuben hadn't shaved for a couple of days and that his shirt, usually ironed and clean, was sweat-stained and dirty. "Where is Susanna, Reuben? She's been gone now for two days, going on the third. What have you done with her?" Aden restrained himself from grasping Reuben's shoulder.

"That's the kind of sister you have, Aden. Hate to tell you. Unfaithful. What kind of mother would run off with her husband's children and never even--"

"Shut your mouth, Reuben, and don't put on that pathetic look. You'll not talk about Susanna like that in my presence. I turned my face the other way, too many times, Reuben Maust. I cared about you, looked up to you and admired you. After that episode at--at--, well, you know where, I had to admit to myself what kind of a man you are." Aden's voice trembled as he found new strength to throw back his shoulders and keep his eyes focused on Reuben's flushed and twisting face.

"Why, you little upstart. Wet behind the ears yet. Didn't even take advantage of what that Alvina was offering you up at the hotel."

"Close your mouth. Don't ever mention *any* of those women in front of me again, Reuben. Now I know. I didn't believe Susanna when she tried to tell me. I sided with you. I looked the other way, not admitting to myself what kind of a man you are. You took advantage of Susanna that night along the Sweetbrier. You, Reuben. You lied to me, lied to the church." Tears crept down Aden's cheeks. He choked back a sob.

"Expect you to side in with your family, Aden. Turn your back on me after all I did for you. Teaching you--"

"You taught me how to lie, Reuben. Lie. Ugly word, isn't it? Hateful word. Taught me worldliness. I behaved contrary to what I was taught and to our church's beliefs. Lord God. I'm going to the front of church communion time, maybe before, and tell the whole congregation how I became a liar just by being loyal to you, groveling at your feet."

"Expect those wishy-washy folks to believe you over me?" Reuben scoffed. "Me giving you work, training you. You ungrateful cur."

"That's another thing, Reuben. Glad you brought it up. I don't work for you or with you anymore. I quit. I'm going up to the lumberyard in town. I'll work there for pennies if I have to, just to free myself from you."

Weldon Hershey heard the commotion by the dairy barn and waddled down from the wide, red-roofed house. "You men have a disagreement out here?" He slid his hands into his pockets, his face creased.

"Yes, Mr. Hershey, we do. I'm looking for Mrs. Maust. My sister, Susanna, and her children. Reuben doesn't seem to know, or if he does, he won't tell any of our family. Have you seen her? Two days ago? Anyone see a dapple grey pulling a buggy? Woman driving with two little boys and a baby?" Aden's eyes searched his face.

"Well, now that you mention that, young man, my wife, Ellie, did speak about a woman she didn't recognize driving by a couple of days ago, headed east. Ellie said she was out pulling red beets in the garden and remembered waving at the young woman driving the dapple grey. Old horse, she said, but the woman kept him kicking dust like she was trying to outride a rainstorm. The day was sunny as I remember it." His eyes swept from Aden's to Reuben's face.

Aden's mind searched. The farm. Who is that eastern lady who takes care of abandoned and abused boys? Miss? Missus? The old Slotter farm. "Mr. Hershey, old Slotter farm about two miles ahead, isn't it?"

"It is. Woman from back east bought it. Home for wayward and homeless boys."

But Aden had already raced back to Prince. Foot in a stirrup, he heaved himself into the saddle. "Let's go, Prince." He galloped down the lane under the cloud-laden sky. His ears caught Reuben's words carried by the wind, "Always knew, Aden Steiner, you didn't have *real man* stuff in you. Go on, whimper down the road, see if anyone cares."

***

Della took a ten-minute break from her class. She stepped out onto the porch to visit with Susanna who supervised Timothy and Aaron rolling on the lawn. "I like teaching math to the boys, Susanna. Once they get over the jolts of moving around they settle in and want to learn. Such bright minds."

"It even encourages me, Della, how you do this. When I have volunteer time, I'm coming over here to help you. May be a while, but someday."

"Don't rush it." Della smiled. "Got your hands full now. Look at the boys out under that walnut tree. Rested and happy."

"Yes. Oh, if it could only continue. This peace and pleasantness. I don't know, Della, how I can ever thank you enough for what you've done for me. I have to go back and try to knit things together." Susanna's sad eyes lifted to her new friend's face, noting the peace and purpose registered there. Then she heard sounds of a horse galloping down the road. She raised herself in her chair and turned to look. "It looks like my brother, Aden, riding Prince. Yes. It is." Her eyes brightened, but only for a moment as she thought of the disconnected threads. What should she tell him? Would he disown her even more? A tremor raced up her spine.

Aden pulled in front of the imposing lawn with the white iron fence and stone gate posts. Prince snorted as Aden tied him to the hitching post. Aden walked resolutely toward the porch. She saw that Aden had noticed Della and her on the wide porch.

"Susanna. Susanna, at last." His voice choked.

Strange the way Aden leaped forward. Susanna stood, a hand lifted to her mouth. Della Delaney rose, her mauve skirt catching the wind, and stood by her side, placing an arm protectively around her waist.

"A--Aden, why, I'm glad to see you." Susanna couldn't hide the rising fear in her eyes.

Aden's foot hit the wide board of the porch steps by the summer hibiscus. "Don't be afraid, Susanna." His sorrowful eyes pled, fixed upon hers.

Susanna inched forward. She lowered her hand from her mouth.

"Susanna. Susanna, my sister." He reached out strong arms and clasped her waist. His eyes filled with tears.

"Susanna, how--how can you ever forgive me?" He broke into sobs.

Susanna reached out and threw her arms around Aden's wide back, one hand rising to the back of his tousled wheat-colored hair. "Forgive you? Aden, my dear brother. I have always loved you." The tears spilled over in her eyes and down her cheeks.

Della allowed them the moment of greeting, her face filled with pain and joy. "Let's all sit here on the porch." When Aden and Susanna stepped apart from each other, Susanna, broad smile beaming through her tears, said, "Aden, this is my new friend, Miss Della Delaney. She directs this home for troubled boys. She let me and the children stay here the past couple of days."

Della extended her hand. "I'm pleased to meet you, Aden. Susanna already told me about you." She smiled.

"Told you? I hope she was truthful. Did she tell you I turned my back on her? That I betrayed her, too? I sided in with..." He started to weep again.

"Aden, I never blamed you. You were caught up in Reuben's wiles. You believed in him and trusted him. That's a good thing, to believe and trust people. I believed and trusted Reuben, too."

A sweet wind blew off the green corn in the field beyond the barn. A mockingbird sang from the top of the red maple.

"Please sit down, Aden, Susanna, until we get this all sorted out." Della pointed to the porch settee and chair. The three of them sat, Susanna clasping Aden's hand.

"He insults you, hits you, lies about you. Susanna, why don't you leave Reuben?" Aden's eyes pled.

"Leave him? For good? Aden, we have three children. I must go back and try. Try to make it work. Pray for Reuben and for me."

"He struck you again, didn't he?" His eyes focused on the purple bruise below her dress cuff, then lifted, surveying the dark abrasion on her forehead.

Susanna's eyes told Della to remain silent about Reuben knocking her down the cellar steps. "Sometimes, yes, Aden. But, we have to love Reuben. I believe he had troubles in his own home when he was a child. Maybe later we will know more."

"Get a divorce, Susanna." Aden's shoulders raised.

"Divorce? Divorce?" The word, like a sharpened butcher knife, sliced through her breast. Divorce? Who in 1903 got a divorce? Why, did she even know a divorced woman? Her brain searched. Well uh--yes, Mrs. Elmo Sandburg over in Lynn Valley, but she was a Presbyterian, wasn't she? Besides, didn't she have to move back to New York because of the shame of it?

"Aden, you know in our community, in our churches, why, divorce, it just isn't done. And Aden, what about our children?"

A cardinal called and branches of the tulip tree swayed in the wind. "No, Aden. I'll have to go back. Take the children back. Reuben needs us all. His heart must be hurting too."

"Then why isn't he riding the roads day and night looking for you? How is it that I found you and he didn't?"

"Considering how I found Susanna, Aden, it is better, isn't it, that Reuben allowed us all some time. We hope his rage has subsided. Are you certain, Susanna, that you do want to return today and try it again?" Della Delaney's forehead creased.

"It's my duty. I gave a pledge. It helps so much," she clasped Aden's hand again, "to know I can talk with my brother." Susanna smiled and rose from the settee. "Come, Timothy, meet Uncle Aden. Aaron, sweetheart, your Uncle Aden wants to see you both."

"Susanna, I've been so--so cold and distant to them. Forgive me." The children, tottering in a circle trying to catch a yellow swallowtail butterfly, laughed in glee. "And, Emily. Susanna, I never even allowed myself to hold little Emily. God forgive me."

WHAT OTHER SECRETS ARE THERE?

26

Three weeks later on a Sunday afternoon Susanna sat with Reuben on the wooden lawn chairs underneath the spreading walnut. Emily snoozed in her perambulator parked by her mother while Timothy and Aaron played Indian, dashing in and out of the spirea. A gentle breeze blew over the cornfield, corn green and promising.

"Thank you, Reuben, for taking the children and me to Lynn Valley Meetinghouse."

Reuben turned, fastening his black eyes on her. "Wondered how you'd take it, Susanna, being adrift for so long." He glanced up at the white clouds sliding by.

"Why, Reuben, I found it refreshing." She wanted to add, "Couldn't we try another Sunday?" But she knew it would be better to wait until Reuben mentioned it again. She realized it was extraordinary for him to try a new church, let alone one that wasn't considered a "plain church." She had learned that in spite of his charm and "hail-fellow-well-met" attitude, he was often uneasy in new groups.

"I found the people friendly. And, Reuben, Pastor Fretz's sermon, *The Christian Community* was an encouragement to me."

"Well, Susanna, I didn't know. Wondered if there'd be any meat on the bones, he a more liberal preacher." Reuben swatted at a fly.

"I didn't know what to think of the organ, Susanna. Little pump organ wasn't, it?"

"Yes, it was, Reuben. Wouldn't have one over in Willow Bend, that's for certain. Small pump organ Luella Baum played. Up in the balcony behind us. Not showing off at all. And the organ sounded so nice when we sang "Rock of Ages." She looked over at Reuben, his skin, dark from the summer sun, contrasting with the white collar of his Sunday shirt.

"I'm going to head out to check the pond in the pasture, Susanna." He stood, stetched his shoulders and strolled toward the yard gate.

"If it wasn't Emily's feeding time, Reuben, I'd love to stroll along with you. All those daisies down along the stream." Susanna smiled, the experience of the morning hours still blessing her day, including the savory dinner of fried chicken, mashed potatoes and gravy, and lima beans. The boys were happy in the new haystack. Reuben evened out, now. She believed that he was better, now that Aden no longer worked with him. Maybe he wouldn't have to strain to impress anyone anymore.

Susanna rose and headed toward the back porch as a sweet wind drifted from the clover along the road. *Have to keep my eyes away from the catastrophe called the front porch. And Reuben won't allow me to touch a single board of it. "Fix it someday," he says.*

***

The next Friday morning Susanna turned from the dry sink where she packed the last of the sliced cucumbers into her blue Bell jars for her bread and butter pickles. She dried her hands on the towel, sweet smell of cloves filling the air. She stepped around baby Emily, playing with a wooden spoon at the edge of the kitchen.

Susanna decided to finish house cleaning today rather than Saturday, as Reuben had promised her they might just ride over to Mt. Blue past Clyde's Corner and look at one of those new leather and oak couches for the living room. She'd hesitated, thinking it might be splurging when the old one, though worn, was quite good enough yet, especially with the two boys.

She retied her apron strings, grabbed the broom and feather duster and ambled into the living room. When she lifted the green roller blinds on both windows, the incoming light revealed the assortment of papers on the open secretary Reuben used as his desk.

What's this? Envelope on the floor. She bent to pick it up, noticing that the letter had fallen out of the envelope and had drifted part way under the secretary. She stooped, reached for the page, careful not to bang her head on the open desk shelf. Her eyes surveyed the official- looking paper.

"Dear Mr. Reuben Maust: We regret to inform you that since we have not received payment for the taxes on your property, forty acre portion of section forty-six, Sweetbrier Township, we have placed a lien in the amount of four hundred dollars on the property. This has only been done as a result of your neglect of the two tax assessment notices we mailed earlier in the year. Yours sincerely, Hiram Mulvane, Office of the Tax Assessor."

"No. He didn't?" When did Reuben manage to have his mother deed the farm over to him? Susanna groped for the back of the straight chair, then eased her body to the seat. Reuben, Reuben, why didn't you tell me about this? Susanna felt the blood drain from her face as her legs grew numb. What other secrets are there? Dear Lord.

***

Ten minutes past eight and Susanna had put the boys to bed in the west bedroom upstairs, Emily in the crib in their own room. She descended the gloomy stairwell, careful to leave the door open in case one of the children called for her. She cleared her throat and lifted her head. *Have to do it. Can't let it pass. Too serious. Involves me. Involves the children.* She stepped into the dining room which they used as living quarters weekdays, saving the living room for

Sunday and special events. He sat in his heavy oak rocker, stockinged feet stretched out on the hassock she had covered with tapestry last fall.

Susanna adjusted the wick of the oil lamp and pulled up a chair from the table. "Reuben, we--we have to talk about something." Why did her heart have to start skipping around? She cleared her throat.

Reuben put down his *Farmer's Home Journal*. "Why are you staring at me, Susanna?" His eyes gave her the once-over.

"Reuben, I hate to bring this up, but I found something on the floor of the living room. In fact underneath the secretary today." Maybe I should have kept it so I could show it to him right now.

"Well, what was it?" He glowered.

"I was cleaning the room. I only picked it up and put it back in the envelope. I didn't bother your things on the secretary, just straightened up a bit." Lord, help me.

"Get on with it Susanna, you're interrupting my reading."

"It was a notice from the tax assessor's office." She clasped her hands. They felt as cold as water in the Sweetbrier in December.

Reuben's dark brows furrowed. "Susanna, you messing in my papers? I told you to leave my business to me. I take care of the bills. You ought to know that by now." He pitched the magazine to the floor, grabbed the arms of his chair and raised himself.

"Yes. Yes, Reuben. You take care of the bills. Only thing, Reuben," she stared straight into his startled eyes, "I didn't know that you, or, we, owned this farm, I thought--"

"Mother deeded it over to me last year, Susanna. I mentioned it to you once. I'll thank you to stay out of my affairs."

"Reuben, how could you do that and not tell me?" Susanna tried to control the shock on her face.

"Tell me, tell me, tell me this, tell me that," his voice boomed. "Susanna, I run this place."

"Reuben, you'll startle the children."

"You made me raise my voice, Susanna, you and your snooping. I should have known."

Susanna realized that she shouldn't respond to the slur about "snooping," as it would only increase his anger.

"Reuben, it's done. I would have liked to have been included. That's all. If I had known, I could have helped us save the money."

Reuben leaped to his feet. "The little woman feels left out? What do you know? Me rescuing her from the streets of Philadelphia. That's where you would have ended up, Susanna, if I hadn't taken you in, making a home for you. Walking the streets. Don't give me any of your lip."

Susanna stood. She clutched the back of her chair, but could not stop the twitching in her arm. She lowered her eyes. "Reuben, I'm thankful for what we have together, thankful to God for our sweet children, but we can't have secrets and build a marriage. I see that the farm is yours, but the money must be paid."

"Secrets? Secrets? You at stinking Silas's blacksmith shop flirting with sissy Leatherman plus setting the constable on me? You?" His laughter bounced from the walls.

Susanna realized that it was time for her to find her way out of the room. She turned toward the stairwell, her legs leaden, her heart like December pond ice. *I musn't show him I'm afraid. Oh, Jesus, Jesus...*

"No, you don't walk out on me, Susanna." A fierce jerk by the collar of her dress whirled her around.

She staggered for footing. "Reuben, please."

"You should have asked me, 'Please, my husband, may I snoop in your business?' You talking of secrets and spending an afternoon in the Rosefield bawdy house? They offered you a job there, didn't they? That's your secret, isn't it?" He howled at his joke and drew her against his chest. His breath hot on her face.

Susanna heard Emily, upstairs, cry. "Reuben, Emily--"

"Why, why don't we just go up and bring the children down here, Susanna? Let 'em see how their mother operates, sneaking off to Madam Carmita's house, and to the Home for Wayward Boys." He hooted. "When's old lady Della Delaney going to open a home for wayward girls like you? Did you tell her, Susanna, that you *had* to get married?"

"Reuben, your arms, you're squeezing too hard. Please let go of me." She struggled to push herself away from his heated body. She could feel the thudding of his heart as the anger raced through his veins.

Vise-like fingers closed on her collar bones as he shook her. Her hair loosened, pins dropped. He continued shaking, this time moving his hands from the collar bones to her neck, pressing in. Her hair cascaded around his hands and arms.

"R-r-r-reu-reu-ben..." But she could not talk, her mind a swirling swamp fog. Pain sliced through her head and shoulders. She could no longer hear the throaty growl of his insulting words. No air. *His thumb--Dear Lord Jesus, I can't breathe*. Susanna lost consciousness. Her body sagged to the floor like a punctured sack of sugar.

LORD JESUS, HELP US SLIP BY

27

When Susanna gained consciousness, a slant of the morning sun shot through her kitchen window, Timothy pulling at her dress, crying, "Mama, Mama, wake up."

"Where is Reuben? Timothy, is your father upstairs?"

"No, Mama, no, Papa left. I heard him calling to Nell as he rode out the lane. There's no one upstairs in your bedroom. Mama, why did you sleep here on the floor all night?"

Susanna, wobbling, leaned on an elbow as she tried to lift herself up from the cold linoleum, her clothes wrinkled and damp. "Mama's all right, Timothy. Come, we must go back upstairs."

Ignoring the pain, Susanna grabbed the edge of a chair and lifted herself from the floor. Staggering, she lurched into the kitchen, bewildered that she'd lost consciousness, and had lain on the floor all night. Dear Lord, and I didn't even hear Reuben get up and leave.

The lamp had burned out, leaving a blackened chimney. A smell of dampness and old limestone filled the house. A red-hot pain seared her throat. Her head throbbed. She reached to steady herself with a hand on a chair back.

Aaron. Emily. "Timothy, Mother must run upstairs. Come with me, hurry and slip on your clothes, then you can have a cookie and a glass of milk." A rooster crowed from the chicken house, announcing the dawn.

It took her only minutes to awaken Emily, who waved her arms and legs while Susanna, still ignoring the pain in her throat and head, changed the baby's wet diaper and slipped her into one of her cotton dresses. She grabbed a baby bonnet and tied it under the child's chin. "We're going for a ride, my darling, don't be afraid." She glanced at herself in the mirror, fallen, tangled hair, pasty face, eyes wide--purple bruise encircling her neck. No time to brush and pin up my hair.

When she'd thought about running away, her heart pounded against her ribs and her breath caught short. "But Miss Della Delaney said I should do it, if ever again..." I must do it. My life. The children. God help me. Reuben, wherever you are, don't return just now.

She stuffed Aaron into his trousers and shirt. "Hold out your foot, dearest, Mama must slip on this shoe." *Dear God, how can this little child keep up? I'll have to carry him most of the way.*

She remembered to poke cookies into an apron pocket after Aaron and Timothy smiled and dunked their cookies in milk while perched at the kitchen table. She opened her dress and nursed Emily.

***

A stiff wind whipped Susanna's grey calico around her legs and thighs. Her head, tied in a triangular head scarf, butted the wind as she leaned, pushing the perambulator. Emily gurgled from under her canopy while the meadow-larks, perched along the road fence, sang to the warming day. Susanna strained to keep the wheels on the packed track. Timothy and Aaron tottered behind, faces grinning in anticipation.

"Mama, my legs are tired," Aaron's upturned face implored.

Susanna bent over and picked him up, shifting him to her left side as she reached for the handle of the perambulator. He smiled proudly and threw up his arms at a meadow-lark that flew across the road in front of them.

"Mama, how far did you say it was to Grandpa's place?" Timothy turned his face up to survey his mother who struggled to keep the baby buggy on course.

"Why, it is five miles, Timothy. We'll rest. See that big cottonwood tree up ahead? The one where the wind moves the branches so? We will stop under that tree and you can have another cookie." *Water. I forgot to bring some water. No time. Everything left behind. All my things, all our clothes. No. Couldn't take Dapple or Duke. Reuben rode off on Nell. Besides, there hadn't been time to round up and harness a horse. And the buggy, that was Reuben's too. On foot. Mother, Father, here we come. Your forlorn daughter and her children straggling home* to roost. *If Sadie Swick hears about this she'll tell everyone, "The dog returned to its vomit."*

Would her parents turn them away? Hadn't she caused them enough trouble? Four more mouths to feed? *God in heaven, where shall I live*? Susanna moved her lips in prayer. Glancing at the horizon she noticed the sun was not yet above the corn. Thank God, only a few clouds now.

"Just a little rest, children." Susanna sagged on the still damp grass along the roadside where the pink primroses bloomed. "When we get to the Sweetbrier bridge, Timothy, we'll step down to the creek for a drink of water." Her heart pounded and though she realized she'd sweated her dress through in the back, the fear made her thirsty. Her hand clutched at her burning throat. She turned her head in its collar of pain as she scanned the road both ways. *What'll I say if someone rides this way? And Isaac and Rachel Weaver's place up ahead. Lord Jesus, help us slip by without being noticed.*

She reached for two cookies, handing one to each of the boys. "We must go. Come, Aaron. No time to bother that butterfly. Some other time we'll catch butterflies."

"Mama, can't you pick me up now?" Aaron turned back his head and fixed his blue eyes on her face.

"When you are tired again. Yes, Mother will help you then. Now see if you and Timothy can walk ahead of me all the way to that little bend in the road." The perambulator wheels started to squeak.

After three hitches of resting and walking they descended the incline through the shade to the Sweetbrier Creek bridge. "Mama, you said I could have a drink of water. I'm thirsty," Timothy said, starting to lag behind. Aaron toddled at his side dragging a forked stick.

"We will. Yes. I'm sure we can find an easy way down to the water." Surprising how hot the sun was after the coolness of the morning. "Yes, children, we'll rest here under the bridge in the shade. We can look for the pretty perch sliding through the water." What if someone came by and saw the perambulator? They would think she was crazy.

Susanna lifted Emily out of her rolling bed, then searched for footing as she eased herself down the creek-bank. "Not so fast, Timothy, don't want to stumble and roll into the water. Hold onto Aaron's hand."

Fortunately, there were rocks and gravel in the shallows along their side. The water trickled, fresh and sweet. "Here, boys, this is the way we can do it."

Susanna, kneeling on a large flat stone that edged out into the shallows, bent over, dipped her hand into the water and sipped from her palm. "See, this is the way we do it today. There is room for you here by Mother where it is safe."

The boys giggled. They dipped their small hands into the water and followed their mother's example.

"Now sit quietly, boys, and perhaps a fish will slide by in those grasses in the water. Surely, if you don't make much noise, you will hear the bellow of a big bullfrog." While the boys sat on a stone, fascinated by the water, the willow fronds blowing in the wind, and the challenge to watch for a fish, Susanna fed Emily once more.

An hour later they approached Reuben's sister and brother-in-law, Rachel and Isaac Weaver's farm. Garden adjoining the road. *Dear Lord, let Rachel be behind her house. If she sees us, she'll grill me about what I'm doing, and lecture me about dragging the children out like this.* Susanna shoved the perambulator faster but the wheels started wobbling.

Emily awakened and cooed when a lark swept low over her rolling bed. Pains shot up Susanna's arm. She reached down to pick up struggling Aaron again, his short legs having given out. "Children, let's see if we can look past Aunt Rachel and Uncle Isaac's barn ahead at that tree top that looms over the hill. Yes. See it grow taller as we walk towards it. Quiet, now, no one talk."

"Mama." Toddler Aaron jerked on her skirt. "Mama, can't we stop at Aunt Rachel's for a drink?" His eyes searched her face.

"Not today, Aaron. We have to get to Grandpa's place, remember?" Lord forbid. The cattle in the barnyard at their left lifted their heads and bawled loudly as the straggly group approached. Then she saw her, Rachel Weaver, white apron flapping over her blue dress, out in the garden alongside the road hoeing her green beans.

Susanna guessed it must be about ten o'clock by the position of the sun. The heavy moisture-laden clouds, sunbeams passing through their edges, and now the hot sun caused her dress to stick to her back. She wiped the sweat from her brow with her arm. "Keep walking, children," she commanded. I'll have to make the best of it. She saw Rachel tip back her sunbonnet, rest her hands on the top of her hoe and stare at them.

Susanna decided to speak first. "Morning, Rachel, fine morning, isn't it?" The baby buggy wheels squeaked, the tired boys waddled from side to side like little old miners emerging from a hole in the earth after a long day.

"Susanna? Why, Susanna Maust, I don't believe it. You out on the road this morning, shoving a perambulator? Where on earth--?"

"Why, Rachel, we all decided it was a great day to take a stroll to Grandpa's. Isn't that right, boys?"

"Yes, Aunt Rachel. How much farther is it?" Timothy stopped, hands in his pockets, and stared at her.

"It's at least two miles yet, Timothy."

Then Susanna noticed Rachel looking at her disheveled hair hanging beneath her scarf. "Why, Susanna Maust, you wearing your hair down? Why, what does Reuben say about that? Her mouth hung open, her eyes widened.

"Boys, come on, Grandpa's waiting. I, uh--I washed my hair and it isn't quite dry yet, Rachel. Nothing like the fresh air to dry one's hair." She yanked the scarf off her head with one hand and leaned in to shove the perambulator on past the garden. She knew she resembled a street waif looking for the Salvation Army mission.

"Something fishy about this, Susanna. Reuben know about this? I don't believe my brother would allow it. But then, those stories, Susanna, I heard about the other two times you ran off. I'd send Isaac right out to hunt for Reuben if I only knew where he was." Rachel stepped over her bean rows to the fence by the tiger lilies. "What kind of a mother are you, dragging those children so far on foot? Well, I never..."

"Keep walking, children. Aaron, want to help me push Emily?" They straggled past the bawling cows, heads hanging over the fence, eyes rolling at them.

Susanna didn't look back. *Believe we made it, keep going.*

When they had gone a quarter of a mile further, Timothy called out, "Mother, isn't that a horse and buggy coming toward us up there by the hedge trees?"

"Yes, it is, Timothy." *O Lord, who is it? We need a ride, but...*"Children, stay on this side of the road. A horse and buggy coming. We don't want to startle the horse." No place where she could turn off the road. No plum thicket to hide behind. Exposed like a pioneer wagon encircled by hostile Indians on a lonely trail.

She could hear the horse hooves clopping on the hard track as the swaying buggy loomed closer. Then Susanna, focusing hard upon the black-clothed figure holding the reins, recognized him. Bishop Weaver. Dear God, no.

The horse snorted, and dust from the rolling wheels drifted around them. The driver leaned forward, his black wide-brimmed hat socked securely on his head, greying hair blowing at the sides. "Whoa, Tobias, whoa." The buggy stopped. The heavyset man leaned out toward Susanna. He stared at her tangled hair cascading down her back.

"Well, I would never have thought it. Susanna Maust out on the road, morning like this? What on earth..."

"Bishop Weaver, just a little journey to the children's grandpa's, that's all." A feeble smile twisted at her lips as she reached a trembling hand to her disheveled hair.

"A little journey? Permabulator with a baby in it and those boys, walking, how far is it, Susanna?"

She ignored the question. "Yes, the children have always wanted to walk to Grandpa's place. Thought today was just the day. Though," she cleared her throat and a nervous giggle ripped up, "I didn't think it was going to get so hot by midmorning."

"Well, I've been wanting to ask you something, Susanna. Now that the Lord's brought us together, have you made your soul's peace with God? Bumpy start, your marriage. I keep looking for you in the congregation, but I guess you have to go with your husband. You're not a member at Edenvale, are you?" He swallowed and placed a fist at his mouth.

"Well, no. That is--" *Why does he have to ask me those things now?* "Brother Weaver, I'm in a bit of a hurry, now, getting later than I thought. Tell Serena hello for me." She reached for the perambulator handle.

"Well, now, Susanna, don't hurry away from your Bishop, guardian of your soul. With those little ones there, you can't keep delaying what you ought to do to put things straight." His eyebrows knit together.

What if Reuben gallops over the hill? Oh, God.

"Bishop Weaver, we'll have to talk about those matters some other time. Right now I'm rolling Emily right on down to her grandmother's place and I'm going to feed her. It's her feeding time." Or did he want her to open her dress right here on the road?

"Why, uh--, guess if a mother has to feed her baby, well, uh--then--. Susanna. Your husband allow you to do this? Drag a baby and two little boys five miles down the road? Hard for me to believe." He shook his wattles from side to side. "And I just as well say it as to say it behind your back, I am shocked a woman with your background, all the instruction about modesty and how a Christian ought to dress, you have the nerve to straggle down the public road with your hair down, no bonnet on. Susanna, I find it hard to believe."

But Susanna had already grabbed Timothy's hand which held Aaron's. Shoving the squeaking baby buggy with the other, she rolled away from the pompous bishop like the Johnny Cake in the storybook who rolled away from the cow, the horse, and all those others, except the wolf.

Bishop Weaver called after her, "Something stinks like a New York fish market, Susanna Maust."

She ignored the bishop's words that drifted in the wind toward her. Dizziness swept over her and the swollen splotch of flesh around her neck throbbed. A hundred feet, fifty feet more. The elm tree ahead. She groaned.

The lane. Up ahead the lane. "Children, look. Grandpa's lane just ahead where the trumpet vine covers the rails. We can make it. I know you're tired, but..." She turned to look behind and dust-covered Aaron had plopped down in the middle of the road. Timothy zigzagged toward her, face sweaty. She let go of the perambulator and trotted back for Aaron, his dead weight like a sack of sugar. She shifted him and reached for the baby buggy handle again, ignoring the blisters that had broken open in the palms of her hands. Behind them, horse's hoofs echoed. Closer. A rider galloping nearer. Reuben? Did Rachel send for Reuben?

"Run, Timothy, run to Grandpa's lane." Aaron, fear in his eyes at his mother's voice, started to cry.

HIS LAUGHTER SCARED THE BLACKBIRDS

28

Aden Steiner rode easy in the saddle as Prince galloped closer. Ahead, the lane stretched toward the slate-roofed house and red barn. Susanna? Pushing baby Emily? And the boys? Surely she didn't walk all the way.... Then it hit him. "Get up, Prince, we're going to have a homecoming."

Ahead, a fear-stricken face turned quickly toward him. "Susanna, it's only me, your brother." He galloped behind the panting woman and the two wobbling wild-eyed boys. "Surely you didn't walk and push that perambulator all the way from your place."

Susanna stopped and turned her sweat-drenched face, her hair hanging in shreds. "Thank God, it's you, Aden. We thought it was Reuben." She bent over and hid her face in her apron, her body rocking unsteadily. Both grimy-faced boys dropped to the ground, too tired to move another step.

"Boys, let me lift you up on Prince, you can ride the rest of the way up to Grandpa's."

Timothy and Aaron stared at their uncle with bewildered eyes as he hoisted them into the saddle, Aaron in front of Timothy. "Here, Susanna, let me push the buggy." Aden felt the blood drain from his heart. His face twisted as he tried to keep back the tears. They walked in silence, he leading Prince.

Ahead, Anna shook a rag rug from the edge of the front porch. She dropped the rug, hurried down the steps and ran toward them, arms open. "Dear Lord, Susanna's come home.

Joseph, where are you? Susanna and her children have come home."

***

By the end of the week Susanna, nursed in bed by her mother for three days, felt her strength returning. She stood, legs trembling, to comb her hair in front of her old dark oak dresser. Who was this lean-faced old woman? The bruises around her neck now were faint traces, but the ones around her heart ached. *Reuben, I had to do it. For your sake, for the children's' sake. For my sake.*

She turned. Her face fell as she viewed a thin body in the now-oversized dress. *Emily. Will I be able to continue nursing Emily? What has happened to me in these last four years?*

She stepped to the east window and glanced out at the spacious lawn. She lifted a finger to her lips as she surveyed Timothy and Aaron below struggling to roll a barrel hoop with a stick. The dog barked at their bare heels. She felt her face break into a smile, even though her heart lay like a chunk of hickory at the wood pile before the splitting axe. Susanna couldn't remember whether or not anybody had asked the question. What was the question? A tremor raced up her back at the thought of it. "Susanna, will you be going back?"

***

"We'll need to watch the gate at the end of the lane, Aden. Reuben's bound to come riding in one of these days insisting on his rights to see Susanna and children." Joseph moved with steadied ease as he tightened the latch on the wide lane gate.

"The gate won't keep Reuben Maust out, Pa," Aden said.

"No, but it'll stop him, at least if we put a lock on it. He'll have to dismount. Give us a few minutes to ride or run down here and ward him off. We can't have him barging in on Susanna and the children at any hour. Not just yet." Joseph's gnarled hands fell to his sides.

"Papa, do you think Susanna will stay here with us?"

"Not sure. She mentioned that when she felt stronger she would look for a place, but, pshaw, I don't see why she can't keep on living here at home." Joseph turned back to his wagon and tossed his hammer in the back.

Two days later, Aden, vigilant in his lookout for Reuben, spotted him riding down the road on Nell, cloud of dust trailing. Aden finished emptying the swill pail into the pig trough, lifted a lean leg back over the rail and loped for the granary where Joseph sat tying burlap bags. "Pa, Reuben's riding up the road. Better hurry down the lane to meet him." His face had blanched. He lifted his hat and ran his fingers through his hair.

Aden and Joseph watched Reuben gallop towards them while they trotted down the lane past the row of lilies along the garden fence. Aden noticed that Reuben wore a smart black suit and a fancy homburg hat. He leaped from the saddle and yanked on Nell's bridle.

"Wait right there, Reuben Maust. Right there." Joseph quickened his run, the brim of his straw hat bobbed up and down in the wind.

"Trying to keep me out, old man Steiner?" Reuben yelled. "I thought you'd be up to some trick." His fingers worked frantically at the lock on the gate.

"Don't bother asking for a key, Reuben." Joseph, his last step leading him to the old oak gate post, looked Reuben straight in the eye.

"Well, that's quite a welcome, isn't it? Who do you think you are, old man? Telling me I can't ride up your rutty lane and talk with my wife? Kiss my children?" Reuben arched back his wide shoulders, his shadowed jaw jutted in the air.

"You better do as Pa says, Reuben. Right now you're not welcome here." Aden crossed his arms and stood, feet apart.

"Listen to the snot-nosed kid. Wouldn't even take advantage of Alvina's offers. Baby Aden had to tell her 'I'm not old enough, yet.'"

"No use to insult us anymore, Reuben," Joseph said. "We know who you are now, we know you have been leading a double life. We know what Susanna put up with. I saw her bruises, Anna had to put her to--"

"Shut up, you old fool. Perfectly legal I get to see my family." He grabbed the gate and shoved, but on the other side, Aden braced himself and pushed back with two strong hands and arms. His father grunted and leaned in, adding the weight of his shoulder.

"We mean what we say, Reuben Maust. You want to leave a message for Susanna and the children, that's fine. We'll tell her for you. That'll have to be all for now. Susanna's too shaken and frightened. I won't allow her to see you just yet." Joseph braced a boot against the gate board.

"You don't realize, Steiner, I can go get the law and have him out here in no time. Don't give me any of your Mennonite lip, either, about 'we don't use the strong arm of the law.'" Reuben spat at Joseph's boot toe.

"Go ahead, Reuben. Constable Crowley is quite acquainted with your ways. Especially after your fine demonstration that day up at Silas Stauffer's blacksmith shop. Had it not been for Silas and Milton Leatherman, you probably would have ended up behind bars overnight."

Reuben seemed stalled for a moment. He turned away, then half-turned back, a crooked grin on his sensuous lips.

"I don't need your soiled goods anymore, old man Steiner. Pawned her off on me. Lucky she got a man at all to give her bed and board. That I did. Bedded and boarded her." He laughed, a harsh, mocking laugh and yanked on a lapel to straighten his fine-cut suit.

"You're not working now, are you, Reuben?" Joseph asked.

"None of your business. Tell Susanna I don't need her company. Tell her there's a woman named Roxanne who moved over to Lynn Valley now, and she invited me to ride over this evening. Tell her I'm riding Nell. Yes. That's what you can tell her, and that Roxanne knows how to treat a man." Reuben leaped into the saddle, slapped the reins on Nell's neck, dug his heels into her ribs. "Hightail it, Nell. Lynn Valley, twelve miles. You can make it." Nell galloped off bearing her rider. His laughter scared the blackbirds that had settled in a hedge tree and sent them flapping and scattering across the pasture fence.

"Pa, that's Susanna's horse, Nell. How is it that he is--"

"That's the way it is for now, Aden. For now." Joseph shook his head and turned slowly back toward the house, his shoulders sagged with the weight of the brokenness around him.

WHEN WILL THE BUTTERFLIES COME?

29

Nine months later, after Susanna had weaned Emily, she and her brood settled in the three-room apartment above the Rosefield Creamery. Rosella Meyers sat in the little walnut rocker Anna had given Susanna, along with two beds, a dresser, chest of drawers, kitchen utensils, and dishes enough for bare-bones housekeeping.

"You're more rested now, Susanna. I worried about you last summer after you left Reuben." She sipped hot tea from her cup as they sat in front of a small pot-bellied stove.

"I'm stronger now, Rosella. The hurt is still there, but the edges are not so raw. Relieved, too, that Timothy enjoys school and it isn't far for him to walk with the other children. Aaron and Emily keep me company." Her hand toyed with her collar.

"Reuben doesn't come around, does he?"

"No, not lately, at least. A part of me is pained by it, but it is a relief that he's willing to keep a distance." She lifted her eyes to glance out the window at the February sky, from which a snowflake drifted now and then.

"Maybe the hardest part is over for you, Susanna. Are you going to carry through with a divorce?" Rosella shifted her weight in the chair at the mention of the dreaded word.

"Divorce?" Susanna turned her head, the tick of the shelf clock broke the silence. "What judge around here would grant a divorce? I'm the one who left my husband. Took his children away from him. You wouldn't believe the list of grievances Reuben has against me, threatening to take me to court. But the very mention of divorce sets him in a rage."

"Pray, Susanna, that it'll change."

"I pray. Yes, and sometimes, Rosella, I can't even pray. Then I must remember that in the silence, no words, Christ understands and is still with me, whether or not I feel his presence."

"You can count on me, Susanna, to help all I can. The plot behind the creamery, surely Rudolph Stover will allow you a garden there. I'll come over and help you plant."

Susanna smiled at the offer. She sighed. "I have to learn to make it on my own." Her voice faded. They could hear the clank of cream cans below. A door slammed, male voices murmured. Susanna smiled at Rosella, "And the smell of cheese. Swiss cheese, Rosella. Don't I smell like curds and whey?" She chuckled.

"Just so long as it isn't Limburger, Susanna. That I would not be able to endure, although Papa always liked it, especially if it had been lying out on the counter to warm." Her nostrils pinched as she squinted her face.

"The worst..." Light faded in Susanna's eyes as she stared at the window pane and the grey sky beyond. "The worst, Rosella, was Nell. My own dear Nell. We'd been together since she was a filly. I felt so responsible." Tears glistened in her eyes while she shook her head from side to side.

"I know. I heard. Brutal. I don't understand how Reuben could have done it."

"He'd been careless with all the livestock. I did my best to keep up, but I had a baby and the boys. I knew he neglected Nell and rode her harder to get even with me." She lowered her chin. "But I never thought...."

"None of us would have thought it, Susanna." Rosella reached across and placed a warm hand on her cousin's.

"Twenty-four miles round trip, that ride he took that night to Lynn Valley and back. Some woman there."

"You don't have to give me the details, Susanna." Rosella's eyes saddened as she watched the grief in Susanna's face.

"No, it helps me to talk about it. His own brother-in-law, Isaac Weaver, happened to meet him on the road at his lane. He tried to stop Reuben. He said Nell was wild-eyed and covered with froth. Reuben beat her. I think he'd had too much to drink."

"Next morning, wasn't it?"

"The next morning. Reuben, determined to ride her again, went to the barn. Found her lying on her side in the lot, dead." Susanna buried her face in her hands. Her shoulders rocked from side to side.

Rosella stood by Susanna, one hand on her shoulder, while with the other she smoothed her hair.

"Such a shock for you and--did the children find out?"

"No. We kept it from them. Sometimes, though, Timothy asks about Nell. I evade the question for now."

"Couldn't you and the children move in with me, Susanna?"

"No. Thank you kindly. We'll make our home here. Grandparents down the road a ways. Reuben's mother here in Rosefield. The children can see her from time to time."

"What does Bertha Maust have to say about it, now?"

"She can't talk about it. I think it reminds her too much of what went on when old Abe Maust was alive. I believe she was a woman who suffered much." A vision of the gray stone mausoleum-house flashed before her. She drew a knitted shawl around her shoulders.

"And it passed on to Reuben? The anger. Like father, like son?"

"Yes, I'm sad to say so." Susanna looked at her worn shoes. "I pray, Rosella, that my boys can break the chain."

"And Miss Della Delaney? She wanted you to stay with her and her boys?" Rosella sat back down.

"She was generous, making that offer. I did consider it, however, we would have been farther from Grandpa and Grandma Steiner. I can work here below in the creamery, earn enough for flour and sugar, a few other staples. I do laundry and house clean over in town. If I plant the garden, that will help. Mother always has an abundance of vegetables from her garden. We won't starve." Susanna smiled. "More tea?"

***

A balmy wind blew in late April. Susanna scraped a small hoe around the lettuce and pale green peas which had broken through the earth and stretched themselves two inches above the ground. Aaron and Emily, wrapped in the sweaters Grandmother Steiner knitted for them, trotted up and down the garden rows.

"Mama, when will the butterflies come?" Aaron yelled.

"It has to get warmer. Be patient, Aaron. Want to run around to the steps of the creamery and see if Timothy is walking down the road on his way home from school?"

Pieces beginning to fit together. What about their father? They did miss him, but she could see they were happier here--not so afraid. *Reuben, Reuben, can you ever change?*

Susanna leaned her hoe against the back of the creamery, reached for Emily's hand and decided to join Aaron in his watch for Timothy. A gaggle of children straggled down the road. Timothy, spying his family gathered in front of the creamery to greet him, waved one hand while clinging tightly with the other to the old belt that bound his books.

"Mother, Uncle Aden just told me some news, and I don't think I like it." He ran past the hitching post, careful not to disturb a team of mules, and leaped up the steps to tell them the news.

A lilac bush on the left filled the air with perfume, the purple spikes nodding in the afternoon breeze. Susanna rose from the steps, reached out her hand to Timothy. "Well, come on upstairs, children. We'll have some cold milk and sugar cookies I baked just this afternoon.

"I want to hear the news, Mama," Aaron said.

"What is news, Mama?" little Emily asked.

"Well, we'll all just have to wait and see." A trace of worry slid over Susanna's face as she glanced down at Timothy's closed mouth and serious eyes. He certainly isn't bursting out with joy. Must have been something he didn't like at school.

AN ANGEL AT HER SHOULDER

Three Years Later

30

"I like it better here on your place, Uncle Aden," Timothy said, bright eyes focused on his uncle.

"That was the news, Aden," Susanna said. "You getting married to Lydia Nyce. 'Course, Timothy approves now. Watch him gobble Aunt Lydia's apple pie." Susanna smiled and raked a finger through the front of her hair where a few strands of grey lurked.

"Well, Lydia and I are always glad for the boys, and for Emily, too. Another year, Susanna, and I'll saddle up a pony and let Emily ride it down the lane."

"It's that they had so many changes and disruptions--things as they were with their father. And cramped, too, living above the creamery."

Three-year-old Emily slid off her chair and patted Aden's leg. "Uncle Aden, do I smell like sour cream?" Her eyes widened.

Aden lifted his chin and laughed. "Lydia, listen to this child. No, Emily, not at all." He bent over, lifted her to his lap and bent his forehead into hers. "You want to know what my little niece smells like? She smells like violets, honeysuckle, and sweet william." They laughed together.

Susanna's eyes swept past the kitchen window of Aden's place, the old forty-acre Swartz farm. She was glad he found the cash for a down payment. They had finished their dinner, all but the apple pie. Susanna ate slowly, savoring the tarty sweetness.

"Mama, when will I be big enough to work here at Uncle Aden's?" Timothy asked, as he waited to be excused from the table.

"Why, son. You are only nine. You'll have to grow some more."

"Well, when I'm ten? Uncle Aden, can I come and live on your farm when I'm ten?"

"Well, now, Timothy. Wouldn't want your mother to accuse me of stealing you. But, yes. Make a good home for you here on this farm." His eyes searched Susanna's face.

"He needs more space, Aden. More to do. But, you know his father..." Susanna hesitated. "Reuben keeps insisting that Timothy come to live with him."

"But Papa never comes for me," Timothy said, a resolve sliding over his face. "I can live here, Uncle Aden, if Mama lets me, can't I?"

Susanna didn't want the conversation to bog down in a discussion about Reuben Maust. She admitted that she was relieved that he kept out of her way. Yet the uncertainty of it. Reuben threatened several times to try to get legal custody of the boys. When he had barged into her creamery apartment, it had been to argue over money. Not the children.

"Well," Lydia said, rising to gather up the dishes and carry them to the dry sink, "we love the children. You are all welcome here." She flashed the children a broad smile.

Susanna didn't want the sadness weighing her soul to spoil the gathering, but she knew that she couldn't hide it completely. She looked down at her faded calico dress and noticed the cuffs were beginning to fray. She drew her scuffed shoes back under the table. She loked at her work-worn hands, betrayed by the broken nails and the lye soap water from the laundries she'd taken in. Sometimes she thought she smelled like furniture polish from all the waxing, polishing, let alone the endless cleanings in town and neighborhood homes.

After dinner Aden took all three children for a ride in the donkey cart out to the pumpkin field to check on the pumpkins. Susanna sat at Lydia's quilt frame and took tiny stitches on her Log Cabin quilt.

"Have you seen the old Maust place lately, Susanna?" Lydia looked up.

"No. I must admit I avoid going by that place, let alone looking at it."

"The front porch fell off in a heap. All the trim work on the old stone house needs painting. One upstairs window is broken. Someone stuffed in some old rags to keep out the cold. One of the hard maples in the front yard died. It's such a shame." Lydia paused to glance at Susanna. "Goats trampled the fence and are often out on the road."

"Reuben has many talents, Lydia. He just seems unable to focus on what is important, especially for a man who has a family. I know a lot of his anger must be at himself. Maybe even his parents."

"Important thing, Susanna, that you drew the line."

"Yes. In some ways, though, it alienated me more in this community. Our marriage getting off to a bad start, the way it did. Then, me leaving with the children. I just couldn't let the children grow up witnessing what I knew would keep on happening." Susanna's hand trembled.

"He dropped out of Edenvale Church, Susanna, did you know that?"

Susanna halted her stitches and looked at Lydia. "I expected them to take him off the membership list if he continued to neglect his Christian life, Lydia. When I left, seems like it all broke open. Everyone found out about his double life."

"The preachers there didn't want to do it. Kept making calls. All they got were threats behind a closed door. Some woman named Roxanne, inside with Reuben. They could hear her laughing." Lydia blushed and looked down at her stitches.

"Still, he gets enough carpentry jobs to keep him from losing the farm. I know it's mortgaged heavily. I wish his mother hadn't signed it over to Reuben. She may lose everything."

"It's sad, Susanna. You don't consider a, a--uh, divorce?" Lydia's voice faltered as if she'd mentioned the unpardonable sin.

"Reuben would never sign for it. Never. He would be even more hostile to me and the children. There's no way."

"Maybe he's not so angry anymore, now that he is older." Lydia threaded a needle.

"I didn't tell you. Papa went over to the old house to get my great-great-grandmother Steiner's chest, the one I used as my hope chest." Susanna's head dipped over her sewing.

"Did he find it?"

"Lydia, he--," Susanna's voice caught. "He marched right upstairs to get it, in spite of Reuben's protests." Susanna stopped stitching and dug in her pocket for her handkerchief. "Papa couldn't find the chest in any of the rooms."

"What happened to it? That was a family heirloom."

"Reuben finally ordered Papa out of the house and told him he had chopped it up and used it for kindling. I know it is true, Lydia." Susanna lowered her head, but she had stopped stitching because of her tears.

***

At four o'clock, Susanna and the children climbed into the spring wagon for a fine October evening ride back to the creamery. The children laughed as they reached for Monarch butterflies and sunflowers along the roadsides. And she? Susanna allowed that she, like Timothy, was glad brother Aden married that pretty Lydia Nyce. A good cook, too.

As they pulled in toward the creamery, Timothy spotted the horse tied to the hitching post by the locust trees.

"Mama, isn't that Papa's old horse, Duke?" His eyes narrowed and he reached for Aden's arm.

"No, Timothy, don't believe that's Duke. But who is that tall man there on the stoop?" Susanna stared. Then she recognized the broad-shouldered man who lifted his brown hat and smiled as he waved it to her and the children.

"Why, it's Milton Leatherman. Wonder what he wants?" Susanna wrapped her shawl close to her shoulders.

Aden drew the wagon in front of the creamery, and Milton stepped forward toward them. "Mrs. Maust, Aden," he nodded to the children. "Afraid I have some bad news for you, Mrs. Maust."

Susanna stared at his face. Now what? The creamery didn't burn down, there it stood before her.

"Sorry to give you bad news, Susanna, or I should say, Mrs. Maust, but Reuben's mother, Bertha, said I should tell you." Leatherman switched his hat to the other hand.

"Reuben? Is it Reuben? Bad news?" Susanna's hand lifted to her mouth. She steadied herself as she climbed down from the spring wagon. The children followed.

"Evening, Milton. You got news for Susanna?" Aden held the reins, waiting.

Milton nodded toward Aden. "It's about your husband, Reuben, Mrs. Maust. Seems he was helping Clarence Rush build a new barn. Somehow he lost his balance and stepped on a large nail. Nail ran all the way through his foot. Happened a week ago. Reuben didn't want any family members to know about it."

"Stepped on a nail? That can be serious, can't it?" Susanna's eyes opened wide. The children stared open-mouthed.

"He's at his mother's place in Rosefield. Doctor Hockman put him to bed there. Pretty sick man, he refuses to go to the hospital. Doctor says it's tetanus."

Susanna stepped back. "Tetanus?" Her shoulders shuddered. "Why, Milton, that can be fatal, can't it? Will they have to amputate a leg or foot?"

"That I can't answer, Susanna. Have to leave the decisions to the doctors and nurses. Anything I can do for you and the children, Susanna, let me know." He held his hat before him, head bent slightly.

Tetanus? Pain rolled through her soul like rocks bowled by a flood in the Sweetbrier.

"Thank you, Milton, for coming down to tell me the sad news. Yes, well--I need to prepare myself. Come, children, let's get inside. Come in, Aden. We have to figure out what to do. *I must go over to see Reuben tonight." O Lord, help dear Reuben.*

***

"Susanna? That you, Susanna?" Reuben awakened from a groggy half-sleep, his voice hoarse.

"It's me, Reuben." Susanna sat in the chair by the bedside, trying to ignore the smell of antiseptic. Something else--stink of rotting flesh. *Reuben. Poor Reuben.* Susanna caught her breath. *I must be strong.*

"Lift my head, Susanna." He turned yellow, bloodshot eyes upon her.

"I'll try to be gentle, Reuben." She adjusted the pillow, lifted his shoulders and head, her hand touching his magnificent hair. "Is that better?"

"Better. The throbbing pain. All through my body, Susanna."

"Reuben, I'm so very sorry." She wondered if she should reach for his hand.

"Don't fret for me, Susanna." His burning hand searched feebly for hers.

"You will be better tomorrow, Reuben. If not, then we must get you to the hospital where--" She reached for his feverish hand.

"No, Susanna. No. Here. If I die, I'll die here. No hospital for me. I wouldn't want them to cut off a foot or leg."

She could tell that it was too much of a strain for him to talk, yet he seemed to persist. "Reuben, rest now. Maybe tomorrow when I come you will be better and we can visit."

"No. Now, Susanna. Now. I have to say something to you." Tears crept to the corners of his sunken eyes.

"What is it, Reuben?"

"Susanna, I always loved you. I don't know why I abused you so. I didn't want to, but it seemed I couldn't help myself. I---."

"Hush, Reuben. You must rest. Tomorrow." Cold fingers encircled her heart.

"Susanna," his fingers pressed her hand. "I don't expect you to forgive me for all the mean things I did to you. I--I let the hate boil up within me. The same thing would happen to Pa, but I--I should have checked it, Susanna."

The tick of a clock measured the time. Susanna's mouth felt dry. Her heart began to pound. Forgive? She let the silence hang and stared out the window. "Reuben, I know I can't live with bitterness in my heart. Yes, you should have done something about the anger. I could have helped you, had you let me." Her breath caught. She wondered if she was going to topple out of her chair.

"Susanna, you are so good. Even your goodness made me angry. No, I wouldn't expect any forgiveness now." He released her hand.

Susanna swallowed. "Reuben, what can I say, you--"

"Don't say anything yet, Susanna." Reuben tried to lift his head. "I'm so sorry. Sorry I was brutal to you. Sorry for the children, I..."

Susanna began to feel as though a third person stood behind her. An angel? There at her left shoulder? Suddenly it seemed as if someone pulled a plug from her heart which had felt like a stopped-up sink. Boiling bitterness began to drain away. *It is Christ? His forgiveness? I must offer it to Reuben in his hour*.

"Christ gives me grace to forgive you, Reuben." She could scarcely see his fevered face through the flowing tears. I won't live with bitterness any longer. Yes, it is the Lord giving me grace to forgive you." She smiled through her tears.

"Did you ever love me, Susanna?"

"I learned to love you, Reuben. It's just that the children and I could no longer live with you."

"Preacher Heatwole from Edenvale Church came yesterday, Susanna."

"Yes. A good thing. He remembered you. Prayed for you?"

"He prayed for me, Susanna. Asked God to take away the burden of hate and anger consuming me."

"I prayed that for you, too, Reuben, many times."

"I knew that, Susanna. I knew that.

"I was unfaithful to you, but I never loved anyone else but you. I know that must be hard for you to believe, Susanna." He tried to press her hand with his thumb.

"Hard, but I believe you, Reuben." Her voice choked.

The clock ticked from the living room. Bertha Maust stepped to the bedroom door, handkerchief at her nose. She watched the couple for a moment, then stepped away.

"Susanna, I have to ask you to forgive me for something else."

"Yes, Reuben, what is it?"

"The old chest from Germany. Your great-great grandmother's, wasn't it? I deliberately chopped it up to spite you. I burned it for kindling in the kitchen range." Reuben began to sob.

"Reuben. I forgive you for that, too." Tears streamed down her face. "It was only old wood. I always treasured it. I have the memory of it in my heart. Sooner or later, we have to give up these worldly goods anyway." She tried to smile at him, but fatigue and the grave illness overtook him. He drifted off into a deep sleep.

TAKE A PICTURE OF YOU, SUSANNA

Two Years Later

31

Susanna straightened the bookshelf in the wide hall by the bedroom. *Thing I like about this Leatherman house is how spacious it is. If I weren't a Mennonite woman, I'd kick off my shoes and dance a jig, all this room.* She shelved Timothy's new book by that California author, Jack London. *Call of the Wild*. She would read it herself, one of these days.

"Hurry, Mama. Father Leatherman says it's almost time to climb in the wagon. He said he would drop us off at the cemetery so we could put these lilies on Papa's grave."

"Tell Father Leatherman I'll be right down. Grab my straw hat and off we'll go." She heard the sputterings of one of those new Henry Ford Model T's as it rumbled by. She glanced out the window to see it teetering dangerously down the road. Don't know if I'd ever want to ride in one of those, Susanna thought, though she'd read in the paper that someone made it all the way from New York to the west coast of the good old U. S. A. in a Packard car in only fifty-one days.

As she stepped off the porch of the imposing brick Leatherman house with the gabled roof and brick chimneys, she realized that after a year and a half, she still wasn't used to such spaciousness. She and Milton planned to remodel the house and enlarge the kitchen. He even wanted to put in electricity and running water. Then folks said the telephone line would be in their community next year. Then she could chat, now and then, with Rosella.

***

Susanna glanced out the window at the granary and the huge red Swiss barn with the stonework on the lower level. She smiled remembering how she and Milton talked about all the remodeling they planned. Times good. Why not invest in home and farm? Livestock--even blooded stock. Pay off in the long run, wouldn't it?

Milton, straw hat cocked at a saucy angle on his head, grinned. "Come on, Aaron, Timothy doesn't want to go. Says he's going fishing with Rob Kulp in their pond. Hold on to the basket of flowers, Emily." He reached to help her up into the spring wagon. Her red hair lifted in the wind.

As they rode down the Leatherman lane, Susanna's eyes focused on the bridal wreath spirea bursting in white along the lane fence. Bride. Bridal wreath. Married again. I never even thought of it. Memories crowded. A glow, balmy as the wind, warmed her heart. How had it been possible? From the bitter to the sweet.

Milton strolled through the Sweetbrier Cemetry to his grandparents' graves while Emily and Aaron laid the bouquet of white lilies against the simple tombstone with the name, "Reuben G. Maust," chiseled on it.

The wind rattled the tree tops. Susanna's hand crept to the front of her dress. She held Emily's hand with the other. Aaron sat on a nearby gravestone and watched two squirrels play in an ash tree.

Susanna stared at the gray tombstone. It seemed that the wind suddenly cooled, blew all the way from the old stone Maust house, down the valley across the Sweetbrier, up the cemetery hill, right through her heart, carrying old pain and sorrow with it. Old echoes from along the Sweetbrier shook her soul. She swallowed, bent over to straighten one lily stalk. *Reuben, Reuben, rest in peace*.

"Come, children, Father Leatherman is waiting."

***

By nine thirty, she and Milton lay on their backs in the bed in the east bedroom for their usual closing-of-the-day visit. Milton reached for Susanna's hand. "I love you, Susanna. Remember the gooseberry pie I bought that day? I thought then you were the prettiest woman in Aaron County."

"Me? At the market? Yes, Milton, I remember. You from the Willow Bend Church. Our family, you know, considered it too modern--our people were wary, Milton." She pressed his warm hand with hers as she thought of how burdened her heart had been that day.

"You're at home there now, Mama Leatherman." He grinned. "The children, too."

"A church again, Milton. You can't believe how at home it makes me feel. Outside so long. So many I cared about, turning their backs on me." She thought of all the rebukes, silent and spoken, the cold shoulders, Reuben's violations of her, the shame of having her name read from the congregation, excommunicated for something for which she hadn't been responsible. "You cannot believe the blessedness of being a part of the community again, Milton."

Light from a near full moon beamed through the spacious bay window. Susanna's eyes searched for the wall motto Rosella had given her long ago: "He careth for you."

She squeezed Milton's hand again, then he leaned over and kissed her on her warm lips.

***

Why not remodel the house like Milton wants? Why should I stand in the way? Besides, with the inheritance from his father, Mose, he says we can afford it. Susanna smiled to herself, remembering what else Milton had said; "Susanna, you, my beautiful bride, deserve it."

Another part of Susanna Leatherman gouged her conscience, the part long used to caution. Particularly in her life in the old stone mausoleum-house with Reuben, the heap of moss-covered rock she'd grown to despise. There I had to pinch pennies, not knowing whether there would be steady income or not with Reuben's excesses, and his hot and cold temperament. Plus the teachings from infancy emphasizing simplicity and moderation. Is this tearing down barns and building bigger that Jesus warned about?

***

Susanna smiled and stepped out on the pillared veranda where the Peace roses climbed on white lattice work at the sides of the porch. Down the lane, Susanna saw Milton wave at her as he sat on the wagon seat above the heavy load of rich-grained walnut and oak planks. "Expensive, yes, Susanna," he'd said. “But, you and I'll live here a long time. And you, four months along, going to bear me a son. We'll name him Edwin, won't we?"

"Yes, Milton. Edwin, if you desire it." Her face wreathed in smiles. *How can it be, love like this flooding my soul? Milton can name his son whatever he wants.* When Felicia, the yellow striped cat, nudged her legs and began to stroke her leg with its neck, her heart purred with Felicia's.

Susanna strode briskly down the red brick sidewalk, intoxicating aroma of the pink and white peonies bathing her in perfume. Her new ivory lawn summer dress with the ecru lace collar made her feel like a country gentlewoman. She reached to smooth her hair, done up today in a French roll with the amber comb in back which Milton had purchased for her in Blessing.

"My lovely," Milton said, "get me one of those new cameras and take a picture of you, Susanna."

She reached the gate by the great block of cement where the carriages and buggies could draw up, stop, and let their passengers step out.

"We'll have the show place of Aaron County, my love." Milton brought his handsome team of matched percherons to a halt, leaped down off the seat.

"Soon's I unhitch these horses, water them and let them pasture, Susanna, I'm going to walk you out here by the barn and show you how I plan to build a large hog house. A new chicken house for your chickens. You said you always liked fancy chickens. You'll have your chance." He stepped closer and placed his warm hand around her waist. Susanna nestled in by his arm, head against his shoulder. The warmth and smell of his body made her cheeks flush, but she didn't pull away.

"Let's do that after dinner, Milton. I made smothered ham with scalded milk, cloves and bread crumbs like your mother used to make. You do like creamy rice pudding, don't you?" She teased, knowing it was his favorite.

Milton pulled off his straw hat with a bronzed hand and drew her closer. Bending his head, he kissed her firmly.

***

Six weeks later Milton finished remodeling the kitchen. Twenty-five feet by twenty. Though Susanna had never been on roller skates, it entered her mind that she might need them to get from one wall to the other. Then, the dining room beyond the kitchen double doors, large enough for an eight-foot sideboard with mirror and a table that would seat twenty-one.

"Gonna feed a whole family, Susanna, gotta have a place to cook it." His warm eyes glistened as he surveyed the heavy chrome and cast iron range against the east wall, and the enameled six-burner kerosene stove with oven along the south wall, the fine dark wood cupboards extending to the ceiling.

“A real sink with a drain. Faucets, hot and cold water. No more dry sink, Susanna." Milton placed his hands on the small of his back.

"Milton, maybe we shouldn't. Electric lines won't be out this way for a while yet," Susanna cautioned.

"Hush, my dove. Hush. That new Delco thirty-two voltage system does it, Susanna. Start up the gasoline motor, charge up those big batteries in the basement--wonderful, isn't it?"

"Yes, almost too good to be true." Susanna had a fleeting image of a dim room, herself on the cold kitchen linoleum, the faintly unpleasant smell of a kerosene lamp gone out, blackened chimney. Cold wind howling at stone eaves.

After noon dinner Susanna, Emily, and Aaron sauntered out the east sidewalk where the hollyhocks strained to outdo the peonies on the other side. She couldn't help but look up at the imposing fourteen-room red brick house with the slate roof, new lightning rods scraping the sky, providing perches for the purple martins.

"There, folks. Between the hard maples and the old plum grove. Nice access from the lane and close enough to the barn. South wind blow the hog smells away. New hog house. It's the go now. You ought to see the round one the Bowman's built last year." Milton pointed.

Susanna clasped her collar and stared at the empty space, where only green grass grew and a few Rhode Island Red hens scratched and picked.

"Plan is," Milton said, "to build it sixty feet by thirty. Two stories. Windows all around. Ought to be large enough, don't you think? Boys big enough to help a lot. Looking into getting blooded Berkshire hogs, Susanna. The best. Markets in Philadelphia only ninety miles away. Blessing even closer. We'll be winners. Have big sales in a barn like that. You better figure out where you'll hang all the blue ribbons."

Susanna watched Milton's eyes glisten. Her love for him overrode questions she'd raised about Jesus and the Gospel.

"Tear down that shack of a henhouse, Susanna. Emily," Milton bent over and clasped her hand, "don't you think you'd like to gather eggs in a brand new chickenhouse? I think it ought to be twenty by fifty feet. Raised front with glass windows letting in the sun, keep it clean and sanitary. You always wanted Barred Rocks instead of those Rhode

Island Reds, didn't you, Susanna? Throw in a few of those fancy Japanese Silkeys and bantams."

"Well, Milton, we'd better check our savings in the bank. That sounds like a lot of building to me, especially since we already splurged on the house." Susanna didn't want to put a damper on anything, but--.

"Already got a loan at the Rosefield bank, Susanna. Pshaw, old Willis Swartley practically clawed at his safe to get the money loaned out. Only seven per cent interest. Way to do it, while we are still young and motivated."

"Whew, Milton. Guess my head ought to be spinning, but it isn't. I guess I don't think of myself exactly as young. I wonder if we shouldn't wait until..." She stared at his even-planed face with the reddish-brown hair falling down over his forehead. Why hadn't she noticed before how one of his ears stuck out like that?

"No wondering, Susanna. None at all. Get those two bathrooms finished in the house, one upstairs, one down, then we'll get the crew in here and start these buildings. Think your brother, Aden, might want in on it?" He beamed and ran a long-fingered hand through his hair.

"Milton, it sounds so, so..."

"So fulfilling?"

"Fulfilling, yes, Milton. And a bunch of things I can't even name yet."

"Exciting?"

"Yes, Milton. Exciting, but--"

"You're thinking of our teachings about simplicity, aren't you, Susanna? Don't you think building up, doing our best, taking good care of the farm, passing it on to the boys is Christian stewardship?"

"Yes, Milton, it can be, I guess. I don't mean at all to criticize." How could she tell him? How would he understand? Those years when she had to pare back, save, worry--locked for a full afternoon in the corncrib. Waking up on the cold basement floor. The commands. The orders. She felt like a slave freshly given her freedom and ushered into a banquet room where a table groaned with roast pheasant, chestnut dressing, buttered vegetables in wine sauces, while she stared in wonderment at a champagne fountain. Once she was like the dogs in the gospel, waiting for crumbs under the table, now she staggered at the spread before her.

"Another thing, Susanna. Going to build a garage to the right by the walnut trees. Easy access to the sidewalk leading to the dining room and to the one up to the front porch. How does the word 'Oldsmobile' sound?"

"Garage? Milton, you don't mean we're going to buy one of those automobiles, do you?" Her eyes widened.

"Quarreling over them in the old church, but yes, Susanna. Folks saying the cars break up the community, young folks spending too much time in town. Driving off to strange places and never returning."

Susanna looked at Milton's flushed cheeks and bright eyes, and said, "Well, I guess you don't believe all those negative things, or you wouldn't build a garage."

"Gotta keep up with the times. No need taking a full day to go to Lynn Valley, Susanna. Why, I could easily drive to Blessing and back in half a day. Save a lot of time."

"Milton, all I can say is I'm not certain that I can keep up." Her eyes lifted to survey the fourteen-room house. "Emily is big enough to help, but we may have to hire an Amish girl."

The next Thursday, just as Susanna guided the horse and buggy into the lane on her way back from sewing circle at the church, she was startled by a large wagon rumbling down the lane toward her with "Mt. Blue Furniture" painted on the side. Two stout men, lurching on the wagon seat, lifted their hats bashfully toward her, and two more slouched in the wagon bed waved half-heartedly as if they'd been caught stealing pullets. Now what? Furniture? She never ordered any new furniture. Milton? What on earth had he done?

She drew the buggy up in front of the house and leaped out, her pink gingham skirts flying in the wind. She grabbed the handle of the dining room screen door and raced in. Sweet odor of the beans and ham on the stove hit her nose.

Nothing new here, just the big table with the bouquet of pink old-fashioned roses Emily had picked that morning. Then her eyes spied it against the north wall of the living room, just beyond the double doors, smack up against the ivory wallpaper with the pink sweeping plumes. "No. I can't believe it." Her heart started palpitating. There stood a tall, shiny, mahogany piano, its white and ebony keys grinning at her. Milton, Milton. He knew she'd always wanted a piano. Susanna reached for a dining chair to keep herself from staggering. How on earth could an old thirty-five-year-old woman like her learn to play a piano?

PUT YOUR MOUTH TO THE MOUTHPIECE

32

It feels like God has a great broom in his hand sweeping everything along, all of us included, Susanna thought as she swept the back steps, being careful not to hit the tops of the begonias on each side of the steps with the broom straws. Begonias and coleus, always beautiful together. She admired her flowers. President Woodrow Wilson up in Washington, D. C. promising to keep then out of the European war. Something about Germany and the Austrian-Hungarian empire. Paper reporting the American ship, Lusitania, sunk by German U-boats. Where was it all leading?

Thirteen-year-old Emily stepped out onto the screened back porch and opened the door, disturbing a swarm of flies. "Mother, the rolls are browned on top. Do you want me to take them out of the oven?"

"Yes, Emily, thank you." Susanna straightened her back. A gentle summer wind whipped the corner of her blue calico apron. A hand swept up to check the comb in the back of her hair. Relief not to have to wear those head coverings anymore, strings dangling and getting in the way, especially when her neck was sweaty. Emily, such a helpful girl. Loved to cook. Got along well with the other girls in her Sunday School class. Determined in her school studies.

She thought of the church and the Sunday School where all four children received fine Christian instruction weekly. Seventeen-year-old Timothy, finishing high school and now living at Aden's place. Miss him? Yes, but he was happy there and had a knack for working with the dairy cattle. "Be a dairyman myself, some day on my own place," he'd told her.

Boy'll soon be eighteen. A hand clutched her throat at the thought of *eighteen. I was that young when...* It was just a flash of an echo in her brain: "Whip poor Willa, Whip poor Willa."

Susanna shook her head to clear it as she pondered her children. Aaron enrolled in high school at Rosefield. Bookish, Aaron was. Be a teacher some day. Maybe a preacher. Milton mentioned college to her last week, but it sounded so extraordinary to her ears, guessed she'd need a little more time to get used to that idea for one of her children. And the way he kept asking about Princeton. Princeton, New Jersey. Think of it. Seminary there, wasn't there?

She smiled, thinking of how easy Edwin had been to raise. A gentle child. Blue eyes and rusty-brown hair like his father's. Sat on the porch and sketched the cattle in the barnyard, birds in the trees. Needed to look into that and talk to his teacher. Never had an artist in her family.

In the kitchen, she noticed Emily had set the pan of dinner rolls on a rack to cool. The aroma made her mouth water.

"Mother, I don't know if I want to keep on taking those piano lessons. I have such trouble with the sharps and flats." Emily turned, a dishtowel dangling in her hands, her red hair, braided and hanging in two braids tied with blue ribbons.

"You'll do fine, Emily. Esther Clemmer is a good teacher. She'll not push you too hard."

"But, Mother," Emily responded, "It makes me feel so dumb, the way you learn to play so fast." Emily leaned against the sink and stared at her mother. "Besides, I get the feeling Aunt Rachel doesn't approve."

Aunt Rachel. Well, thought Susanna, what does Reuben Maust's sister have to do with rearing my daughter? What could she say?

"Aunt Rachel has a long face, Emily, but really she's good at heart. That's where we have to look, the goodness in her heart."

"Well, Mother, if it's goodness, then why does it have to come out like sour pickles?"

"Some people are cautious about change, Emily. And when you look at their cautions, there are some good reasons behind them."

"Well, I wish I could get the hang of it like you, Mother." Emily's red hair glistened in a sunbeam from the window.

"Reading music was always easy for me, Emily. Guess I may have a knack for it. Your grandfather Joseph Steiner is musical. Tell you the truth, when I sat down at Esther's piano the first time, though, I wanted to get up and run home. That's how scared I was."

"But, Mother, you're already playing *Now on Land and Sea Descending*, three flats. Why, soon they'll be asking you to play the organ in the balcony at church."

"I doubt that, Emily. But, it does warm my heart to play those hymns from the hymnal."

"Well, I want to learn the hymns, yes, Mother. But couldn't I learn to play some other music too? You know, 'O, Susanna,' and 'There's an Old Spinning Wheel in the Parlor,' or 'In the Gloaming'?"

"Oh, yes, Emily. Yes, you can learn to play other music besides hymns. In fact, I'll help you."

Emily set the table with the everyday china sporting the bluebirds, while Susanna popped a lattice-covered apple pie into the hot oven. Then she picked up a paring knife and began to peel potatoes. Her eyes glanced up at the calendar from Stover's Mill. June 1916 already. Where has the time gone?

***

Susanna sat on the round piano stool, eyes straining at the notes of "Joyful, Joyful, We Adore Thee." One more time and she'd have it. She didn't forget the sharp. Her strong fingers struck the keys with determination and the music resounded through the room and up the ivory-papered stairwell.

Only when she stopped did she realize someone was pounding on her door.

She leaped off the stool and hurried for the dining room. On the porch stood two grinning men, one of them clutching a strange-looking wooden box-like thing with an ugly black snout sticking out of it. What on earth?

"Telephone, Mrs. Leatherman. Your husband ordered this new telephone. All you gotta do is to show us where to plaster it on your wall. Call up Clara Swick in no time at all. No time at all. You still talk Dutch, Mrs. Leatherman?"

Now what on earth has Milton done? "Why, uh, yes. Why, come on in." Where was Milton? Let him decide where to hang the ugly box. Springing something like this on her.

"Met your husband on the road going up toward Rosefield. Mr. Leatherman said for us to put it wherever you want. All right if we lay it right here on your dining room carpet until you pick a spot?" The one sweating profusely dug for his handkerchief as he smiled at Susanna.

"Why, uh. Where is the best place?" They'd think she was dumb, asking a question like that. Let's see. Space between the sideboard and the double doors going into the kitchen? Put it in the kitchen? Where do I spend most of the time?

"Well, uh, I'm sorry, but I didn't get your names." Susanna, cheeks flushed, turned to the men.

"Calvin Hodge here, Ma'am, and this here's Frank Clemens of the new telephone company."

"Well, pleased to meet you both. I think I'll have my telephone in my kitchen. Yes. There on the north wall next to the porch. Space there between the window and the door." *What if* I *make a mistake? What will Milton say*?

"Good spot, Mrs. Leatherman. Outside wall. We'll have this contraption mounted on your wall and hooked up to the line we'll string this afternoon down to the poles by your lane gate. Pretty swell place you got here, Mrs. Leatherman." The heavy-set man, Calvin, smiled as he eyed the spacious rooms, fine cherry corner cupboard, walnut sideboard with carving at the top and in the parlor beyond, the elegent Duncan Phyfe sofa with spreading wooden arms.

"After we string her up, we'll come back tomorrow just to see if you are getting the hang of it." The short one, Frank, tipped his striped cap.

"Hang of it? Nothing to do, Mrs. Leatherman, 'cept give that little handle a turn and get your mouth up to the mouthpiece there and tell Central the number you want. Gotta hold that earpiece close to your ear, the receiver, you know."

Receiver? Turn the crank? "How will I know someone is ringing for me?" Susanna hoped they didn't think she was completely ignorant.

"Jest about to tell you. Says here in our papers your number is six-on-two. You're on a party line. That means when you hear two short rings and a long ring, better empty the potato peelings in the swill pail and hurry to your phone." Calvin laughed.

"Guess you knew, Mrs. Leatherman, we got your folks, the Joseph Steiners, already hooked up. Weavers too. Isaac and Rachel Weaver relatives of yourn, ain't they? Don't want to talk to Clara Swick, you can get on the line this afternoon and ask your mother for one of her recipes. Ain't it a marvel?"

"Clara and Sadie Swick? They're on this line?" Susanna felt her lips tighten. "I'll bet Rachel and Isaac Weaver are on this line too?"

"That they are. Good thing, having friends and relatives at your crank and call." Calvin laughed at his remark.

***

In the afternoon, Susanna and Emily sat on the side porch, fingers busy stringing beans, while they watched the telephone crew run the line from their house down the lane to the poles with the crosspieces and the funny-looking little green glass spools they stretched the wires around.

"I think it is just wonderful, Mother. Now I can call up my Sunday School friends. And, won't it be nice, calling up Uncle Aden's place and talking to Timothy now and then?" Emily reached for another bucket of green beans.

Susanna kept thinking about Clara and Sadie Swick and Reuben's sister, Rachel. She'd forgotten to ask the men if someone down the line could pick up their receiver and listen in on her conversations. She concluded that if she was going to be a modern woman, she'd take the bitter with the sweet.

***

After a few days, Susanna found the courage to call Rosella and her mother. Had to ask her mother to kindly speak up a bit, but Susanna realized her mother was probably intimidated by the ugly snout and earpiece. Then, too, Milton came up behind her as she was asking Rosella about her new baby chicks and placed a warm hand on her waist.

"Susanna, pipe down. You really don't have to yell like that."

Well, she'd giggled about it. Had to learn to lower her voice. But her heart beat steadily with pride at the marvels of 1916. She looked across the pasture and saw dust rising behind an automobile. Seemed like there were getting to be enough cars to cause a real nuisance. Kicking up the dust like that. Those horns, u-u-h--o-oo-ooo-gah. Ugliest sound she'd ever heard. Scaring the birds. Horses shying. Had to get out of her buggy and hold Beaut's bridle when Sam Strohm whizzed by in a big shiny thing called a Packard. But she remembered that the neighbor down the road, Emma Stauffer, snorted and called it "nature's mistake."

SUSANNA WEARS THE PANTS

33

"You gotta be careful lifting the receiver when Susanna Leatherman's number rings," Sadie Swick said. She leaned forward, elbows on the red-and-white checked tablecloth covering Rachel Weaver's breakfast table. Sadie and Rachel spooned spicy apple butter and spread it on thick slices of Rachel's bread, freshly drawn from her oven.

"Careful? Well, it doesn't sap any more strength from the lines than if you'd listen in on anyone else, Sadie." Rachel swept her eyes over Sadie's wide face, hair parted in the middle and drawn back tight enough to make her look Chinese. No wonder Sadie couldn't catch a man, giving such little attention to the way she looked. Why didn't she try to sit up at the table? Heavy-breasted woman shouldn't slouch like that, not at her age.

"Well, you know how it is with those Leathermans. 'Twas Milton Leatherman's grandfather, Elias, who Pied Pipered that group out of our church. Before my time. But, Rachel, my mother always said those Leathermans were as tight as a buffalo's hind-end on a wooden nickel." Sadie wiped a smear of apple butter from her chin with the butt of her palm and took a gulp of hot mint tea. "Except for the one Susanna married, Rachel. You oughta know that. Look how they splurge. Ever see anything like it?" Sadie's eyes bulged. "That Milton is sure a dandy."

"Have to admit they act like they are related to President Wilson. Milton doesn't even caution Susanna when she climbs into that big Overland and guns it down the pike toward Blessing." Rachel glanced at Sadie, making sure that her face reflected shock enough to keep Sadie diddling in the gossip. "Next thing she'll join those women squawking for the vote."

"Ought to be a law against it. I hear the bishops of the church districts are concerned about how some of the sisters drive around in cars. But you know how things are in that new church, women sporting hats. Coverings out the window, too. I think it's a real shame, woman flaunting herself like that." Sadie swished her mouth with another gulp of tea. "And at Susanna's age, too."

"Never catch me with one of those hats that look like a mushroom turned upside down. Funny scarf tied over it and under her chin. Gripping that wheel with her kid-gloved hands, leaning in like she's going to the Republican convention."

"And the coat. They call those long coats with high collars dusters." Sadie lowered her eyes, as if seeking approval for her wisdom.

"My Isaac went over to Milt and Susanna's place month ago. Isaac putting in a bid on six of those big Berkshire hogs Milton had for sale. Fine hogs, I have to admit that. But when he come home he just sat in his leather chair and shook his head."

"Shook his head?"

"Yes. Why, I didn't know until he told me. Said it was Susanna herself that goaded Milton into putting up that stone wall all around the barnyard. Cost a fortune. No wonder brother Reuben never could get a toehold on his place. Then she made him haul in those big spruce trees and sock them on each side of a well she'd insisted he dig." Rachel rose to slice more bread. "Oh, yes." She turned. "Fancy lawn furniture out there by the well and spruce trees. I'd call it plain waste." Rachel steadied her chin with a fist. "Besides, who has time to slouch around in lawn chairs?"

"Well, Rachel, with a war on, don't you think people ought to be cutting back?"

"I wouldn't criticize Susanna because of the war, Sadie. Not with her oldest, Timothy, drafted into the Construction Engineers up there at Fort Pitt, serving his time for his country. Thank God he's not shipped to France or Germany and having to carry a gun."

"Well, you're right on that, Rachel. Not criticizing Susanna for that. Young men of our churches having it hard. No place made by the government for conscientious objectors. Out west, I hear, young men of our faith have been imprisoned."

"Well, I still have to wonder what Reuben would have thought." Her face dropped at the mention of Reuben.

"Well, I remember years ago when Mama and I unloaded our market produce up at Rosefield, Susanna and Anna always got there first to grab the best spot. I especially recall one day how she simpered and put on when Milton Leatherman sidled up, asking about gooseberry pies."

"Well, I expect the Steiners had gooseberry pie, old Anna always liked it." Rachel leaned forward at the mention of the long-ago event.

"Yes. That was when Susanna was-- well, you ought to remember. It was your own brother, Reuben, caught in the mess." Sadie's eyes shifted.

"Caught in the mess is right. He made it right in the Edenvale Church, though. Susanna balked. Never did go forward. Stayed outside the church till the day Reuben died. It was sad. Very sad." Rachel dug for her handkerchief.

"That's why I even wonder if it's right, she being a member now over at that *new* church."

"Well, we'll have to leave that up to the Lord, Sadie. You say Susanna was sporting around in that Overland car?"

"They could have bought a Ford," continued Sadie. "Ford good enough for most folks. They make them with two seats, touring cars, don't they?" Sadie dug for more apple butter.

"That they do. But, you ought to know Susanna'd never ride in an ordinary Ford. Why, I got it from Stella Baum that it was Susanna herself took the lead at the Overland dealership down there in Blessing. Said she followed Henry Hunsberger around, battering and haggling about the price. I don't know why Milton doesn't keep her on a tighter leash." Rachel sighed.

"Well, Rachel, I lifted my receiver last week, Tuesday morning to be exact. Susanna harping to Ernest Miller up at the store about the canned Mandarin oranges she'd bought, claiming they were poor quality and would spoil her salad."

"Well, I've bought groceries at times not up to quality, Sadie, can't fault her on that." Rachel straightened her shoulders and pulled down her calico apron.

"But what I'm telling you is that behind her conversation with Ernest, my ears had to endure those shrieks and brassy blasts coming from that big black Victrola they got socked in the parlor. Think of it. Lid up like a hippopotamus with its mouth wide open, music blaring, in the morning, too."

"Are you sure that's what it was?" Rachel's eyes widened.

"My own mother saw it when she went over there last summer for raspberries. Susanna asked her if she'd like a glass of iced tea. Mama stepped right on into the dining room. She said there it sat in the parlor with that big ugly horn-of-a-thing on top." Sadie licked a finger.

"You heard the music over the telephone? What was it playing?" Rachel tried to register shock.

"I couldn't make it out, Rachel. It was kind of brassy with horns playing, and some violins. That red-headed Emily, probably sitting there in front of the Victrola endangering her eardrums when she'd ought to have been out hoeing the beans." Sadie shifted in her chair.

"Probably some of that new music I read about in *The Intelligence.* Man up in New York named Irving Berlin writes it. No wonder the bishops are worried."

"Next thing you know that feisty Emily'll be pounding it out on that big mahogany pi-anna plastered up against the wall in their living room." Rachel's face tightened. "And, you say they have an icehouse?"

"Yes, they do. Why on earth would anybody out here in Pennsylvania need an icehouse? What a waste. But then, I guess Milton Leatherman's cowed by the woman he married. Evident, Rachel, that Susanna Leatherman's wearing the pants in that household, much as I hate to say so. Poor brother Reuben. I guess I never knew what all he had to endure." Rachel sighed.

Sadie Swick stood up and brushed the crumbs from her ample bosom. She lifted a hand to see if her covering was still correctly perched on her head. Then, surprising Rachel, she turned and smiled across her wide, front teeth. "Rachel, there is some news I'm obliged to share with you. Wouldn't want you to hear about it on the line before I told you." She arched her shoulders as if she were going to announce the entrance of the Governor of Pennsylvania.

"Why, news, Sadie?" What on earth kind of news would a plain spinster like Sadie Swick have to offer, anyway?

"Why, uh--," Sadie blushed. Beads of sweat appeared at her hairline where wisps curled and wouldn't stay poked back in her covering.

"Why, Rachel, your father-in-law, Bishop Weaver, has asked me if I'd like to go to services next Sunday evening over at Fairfield Glen." She smiled triumphantly, her trembling fingers clasping the butter knife.

"My father-in-law? Why, Mother Weaver hasn't been dead that long...." Rachel's eyes looked like burnt acorns. She gaped pop-eyed. "Sadie, why, I--I--"

"Now you know your dear mother-in-law has been gone now almost two years, Rachel. Bible says it isn't good for a man to be alone, especially a bishop. 'Husband of one wife,' to be exact. Solomon already took me to services two weeks ago Sunday evening at Edenvale." Sadie's hands trembled; her cheeks took on a high blush at the mention of his name.

"Why, uh, that sure is nice, uh, uh, Sadie. And Solomon owns a right nice eighty acres with two barns and a ten-room house, too." Her face fell at the mention of her husband's old home place. Rachel stood, legs trembling as she stared at the empty apple butter jar.

"That he does, Rachel. That he does. Everyone says your father-in-law is well off with a good bank account. Comes from disciplined living. Christian living. And I don't know if you realize this yet, Rachel, but the Bishop says he's looking for another eighty, or a hundred acres with nice buildings in a few years." The beam of Sadie's eyes transfixed her plain face.

Rachel's lips turned down as if she'd bitten into a green persimmon.

THE QUEEN OF THE HILL

34

Susanna swung her basket as she sauntered in the June evening out to the long henhouse which loomed up in front of the plum thicket. Her mind clung to the letter she'd received from Timothy at Fort Pitt. She could see his face, serious, lips in a straight line, his blue eyes fixed on hers, full of apprehension and love. His words echoed in her heart.

"Mama, they're drafting me along with a half-dozen other young men from our community."

"Our peace position, my son..."

"Mama, I love you. And I love Aaron, Emily and Edwin, Father Leatherman, too. He's been a real dad to me through the years. I have to decide this for myself, Mama. If I refuse, I'll have to go to prison. If I opt for the Construction Engineers, I won't have to carry a gun, Mama."

Why did the choices have to be so heartrending? Where was God in times like these? Mothers grieving. Fathers bending their backs to get their farm work done while their sons are shipped off to Germany and France. Her heart felt like someone had attached a leaden weight to it, her steps slowed.

The years. Where had they gone? Only occasionally did the old dream disturb her sleep, those crazy whippoorwills screaming, the wind, the roar of the water in Sweetbrier Creek.

Milton's warmth. His embraces. His love for order and beauty. Good children. Obedient. Church loving, too.

Timothy and Aaron's agony with their father, Reuben. What did they remember? Emily--too little to remember.

Guilt banged against her heart, though, for going ahead after Timothy was drafted and entering their livestock in the county fair. She'd encouraged it, in spite of reservations. Even glad that Milton went along. The trophy, the blue and red ribbons now seemed mere trinkets against the backdrop of Timothy and the draft.

***

Though Susanna rejoiced that Timothy seemed well, she could detect in his letters his uncertainty about the war and what would happen to him. She looked down at her feet, careful not to trip at the door of the light-filled henhouse where her two hundred prize Barred Rocks cackled, roosted, laid their eggs, and courted with the dozen strutting roosters. "Dear Lord, take care of my boy," she prayed.

Beams of light shot through the dust motes illuminating the rows of box nests where a few late fat layers still snuggled down into the straw.

Four of those hens wanted to brood. Had to jerk them out of the nest soon and close them in a pen until the cycle passed.

The acrid ammonia smell of the chicken manure and straw engulfed her as she reached into the nest to the left to search for the eggs. Six fresh brown-shelled eggs from one nest. Susanna smiled, proud of her henhouse. She would gather more than a hundred eggs today. They should have brought another basket.

"You, my beauties," she cooed to the hens circling her shoes, then she brushed them away with one foot. "You weren't content with one prize at the county fair. No, you had to bring me four." Susanna's smile widened as she thought of the three divisions she'd entered. Red ribbon on her young hens. Blue one with the mature hens fluffing themselves and clucking at the judges. And a gold-toned trophy mounted on a block of walnut for best overall laying hens in the county.

Milton had entered five of his Berkshire hogs. How he'd beamed as he held up two blue ribbons, a check for fifty dollars, a red ribbon and a trophy for "Best in class." She saw in her mind's eye Milton filling out the papers to enter these winners in the state contest. He'd paid to follow through with her suggestion that they stay with blooded livestock, even though the initial investment emptied their pockets for a while.

That was another thing, paying back those two loans. One from the Rosefield bank and another from the bank at Blessing. Milton, sure of himself. In command.

"My darling, farm like this is a county show place. Good bottom soil bringing in fine cash crops. Blooded stock, the big brown-eyed registered Guernseys, those heavy stubby-snouted Berksire hogs. Took a while getting all the papers on them." Milton planned to sell another fifty as soon as they gained twenty more pounds.

"Prices good, Susanna. With the hog market up and the big-bagged Guernseys emptying out bucketsful of milk like they do, get both bank loans paid off come next year." Milton smiled, his strong hand clasping her arm.

A flock of Susanna's Japanese Silkey bantams circled her feet and pecked at her shoes. "Not feeding time yet, my pretties, you'll have to be satisfied with grasshoppers until four o'clock."

Egg basket full, she turned toward the well-cropped yard, glad they had planted those spruce trees on each side of the well. She gazed at them now, almost forty feet, in such a short time, too. Susanna's eyes surveyed the fourteen-room house with the slate colored shutters matching the roof--three-dormer windows in front, imposing brick chimneys looming up, well-proportioned, not at all like that old stone...

Guilt stabbed her again. Was she showing off? Milton wasn't responsible for all this luxury. He never would have chosen blooded stock had she not suggested it. *Me. My pride.*

Then, as a chunk of soil falls loose from a roadbank and crumbles into the ditch, a fragment let loose in her brain and nudged her mind. *Am I doing all this to show them? Those women who turned their backs on me, eighteen years ago? What did it say in the Gospel about tearing down barns to build bigger ones?*

Then Sadie Swick's remark to her mother, Clara, in front of Ernest Miller's store last week raced through her brain. "Don't stare, Mother, but here comes the *queen of the hill."*

Clara had turned and stared at her. Susanna knew Clara didn't approve of her brown velvet hat with the bird wing decoration at the back, purchased at Shawnasee's in Blessing. "Afternoon, Clara. My, I haven't visited with you for, how long has it been? Ages, hasn't it?" Susanna deliberately made red-faced Sadie and fidgeting Clara stand there, feet shifting up and down.

"Let's see, we all used to market our produce and baked things together, didn't we? Last I remember, we shared space under a hackberry tree. You had such a busy day selling your potatoes and radishes we didn't get to visit much, *did we*?"

"Why, Susanna, no, why--us both on the same line, I been thinking of ringing you up. Sadie here, real good at baking a coffee cake, so's you could drive up in your, er, what is it, an Oldsmobile?"

"You once called me 'Hester,' Sadie. Remember? The car, Clara, it's an Overland. Your husband, Hank, bought one of those two-seated Fords, didn't he? One with a top that folds down and looks like a *buggy*?" *What is the matter with me? Susanna, bite your tongue.* But a need to goad rose up like water in their artesian well. Her tongue refused to hold.

"Why, uh, yes, Susanna Leatherman, it's a Ford." Clara's mouth drew tight.

"Another thing I might mention, Clara. When I'm calling up the veterinarian about my *blooded* livestock, like that time one of my Guernseys swallowed a piece of wire, I'd appreciate it if you'd hang up your receiver so's I could hear better. Important call like that, I need to write down what the veterinarian says. Believe you and Sadie understand that."

Sadie and Clara shuffled their feet as Susanna watched Sadie surveying her beige summer linen dress with the gored skirt and ecru lace collar, and the amber brooch Milton had given her for her birthday.

Sadie dipped her head in her black bonnet and tried to step behind a rack of garden tools in front of the store.

"Oh, Sadie does get carried away sometimes on the phone. Think it's she wants to get out of shelling peas or breaking beans." Clara attempted a chuckle at her daughter's expense. "You'd be glad to do that, now, wouldn't you, Sadie? You be leaving me soon anyway, engaged to Bishop Weaver." Tears crept to Clara's eyes. Then she turned. "Susanna, the way your own mother must have felt when you married Reuben at such a young age, why, I can still see...."

Susanna's face flushed. The Bishop and Sadie? Right in the middle of this community and she hadn't heard about it? She felt her pulse throb at her neck. She sucked in her breath as she smelled the bitter coffee beans Earnest ground inside the store. The nerve. How could she bring up what happened to me and Reuben?

"You needn't bring up a subject like that, Clara Swick. As I remember, you and Sadie both crossed the street in town whenever you saw me approaching. You did it when I was young and married to Reuben Maust. It hurt, Sadie. You and I used to be friends, before my name was read from the pulpit. Excommunicated." Susanna bit her tongue to hold back her response about Sadie and Bishop Weaver. She only hoped her eyes hadn't crossed.

Sadie cleared her throat, her eyes rolled upwards. "Why, uh, Susanna, it was just a, a--we was just following what Bishop Solomon taught us, shun the--"

"*Hester*, the fallen woman, like in *The Scarlet Letter* book? That what you both meant in those times? Well, now that you bring it up, the hurt still pushes up in my throat. But I do know I can't live with bitterness in my soul. I have to let it go."

"Why, Susanna, you must have misunderstood our--"

"It wasn't a misunderstanding, Sadie. You shunned me. You, Beulah Byler, Dorcas Hershberger, and most of the girls my age at Willow Bend Church. Nobody in this large community of people of my faith dared have a shower for me. But tell you what. You go ahead and bake that coffee cake and ring me up on your telephone. I'll hop in my Overland, maybe even walk the three miles over to your house if it's a good day, and we'll catch up on all the years. Ask Dorcas and Beulah to come, too."

"Why, uh, uh, of course. Yes." Sadie's lips turned down as if she'd bitten hard on a rock in her spoonful of beans. Clara's hand shook as she attempted to yank the brim of her bonnet closer over her eyes, the other hand nudged Sadie to plunk her feet on down the sidewalk toward their mud-splattered Model T.

Susanna's phone rang, dozens, hundreds of times. The invitation never came.

OUR WORK MUST BE PRAYER

35

"I'll ride along with Ephraim Wise in his Chevrolet truck, Susanna. We'll load up the two beeves we butchered, plus all the canned meats and vegetables from the people of both churches."

"Folks sure gave generously, Milton, didn't they? Terrible thing Della Delaney and her boys going through. Influenza epidemic. Quarantines everywhere. Can't let Aaron, Emily, or Edwin go over there. Too dangerous. Three of Miss Della's boys dying last week. Six more down in bed. Dear Lord Jesus, reach forth your hand...."

Susanna started up the Overland with the nickel-plated headlights and the big spare tire in its niche by the front door and fender. The engine, in spite of the cold, roared, then evened into a smooth, rich rumble. Susanna turned to glance at the back seat. Boxes of carefully packed canned goods rested on the floor and back seat, along with bags of flour, salt, sugar. She surveyed the smaller bags filled with medicines, cough syrup, jars of Vicks and Mentholatum. Lemons, couple bottles of whisky for hot toddies and racking coughs. Aspirin. Mustard for plasters on congested chests.

Edwin, his blue-green eyes shining, hair curling beneath his wool cap, leaped down the front steps, red scarf Susanna had knit for him swinging behind him. "Mama, can't I drive you over to Miss Della's?"

Susanna opened the window. "No, Edwin. I won't allow it. Influenza's too contagious. You keep the home fires burning until Father and I get back. If we don't come back tonight, we'll be home the next evening sometime. Tell Emily she can bake a cake if she wants to. Roast beef in the oven. Potatoes on the stove."

The shiny car roared down the lane, Susanna grateful that there was only an inch of snow and not drifted like two weeks ago. Couldn't have made it through the drifts then. In her rear-view mirror she saw Milton and Ephraim in the truck, wending their way toward Rosefield, then they'd take the road eastward to Miss Della Delaney's Farm School, now famous in the county and state for her achievements with her boys.

Approaching the junction in Rosefield at Main Street, Susanna glanced down the block to the left at The Three Blossom Hotel. She noticed that the sign needed painting. The girls. What ever happened to them? She knew the constable shut down Madam Carmita's business. Rumor had it that pretty Elvina married Chester Langwalter and lives over in Mt. Blue. Bore him three strapping sons.

Susanna guided the heavy car past Silas Stauffer's blacksmith shop. Through the opened door, he lifted a hand holding his hammer as she roared past. A flash of shame swept over her at the remembrance of the humiliations she'd once experienced there. Reuben shocking her with his unreasonable demands. Slapping her. Threatening all three of them, Silas, her, and Milton.

But thoughts of the epidemic overshadowed the brief recall. Susanna thought of the three times she'd driven over to Della's place to help her kitchen staff can corn and green beans grown in her two-acre garden. Then the time she came with a church group to lead services on a Sunday afternoon. Miss Della insisted that she, Susanna, sit down at the piano and play for the hymns.

Her mind caught on the funerals in the churches the last three weeks. Three-year-old Tobias Hershey, seventeen-year-old Frances Stahley. Ruby Kauffman dying within three days of the first symptoms, leaving poor Emil and five children. Lord. Lord.

Preachers so busy they hadn't time to prepare the sermons and do their chores. And the terrible war news. Young men falling in France, Germany, the Netherlands. Western Union boys knocking at folks' doors, reading telegrams that transformed blood to ice water in people's veins.

And the community worries. Who knew who was spying on whom? Forbidden to speak their Pennsylvania Dutch or German on the telephone, or in public places. Aggressive, demanding drives forcing people to buy war bonds. Quaker, Brethren, and Mennonite young men in prison. And, the new war songs chilled her soul; "Over there, over there...," and "The Yanks are Coming," and that other disturbing one about "Lighting your fag," whatever that was.

Susanna tightened her grip on the wheel of the surging Overland as the strange, doom-laden words in the papers clouded her brain: The Meuse-Argonne Line, Ypres, and the soul-aching sound of a place called "Verdun."

Would Timothy be spared? What if he was shipped, after all, to Germany or France?

***

Two days at The Farm School and Della Delaney had slept on a couch in the hall alcove for only three hours.

"It's little seven-year-old Carlisle, Susanna. He has the soul of a poet. When he comes out of his fever and opens those blue eyes at me so trustingly, I cannot stand to leave his side. His lungs, how they rattle. I couldn't bear it if--he has no one, you know."

Susanna reached out and drew Della's head to her shoulder. "You have to rest, Della. You wouldn't want to come down with the flu yourself. Unless you rest, you'll only weaken yourself. Milton and I'll sit by the sickest children's bedsides. We'll attend them when Dr. Trimby makes his rounds. I know how to make cough syrup with whisky, sugar, and water. Milton can keep the furnace burning." Susanna guided Della, dark circles under her eyes, hair falling from under her combs, to the alcove where she tried to rest at intervals.

Four Quaker women and several from both Sweetbrier churches divided the labor: a half-dozen in the kitchen, baking, stirring great kettles of chicken soup. Others, white-aproned, white scarves over their heads, ascended and descended the stairs with spoons and bottles, tonics, and mustard plasters to be re-heated in the oven. A stout woman, covering strings flying, tromped down the steps and headed for the bathroom with two chamber pots.

In the spacious washhouse annexed to the kitchen, steam boiled up as Presbyterian and Methodist women, long sticks in their hands, poked at the sheets and undergarments in the copper-bottomed boilers on the stoves.

Then Susanna spied Rosella Meyers, hands gripping the lever of one of the big-barreled washing machines. Sweat broke through her dress in the back as she heaved to and fro on the handle.

Susanna placed her hand on Rosella's shoulder. "Rosella, when did you come?"

Rosella turned but kept on pushing her wooden handle. "Oh, you startled me, Susanna. I've been here four days now." Her brown eyes filled with tears. "How does God allow it, Susanna? The undertaker came for two yesterday, a fourteen-year-old named Anthony, and a handsome Italian boy from Lancaster, named Alonzo. I wonder how much longer Miss Della can endure it." Rosella sobbed, but never stopped heaving her machine handle.

Steam engulfed Susanna's head along with the smell of the lye soap and bleaches. "I'm here to do my part, Rosella. Right now, I promised Della that I would sit by the bedside of a little boy named Carlise, while she snatches a bit of rest. We must pray for Miss Della and her boys."

"Yes, Susanna, pray. Even our work must be prayer."

***

Susanna wrung out the cloth in cool water and brushed it carefully across little Carlisle's forehead. His curls glistened with his sweat. His mouth open, cheeks flushed. "Our Father who art in heaven..." Susanna whispered as the tears streamed down her cheeks. She could hear Milton and Ephraim stacking wood in the basement, then the clang of the great furnace door as they opened it to stoke the fire, then close it.

Why, Susanna thought, when plague like this struck did even the earth weep? The grey clouds outside hung like funeral crepe. Ghoul fingers of fog rising from the ponds and creeks seemed to reach for newly-opened graves. Heavy mud silenced the horses' hooves and muffled echoes from exhausts of automobiles snaking by in the crooked ruts. Even Mother Nature wept. But, Susanna thought, *Mother Nature herself is completely obedient to God. I must be as obedient, myself.*

The child's breath caught; he coughed. A rattle like heavy flapping paper rose from his tiny throat. "Dear God above, stretch forth your hand." She rose to descend the stairs. "When will Dr. Trimby be here again?" Susanna called, her eyes ached. *Dear God, make it soon.*

***

Three lads died in the forty-eight hours Susanna and Milton enmeshed themselves in the work and life of Miss Della's Farm School. Milton guided the mud-splattered Overland into the lane as they rocked in silence. Only a moment before, a shaft of light had burst through the gray, thinning clouds, illumining their house on the rise. The great spruce trees, flocked with traces of snow, swayed in a sudden wind. A slow drift of wood smoke swept eastward toward the oaks and the barn. Then gloom descended as the clouds again slid over the sun.

"Milton, who is that?" Susanna rubbed a circle through the steam on the windshield and leaned forward for a better view of someone on a bicycle, obviously struggling through the wet sand at the curve by the front gate.

"Someone on a bicycle. Wouldn't have thought a bicycle rider would have made it out with the roads like they are." Milton guided the car closer.

"It's one of those Western Union boys." Susanna's eyes widened. Her throat constricted.

Milton brought the car to a halt, half-opened his door and called out. "Looking for me and Mrs. Leatherman?"

The teen-age boy with the billed cap and uniform held the handlebars of his bicycle as he rolled it over beside the Overland.

"Telegram for Mrs. Leatherman, sir." He dug in the leather case attached to the bicycle frame.

"I'm sorry to hand this to you, but, as you will understand, it's my duty." The boy's pain-filled eyes lowered.

"Duty? What duty? What can he be speaking of? On a day like this?" Susanna's heart palpitated. "Open it, Milton."

Milton ripped open the envelope and withdrew the yellow half-page. Steadying it, his eyes scanned the page. His jaw fell.

"Milton, let me see." Susanna grabbed the telegram as her burning eyes swept over the words.

> ...Army of the United States of America... The Construction Engineers... We regret to inform you that your son, Timothy Johannes Maust, died yesterday at six o'clock, P. M., from influenza. We extend our deepest sympathy....

Susanna groaned, her hands closed over her weary face as Milton reached over to draw her head to his chest.

"Susanna, my love." His tears blended with hers.

PENNSYLVANIA SHOW PLACE

36

Susanna drove slowly in the new, green 1921 Buick Milton had purchased in Staunton in early spring. She was on her way back from the cemetery where she'd sat for an hour after placing a bouquet of summer roses on Timothy's grave.

She glanced at the bachelor's buttons along the road and thought about how life renews itself. Winter, cold, rotting leaves, death. The miracle of spring with April showers, the sheen of summer, followed by autumn harvest.

Even though Susanna knew in her depths that she was mysteriously tied to it all through some wisdom of God, still a sadness clung to her heart.

I'll have to give the others up soon, too. Aaron, in college at Penn State--writing home about Albert Einstein's new relativity discoveries. Science? Where will it lead him? A doctor, maybe?

Emily, seventeen--last year of high school. Wrote for information about Bethel College out in Kansas somewhere. Music. Emily would surely study music. The strains of "Blue Moon" Emily played last night echoed through her head as she turned in to their lane. Women? Doors opening. Why even the U. S. Congress now presided over by that woman. What's her name? Republican from Oklahoma--Alice Robertson. Would the boom times and the wonders never cease?

Edwin. Sixteen in July? Her heart warmed at her remembrance of Brother Fry's words to her a month ago: "That boy, Susanna, interest like he has in religion, ought to soon be thinking of a theological seminary. Keep your eye on him."

Well, she would. Milton, too. Had they done their best?

"Boom times, now, Susanna, after the war. Ought to add to the Guernsey herd this year." Milton's enthusiasm bubbled up like water in their artesian well. "I'm glad the farm's productive. We're successful. Berkshires won the Lancaster Cup in last year's showing, now on to the state fair. Maybe to the American Royal out there in Kansas City."

President Harding up in the White House, grinning with that rope-twirling Will Rogers, who made everyone laugh, even here when he'd said over the radio, "Everything is funny as long as it happens to someone else."

Well, Susanna admitted that she did more than snicker when two years ago Bishop Solomon Weaver married dumpy Sadie Swick. "Deserve each other," she'd grumbled to Milton before she saw the humor embedded in such a mismatch. Then she chuckled in a low, throaty laugh.

Smiling Milton, often reaching for her hand, his warm voice softening her heart. Together they were a team, weren't they? She glanced at the tall silo Milton'd built behind the barn. The place, a showplace of Aaron County. Reporter from "The Country Gentleman" interviewing them both a few weeks past. Pictures--inside the house and out. The cover spread of the palatial house taken at an angle showing the magnificent spruce trees at one side, and the hard maples at the other. The double-page spread displaying the table set with her Dresden china and Fostoria crystal. Her big platters and bowls loaded with appetizing, color-contrasting food, the famous "seven sours and seven sweets" of the Pennsylvania Dutch. Emily's bouquet of lilies and roses in the center.

The reactions at the church. Pats on the shoulder. Smiles, congratulations on such successes. Words like--"Aren't we all honored to have a Pennsylvania showplace in our community, here along the Sweetbrier?"

Susanna felt the tension between the honor and exposure of their material successes, and the long-heard messages from home, Sunday school and the pulpit on "We ought to simplify our lives in order to have more to give."

Susanna spied the cover of the new book she'd been reading, *A Daughter of the Middle Border*, lying on the end table by the walnut radio.. Maybe that's where she was, straddling a "middle border." Maybe she ought to caution Milton about holding back on adding to the blooded stock.

She reviewed in her mind the last bank records and the amount they still owed on those two loans. Then another part of her loomed its impish head and said, "My, Susanna, wouldn't a few splendid, green-gold peacocks grace your front yard? How about one of them flying up on the roof of your barn and spreading its tail just when Sadie Weaver the bishop's wife drove by?"

Susanna pushed back the thought. *Well, if you ask me, Sadie Weaver could use a little beauty.*

***

Thursday next week, Susanna in her blue smock, sat at the secretary in the dining room digging in those little cubicles. Where was it--the statement from the Blessing Bank? She had the account summary from the Rosefield Bank before her. Beads of sweat broke out on her neck as she remembered banker Willis Swartley's turned-down mouth. *We owe that much? On that building loan? Why, I thought Milton...oh well, it's me, too. I never put on the brakes. Twelve thousand dollars is a pile of money, even in boom times.*

Her fingers raked past the bound breeding records. Yep. Always like to keep the animal husbandry records. Leave it to easy-going Milton--no telling when the Guernseys would be calving. Was it time to sell Buford and bring in another bull?

She heard Milton's steps behind her as he sauntered across the dining room. The heat of his hand on her shoulder melted her body, softened her spirit.

There it was. She spread the account sheet open.

"Milton, look at this. We only paid eight hundred on this Rosefield loan last year. Willis Swartley's going to blow a gasket."

Milton, smelling of sweet alfalfa hay, leaned over and kissed her on the neck. "No, my beauty, Willis's not going to blow any gasket. I told you he practically gave the money to me."

"But he's raised the interest to eight percent, Milton. Hadn't you noticed?"

"Sell those twenty two-hundred-pound Berkshires at the market come August, Susanna, and we'll cut a swath right through that Rosefield loan." He massaged her shoulders tenderly.

Susanna smiled, and she couldn't help turning her head and kissing his arm below the shirt cuff.

"We'd better fix our eyes on this Blessing one, Milton. Easy to shove these things in a cubicle and...."

Milton reached across and picked up the statement. "Fourteen thousand three hundred? Susanna, that right? Thought we knocked three thousand off that last April."

"We did, Milton. We did. But are you forgetting your sally into the city and the seven-passenger green Buick you drove back?"

"Guess I did, Susanna. Had to add a couple thousand to the loan. Banker Stutzman happy to accommodate us. He knew our place was the showplace on this side of Aaron County."

He cleared his throat, turned Susanna around on the swivel chair. "Besides, my pretty one, the car was for you. Green to match the peacocks you ordered."

"Well, the Overland was good enough for me, and I admit, the Buick is easier to drive, but Milton, did we have to have such a large car?"

"Never know when one of our young'uns gonna break loose and marry. Bring in a passel of grandchildren. You do want to drive your grandkids to a picnic over to Lynn Valley don't you, Susanna?"

"Milton, Milton. You're the death of me. I believe you, these are good times, but we're going to have to be a little more serious about these bank statements. August, you say? Selling the fat shoats?"

"August, Sweetie. Want to go out and watch them eat tonight?" Milton grinned.

"Not tonight. But if we don't get a couple of thousand knocked off one of those loans and make a good run at the other, I'm going to have to learn to play that piece Emily's been pounding out on the piano, "Blue Moon."

Just then Edwin, looking worried, strode through the dining room door and dropped his books on a chair.

"Father, I walked past the Berkshire pens on the shortcut home. Some of those biggest hogs are walking stiff and funny. Coughing, too, Father."

"YES, WE HAVE NO BANANAS"

37

Veterinarian Rudolph Miller shook his head and reached to steady the brim of his hat in the sudden gust. "You can try it, Milton, separating the ones that still show no symptoms, but I have my doubts, not with cholera."

"In these times? No cure? Surely..." Milton's eyes glazed as he stared at Dr. Miller's drawn face. Then he glanced at Susanna leaning over the white-painted fence-rail, forehead creased, chewing on her lip.

"Let me climb in there and help, Milton. At least we must try. O dear God. Why this? Look at their purple, swollen bellies." She struggled through the hogs to turn on the water faucet to fill a trough. "They're so thirsty, too. That go with it, Dr. Miller?"

"Part of it, Susanna. Milton, I'm afraid these thirty-five I've already isolated will have to be shot. Earlier, the better."

Susanna's stomach knotted. Milton, how he'd hate doing it. Did they even have enough rifle shells? How did it happen with all the care they'd given the hogs? Blooded stock. Twice the price of the ordinary run. The August market. The check for the two-hundred-pound shoats. The bank loans. Mercy, mercy.

"Shot? But Rudolph, these hogs cost..." Milton's face paled.

"And I suspect by tomorrow these others here'll be showing symptoms. Hog cholera spreads like wildfire, Milton. Like I say, no cure. These shoats must have been born from sows that were infected. That's what usually happens."

"How'll we get rid of the carcasses, Rudolph?" Susanna stared, open mouthed.

"Hafta hire a big tractor, or steam engine with one of those graders like when they dig a pond. Open up a big trench out back on your property. Throw lime on the carcasses, or if you have enough brush and dry wood, you could try to burn them."

A tractor? Steam engine? That'll be another two hundred dollars, job like that. Milton's and Susanna's eyes met, their faces froze.

***

The purple and orange clouds wove around the setting sun. Foliage on the trees turned dark green tinged with gold and orange. Cicadas chirruped and frogs in the cattails at the edge of the pond croaked lustily.

Susanna, hand braced against a carved porch post, looked westward toward the far end of her pasture and the hedgerow. The ugly cloud rising from the lime truck lingered, white drifts catching in the wind. The rich, opened earth--the bloated carcasses of their prized Berkshires...

She knew that tomorrow the others, too, would have to be shot. Dr. Miller had only held off, seeing Milton's grief. In the morning, he'd be back, shaking his head, saying, "Mr. Leatherman, I really am sorry. Better load up your rifle. I brought one of my own to help you if you wish. It's the only way."

Would Milton even want any supper? She'd mixed a fresh lettuce salad with her sweet-sour dressing. Celery and onions in the steaming potato soup filled the house with a rich aroma. Milton definitely wouldn't want any ham with his supper this evening. Certainly not.

Susanna wiped tears with her handkerchief as she spied him and Edwin, shoulders slouched as they trudged back from the raw trench, the team dragging the empty sledge behind them. Was there yet another load?

Then the largest of her three peacocks bounced across the half-acre front lawn, stopped, danced in a circle and shuddered all over as he spread his magnificent gold-blue-green tail before her.

Display your finery, my pretty. About the only one around here for a while that'll be doing that.

She turned toward the kitchen to join Emily in setting the table.

***

Two days later the wind whistled through the open pig pens and the grand, round hog house. Milton, bracing back the doors after the day of fumigating, waved at her as she turned the Buick down the lane toward Rosefield.

The bank. She had surprised Milton by plunking down her prize chicken money she'd been saving for...just what was it? New china? Why, the ecru and pink Rosebud bone china was surely good enough.

"I know it was a foolish thing, Lucille," Susanna said to the bank clerk assisting her with the deposit. "A lot to count. My chicken prize money. Ought not to have saved it in my bureau drawer. Bit risky, wasn't it?"

Lucille twisted her lips, her glasses drooped on her nose as she counted the bills, then the change. "You got one thousand two hundred and fifty dollars here, Mrs. Leatherman. I'd say it takes a disciplined woman to save that much chicken money. Your husband know about this?"

"No, Lucille, he doesn't. Surprise him by lopping off the next layer on that loan. Could you kindly tell Mr. Swartley I'd like to see him personally?"

Lucille led Susanna through the varnished gate into the sunlit office where Willis sat glowering over the financial page of the newspaper. He looked up, then stood.

"Susanna Leatherman, what can I do for you?" He pointed to the chair before his desk.

"Good morning, Willis. Fine morning, isn't it?" Funny how she couldn't get the refrain of that silly new song out of her mind just now, "Yes, We Have No Bananas." Foolish, foolish.

Willis stared at her as if he wondered if she was dressed conservatively enough. He harrumphed, not moving his steel-blue eyes and set face, waiting.

"I'm going to write you a check for twelve hundred dollars to put on that building loan, Willis." Susanna unscrewed the cap of her fountain pen and turned back the cover of her checkbook.

"Well, now. That's knocking it down, Susanna. You and Milton took quite a blow on those blooded Berkshires, didn't you? Sure you want to go ahead and make that size of a payment?" He smiled.

"Certain of it, Willis. My money, and a surprise for Milton. He's discouraged right now. Out there fumigating pig houses. We've got to get the soil in the lots sterilized yet."

"Serious financial loss, Susanna. Serious." Willis drew his lips into a pucker and stared above his wire-rimmed glasses at her. "Really don't know how much longer these boom times'll hold, one of these days, maybe...." Banker Swartley slapped the edge of his desk with his wide palm, then stood up, dismissing her. "One of these days..."

***

Susanna carried her bag of groceries up the sidewalk to the car. Why couldn't Swartley have been a little more friendly? Anyone putting herself out like she'd done deserved at least a generous smile and a word of encouragement for being responsible, didn't they?

She glanced across the street at the old Three Blossom Hotel. Hummm...scraping the paint off the weathered boards. She wondered who bought it. A fleeting vision of Madam Carmita's face appeared in her mind. A pain stabbed somewhere within. Suddenly, she saw, instead of a paved street, a wide muddy expanse, and a well-suited dandy sitting in a new buggy, tipping a new homburg, baby Timothy, wrapped in a blanket, leaning against him. A chill gripped her entrails. And then that song started circling again in her head, as though it was playing from a warped record, *Yes, We Have No Bananas.*

WHIPPOORWILLS STARTED SCREECHING

38

Susanna lowered her eyes to read Emily's letter: "Mama, I loved my studies at Bethel College, especially piano. Now that summer's here, I'm taking a waitress job in a restaurant in Manitou Springs, Colorado. Why don't you and Papa drive out in the Buick...?"

Susanna lifted her glasses and placed them on the dining table as she tried to envision the flat plains of central Kansas. Off to the mountains? She'd always wanted to see the Rocky Mountains. Well, she would discuss this with Milton. She'd have to get a letter off to Emily this afternoon after she'd finished making her lime pickles.

Should she tell Emily they'd asked her to play the organ at church on alternate Sundays? A letter to Edwin, too, over at Ohio State, studying English and languages. Would he go to seminary after he got his degree? Wrote to Aaron at Penn State last week. How much was still in that college bank account?

She heard her teakettle sing and stepped briskly into the kitchen which she'd papered with red-cherry-patterned wallpaper above the oak wainscoting last spring. Glancing toward the barn, she saw Milton poking around with the Guernseys. Then she remembered, today was churning day, too.

While she scalded her pickles the kitchen screen door squeaked open. Milton stepped in, pants soiled near the cuffs of his dusty shoes. He lifted his straw hat, showing his white forehead and shock of gray hair. Why is he blinking his eyes like that?

"Susanna, better shove those cucumbers back on the side of the stove and step out to the barnyard with me. Think maybe we'll have to call the vet again." His voice was gravely and tight.

Milton opened the gate to the barnyard where the big yellow-brown Guernseys clustered in the shade of the locust.

Why were several of them lowering their heads and drooling? "Milton, what is it, something's wrong?"

Milton stepped close to a panting cow, feet wide apart, bracing herself. "Noticed last two days, Susanna, how these cows been letting up on the milk. Didn't think much about it with the summer heat, but look at this." He reached over and lowered the lip of the panting cow. "See those blisters?"

A wave of acid rolled up in Susanna's stomach. She bent over to look. "Why, Milton, her mouth is broken out." Glancing to the cow at her left she could see the rim of blisters around her lips, too. "What on earth is it?"

"Look down here." Milton lifted a hoof of the patient Guernsey. "If you look closely through the dust you can see those little sores right in the tissues between the split in her hoof."

Susanna stared. Her eyes widened. No. It couldn't be. More than ten thousand dollars tied up in this herd. It simply can't be.

"I'll run and call Dr. Miller, Milton. O Lord, let it not be the prized Guernseys." Susanna loped toward the house. Glancing back she saw two or three of the cows struggling to approach the shade of the locust. How they staggered in that stiff walk.

***

"All the symptoms, Milton, Susanna." Dr. Miller cleared his throat, his eyes telling the story: *Why do I have to break such heartrending news?*

"It can't be...," Susanna started to say.

"Foot-and mouth-disease? No. Absolutely not, Rudolph." Milton tipped his hat and wiped sweat with a red handkerchief. "Why, I got papers on all these cows."

"Classic symptoms, Milton. No doubt about it. Spreading over southwest by Staunton, too. Never know how it got started. Some blame the wet spring."

"Foot-and-mouth disease? First the Berkshires with cholera, it just can't be...." Susanna's face paled. The acrid smells of the barnyard engulfed her nose--how could she work with pickles now?

"Afraid you got it right, Susanna. And like you say, only a little over a year after that cholera outbreak, it's gonna be a blow." Rudolph looked down at the ground. "You folks took a cleaning on that disaster, I know."

"You mean, there's no medicine? You can vaccinate them, can't you? You know, Rudolph, these are blooded Guernseys. They brought in a pile of prize money, let alone the milk. That's our living, Rudolph, our living."

"Afraid you're going to have to get that rifle out again, Milton. Sorry to have to say it. Really sorry. You know we'd better get it done, the sooner the better. You're going to need some help. I'll stay and give you a hand like the other time."

Milton stared open-mouthed at Susanna, his face pale. "Maybe you'd better go on back to the house, Susanna."

She knew what he was thinking. How much was that loan over at the Blessing bank, thirteen--fourteen thousand? Dear Lord, dear Lord. Susanna wrung her hands in her apron; her feet kicked the barnyard dust as she shuffled back through the gate and on up the walk past the spireas to the porch. The telephone. Better call that tractor and grader man. Another gulch at the back of the farm? Cows were big--how big a ditch would it take? Mercy, mercy. Or did Milton or someone say they sent out the "dead truck" nowadays? What will Aaron, Edwin, and Emily say--all in college?

Suddenly those whippoorwills started screeching in her brain again--she hadn't heard their squawks for years: "Whip poor Willa. Whip poor Willa." Her pickle-stained hands reached up to cover her ears.

COUNT YOUR BLESSINGS

39

"Glad you decided to spend a few days at home before going back to Kansas, Emily." Susanna, in a pink calico shirtwaist that flattered her still slender form, gave Emily a hug and kissed her on the cheek.

"We all worried about you and Father, Mother. You simply will have to let the three of us hoof it on our own now. We've applied for scholarships. Edwin's already received his at Ohio State. Aaron's always looked after himself, Mother. Don't worry about him. I can have the job as assistant to the president's secretary at Bethel College. So you see, we all learned how to manage from you, Mother." Emily kissed her mother on her flour-dusted cheek.

Aaron, an inch under six feet, strolled in off the porch. "The gang's rolling in, Mother. Grandpa Steiner amazes me, the way he keeps his Chevrolet polished."

Susanna glanced out the window at Joseph and Anna, now in their early eighties. Joseph steered the car under the locust by the yard gate. "I just know Mother brought her famous rice pudding."

"I hope so, Mother, and did you bake that elderberry pie? Lots of elderberries this season."

"That I did, son. Grape pie, too, and apple." Susanna hurried out to her big range to check on the beef roast in the oven. She needed to get those fryer parts rolled in flour and seasoning and into the cast iron-skillets. She felt the pulse of her heart--alive, family descending on her and Milton today.

About time--she'd insisted on it. Enough misery and blues with the hog cholera, and the foot-and-mouth disease wiping the cows out. But the peacocks and the chickens, screaming and cackling, couldn't fill the silence. Susanna longed for the lowing of a milk cow. Even the pigs' grunts at the trough had been exhilarating, hadn't they?

She rolled a fat chicken thigh in flour and dropped it into the skillet, nimble fingers working automatically. She heard the gentle voices of the grandparents and Emily, Aaron, and Edwin greeting them.

Susanna's mind caught on those sad bank accounts and their recent trip to the bankers concerning them. She and Milton had gone over the accounts a hundred times. Owed almost twenty thousand at the banks. Markets on the down-slide. Place sunken in mortgage like the Buick's wheels in last February's mud. Willis Swartley's down-turned mouth. She'd seen him last week park his burgundy Chrysler out along the road by the pasture, get out and survey the farm as if he already had a buyer for it. And Silas Stutzman's drawn face at the Blessing bank. They'd explained how they could cut back--sell almost everything to keep the farm. He only thumped the edge of his desk and frowned.

"Way I look at it, the seesaw down on one end, Mrs. Leatherman, and you and your husband happen to be on the high end and sliding down, greased plank, too. You went overboard, Mrs. Leatherman," Silas had said in that gravelly voice of his as he gripped the edges of his desk. "You and Mr. Leatherman ought to have had more checks and balances. Sure, you got a showplace. Big spread in national magazine--you realize we at the bank do have to protect our investors."

On the way home, Susanna had brought up selling the Buick and going through the house and getting rid of half of the furniture. "It's mostly my fault, Milton--I don't know why I seemed so driven to, to...." What was it? Why hadn't she finished the sentence? "To show those women who shunned me that I really was somebody?"

"No, Susanna. Remember--I pushed building the hog house, the new henhouse, and insisted on all that house remodeling," Milton said, placing his arm around Susanna's shoulder.

There'd been little sympathy, but who was she, Susanna Leatherman, to expect any sympathy? She'd cried a lot at first. No, they couldn't sell the farm. And Milton--arm around her, big hand holding her head on his shoulder--well, as long as they had their love, maybe land and opulent buildings weren't so important after all. Still healthy. Always knew Milton wasn't really a farmer at heart, anyway. Talking now about a town job. She rolled the wishbone piece and tossed it into the skillet as the grease popped.

Susanna turned, glanced through the double doors into the dining room as Cousin Rosella stepped into the room, napkin-covered dish in her hand. She bet it was a pan of her butterscotch rolls.

Susanna held Milton's warm hand as Grandpa Steiner said the blessing. She lifted her eyes and surveyed the hungry brood. Her three children, clean, grinning across white teeth, intelligent, wide-open eyes. Rosella beside her on the left. Dear Rosella. Said she had important news today. How old is she? Fifty-five?

Brother Aden and golden-haired Lydia beside him. Their two boys and little Sally Ann beside Lydia, eyeing the fried chicken through the Fostoria goblet in front of them. Table spread with her ecru linen with matching napkins. Aroma from Grandma Steiner's rice pudding making the saliva flow.

"Well," Milton said, reaching for the fried chicken platter, "sure there's lots more news than what Susanna and I have to share." He looked at Rosella. She blushed. "Start with you, Rosella. You keeping secrets from Susanna?"

Everyone giggled as Rosella's cheeks blushed even redder. She reached for her goblet and took a sip. "Now, don't rush me, Milton. You wouldn't want me to talk and eat at the same time, and right now I'm just ravenous."

"I know what it is, Mother," Emily said as she lifted the big Dresden bowl with the green beans. "I saw Rosella Meyers and Elam Wasser standing in front of the jewelry store in Blessing. Then, Mother, your dearest cousin sidled over to the edge of the sidewalk and got into his yellow La Salle. Pretty spiffy car, if you ask me."

"Why, Rosella. Elam Wasser? Really? What a nice man. College educated too. But Rosella, he goes to the new church. Mean a lot of changes, wouldn't it?"

Rosella giggled and sunk her teeth into a golden chicken thigh and refused to answer any specifics.

Finally brother Aden chimed in. "Glad you decided to have us all, Susanna. Lydia said it was our turn to get the gang together. We'll do that Thanksgiving. You collegians gonna be able to come? We've got the turkey, goose, too."

"Afraid not, Uncle Aden. Sure like to. But we'll all try to make it for Christmas. Mother, you going to put up a big Christmas tree again in the parlor? Emily'll play the carols on the piano." Edwin forked a drumstick.

"Not until Mother plays first. Never thought my own mother'd be playing the organ over at Lynn Valley Church," Emily said, eyes filled with pride.

"Well, I want to know what Rosella and Elam were looking at through the glass there at the jewelry store. Couldn't have been a wedding ring, could it, Rosella?" Susanna said, color rising in her cheeks.

Rosella finished chewing her green beans and, forgetting herself, forked a hefty slice of the roast beef from the platter in front of her plate.

"Well, if you all are going to goad me, I might just as well tell it. Yes, Susanna. That's what it was. I only wanted a simple gold wedding band, though. No diamond."

They all chorused together, "Rosella, marriage?"

"I think it's just great, Rosella," Edwin said. "And if I were an ordained man, I'd even offer to perform the ceremony without charge, even if Elam Wasser is a well-to-do man."

For a moment Susanna's mind caught on memories of yesteryear: plain, they were the plain people. The clothing, no ornaments, no jewelry, not even a wedding band. She looked up at her sideboard mirror, and it seemed as if she caught the word flashing there: "Excommunicated."
She groped her way back from the darkening tunnel.

"Why, Rosella. I'm delighted. You'll be joining our church then? You know you can't..."

"Yes, Susanna. Yes, I've talked to Pastor Fry."

"From Lynn Valley?" Milton's voice was serious. "It'll mean a lot of changes, Rosella."

"And, Milton, most of them quite welcome. Grandma Steiner, please pass your rice pudding. I simply can't wait any longer." Rosella smiled.

"You can tell she's going to be a bride. Brides always get ravenous just before the ceremony," Aaron said, a teasing grin on his face.

***

Following the sumptuous feast and after the young folks cleared off the table and washed the dishes, the whole gang gathered on the wide porch outside the dining room windows.

"I want us to go into the parlor sometime this afternoon and sing from the new hymnal," Emily said.

"We'll do that this evening, Emily. Yes, we must sing together. Unites a family when they sing together." Susanna, sitting on the wicker settee, clasped Milton's hand. "We have some other news, folks, we need to share with you. Milton, you want to start?" She squeezed his fingers.

"No, you go ahead, Mother, you got the right words." A warm breeze blew off the silver lace vine spreading its sweetness. A cardinal called from the top of the red maple.

Susanna's eyes surveyed the sloping emerald yard; and the immaculately trimmed fence rows; the flower beds on each side of the walk, crazy with late summer phlox, sweet peas, zinnias, dahlias, petunias, cockscomb, and marigolds.

She looked over right and saw the grand hoghouse, now empty. The big bank barn with the towering silo behind it. A sudden gust of wind rocked the boughs of the hemlock. Peaceful here. Family. Most important thing, family gathered around. Sure, they'd soon be scattered, but family--that's something that can be kept in the heart. Through it all she'd built it, family.

"What is it, Susanna? You're going to break some news?" Grandma Anna leaned over, her covering hardly showing at all on her snow-white hair.

"Now let her tell it in her own time, Anna." Grandpa Steiner's deep-set eyes twinkled.

Susanna cleared her throat. "Milton and I are going to have to make some rather drastic changes. We don't want you to feel too badly about it. Maybe get used to it in the next couple of weeks." Susanna looked down at her work-worn hands. Would her voice start to quiver?

"Your Father and I've had to take stock of our finances and the farm here since the livestock disasters." Her lips twisted.

"Terrible, Mother. Wish I'd have been here to help Father when all those guernseys died, but...." Edwin's face fell.

"It was all right, Son," Milton said. "What your mother's trying to tell you is that we're going to have to--uh, to sell the farm." He forced a smile.

"Sell the farm?" They all chorused together, leaning forward, eyes widening in disbelief. Anna Steiner's head shook with her palsy.

"We've been over all our finances many times. Both up at the Rosefield bank and over at Blessing. Doesn't seem to be any other way out. Too many losses. We had too large a debt."

"Father," Emily sat on the edge of her chair, "This is our home. Why, why...."

"Our home, but we'll have to make some changes. The banks are foreclosing on our place, children. We can't stop it now, though we've done everything possible. Sheriff

Spengler, actually a cousin of mine, will bring an auctioneer and the farm'll be sold two weeks from today. Big sale. Everything spread out on the lawn and in the lot out front. Moving to town." Susanna reached for her handkerchief.

Suddenly she saw a fatigued young woman in the dim light of a dingy upstairs creamery room, a baby in a perambulator, and two hungry toddlers. A chill crept over her heart.

"Why, Susanna," Joseph Steiner said, "you didn't even tell us."

"I wanted to, Father, but I just couldn't find the words. I wanted us all together. That way, with you all here, it, it...."

"You did the right thing, Mother, waiting for us all. Can we help? Uncle Aden, did Mother come to you?" Aaron looked at his ruddy-faced uncle.

"She did, Aaron, but you know your mother. She didn't want me to sell part of my herd, or take out a loan. You know your Mother, she has to climb Mt. Blue on her own strength." Aden shifted back in his chair.

"Those bankers, couldn't they do something?" Edwin asked. "That's old Willis Swartley up at Rosefield, tighter than a--"

"No, son, it's not Willis Swartley's fault, grouchy as he is. We only have bad luck and ourselves to blame." Susanna tried to smile.

"Where will you live, Mother?" Emily asked.

"Go ahead and tell them, Milton." Susanna smiled through her tears.

"Well, I'm taking a job in marketing at the pretzel factory in Blessing. Put a down payment on a nice new row house there on Myrtle Street. Room enough for your mother's piano, too. One of our churches three blocks from our house." Milton glanced at Susanna.

"Blessing? Well, it's a pretty town, but the farm, the beauty here, all the room--"

"Well," Rosella said, "Susanna, I want you to stand with me at Marvin's and my wedding. That I do. And when we get back from our trip to Oregon, you can bet your bottom dollar I'll be there to help you get your curtains up."

A silence hung as the news settled in, broken by the chirp of a lonely cricket somewhere under the porch.

"Now let's not have long faces. Why don't we just march right on into the parlor now and open the hymnal. I think it's time to sing 'Count Your Blessings.' That was one of Timothy's favorites, remember?" Susanna's hand lifted to her chin at the mention of Timothy's name. She rose from the settee, stepped over and put her arm around Aaron's waist, drawing him near. A sudden ache squeezed at her heart as she saw Aaron's downcast eyes. What is he thinking? Does he remember? Oh, he surely misses Timothy, too-- The old perambulator--running, fleeing along a lonely road.

WE WOMEN HAVE TO BE HEARD

40

Well, here goes, Susanna said to herself as she untied her pink apron and automatically brushed the sides of her graying hair. *Thank God it's a sunny day. Hard enough propping my spirits up as it is. Don't need a thunderstorm.*

She and Milton had gotten up early. While they had coffee, Milton had read from Psalm 27: "The Lord is my light and my salvation: Whom shall I fear? the Lord is the strength of my life; of whom shall I be afraid...? Wait on the Lord; be of good courage...."

She'd slipped her straw hat on her head to protect her eyes from the glaring light, and her face from the August sun.

What'll I do next to get through this day? She decided to stroll out on the lawn amidst the lined-up furniture, though her back ached and her calves were sore from heaving boxes and moving household wares. How many bushel baskets of fruit jars had she carried out of the basement? She could hear the rumbling of trucks and cars down the road and see the cloud of dust rising. Soon the pasture beside the barn would be lined with parked vehicles, a few wagons and tied-up teams.

Why did it have to be this way, humiliating foreclosure? Second Cousin Sheriff Ted Spengler strutting out there by her spruce trees, badge on his shirt pocket, pointing to her mahogany block secretary desk. Probably working out a deal with auctioneer Cobb over how to land it in his own truck at a bargain price.

Dozen cars already parked by the barn. Sadie and Bishop Weaver? Yes, should have expected them among the first, Sadie already pawing over her tablecloths, rummaging through the pillowcases and sheets.

Drawing nearer, Sadie failed to hide her enthusiasm, eyes bright as if she expected great bargains. She squawked, "Why, good morning, Susanna. My, don't we just thank the Lord for such a perfect day for the sale?" She reached for Solomon's arm: his shirt-buttons barely closed over his portly belly.

"Why, that we do." He tipped his black hat. "Morning, Susanna. My, my, you and Milton unloading enough to keep the trucks backed up at Sweetbrier bridge 'till ten o'clock tonight." His ruddy face spread in a thick smile. "I do, Susanna, extend my sympathies. Foreclosure, most unpleasant for you folks, to be sure." His wattles shook.

Susanna cleared her throat and forced out the words. "Morning, Sadie, and Reverend Weaver." There, she'd said it, acknowledging his high church status. Ignore the dizziness that twisted her head as her lips formed the words. "*Whom shall we fear*?" Let bygones be bygones and march on. But a part of her felt like she'd been stabbed with a newly sharpened pencil when Solomon rasped, "You and Milton think the farm'll sell at the going rate? Land bringing eighty an acre around here. Seems high, but with that spacious house and those fine buildings...." Bishop Weaver's round eyes widened as he placed his hands in his hip pockets and surveyed the stately house, sturdy barn, and fine out-buildings.

"Mercy, Lord, give me mercy," Susanna mumbled to herself, moving on past the sewing machine, an old dry sink, stand tables, and kitchen chairs where Dorcas Hershberger Shenk stood with her frail husband, Ezra. Had to ignore it, get used to it. She lifted her eyes away from them when she saw Dorcas open the double doors of her carved mahogany highboy--*Dorcas once crossed the street in Rosefield so she wouldn't have to face me back when....* Lord, Lord, Susanna prayed.

Everywhere now. Plain people. White straw hats, black hats, shawls, bonnets. English people from town, too, stomping through her flowerbeds. Antique collectors, eyes glassy for the bargains. "Some of the finest furniture this side of Lancaster," the ad had announced.

Susanna caught her shoe on the five-gallon crock by the pump. She reached out and braced herself on the edge of her combination electric-and-wood range. Milton. I need Milton to walk through this with me. But she knew he was down in the barn with Aaron, making sure the two teams had enough water and oats--keeping them calm for their ordeal. Drag them out, people circled around, the auctioneer Cobb's raucous, monotone mumbling--she couldn't understand them, nor keep up with them. Miracle, who ended up with the goods. Glad that Aaron sacrificed to be here with them. Her heart ached at his downcast eyes, trying to hide his shame, though she knew he struggled to be upbeat, especially today.

Someone pulled at her dress sleeve. "Fine day for a sale, isn't it, Susanna?"

Susanna turned. "Why, Rachel. Rachel Weaver. Yes, well, Isaac's here, too, isn't he?" She knew Isaac had some interest in buying the place, though she doubted if he and Rachel could swing it.

"Oh, yes, Susanna. Isaac wants to know if you're going to back out the Buick and...."

"No, Rachel. We're keeping the car." The nerve. How could she ask such a thing? Wasn't there enough here to satisfy Rachel without asking if they'd sell the car?

"Just thought I'd ask, Susanna: we both thought with you and Milton having to scale down, and we do feel sorry about that, the Buick would be--"

"Too fine a car for us? Well, maybe you're right, Rachel. Maybe it is too fine a car for us. You'll just have to forgive Milton and me that excess." *Lord, help me hold my tongue.*

"Well, Susanna, I know this is a hard day for you and Milton. If you'll allow me, I do want to inquire about one more thing. Is that my brother Reuben's ripsaw and carpenter's square mixed in with those other tools out there on that table?" Her one eyebrow was raised with a questioning slant as she pointed towards the spirea bush and a table loaded with garden tools, old saws, hammers, and all those "miscellaneous things too numerous to mention."

The nerve. How could she ask such a thing? Susanna felt like her feet were going to root in the ground. She turned, her nostrils flaring. *Lord, give me patience*. "When I walked away from that mausoleum that day, Rachel Weaver, I took nothing but my children and the clothes on our backs." She felt her fingernails dig into her palms.

"Well, just wanted to make sure, Susanna. Don't have to get in a huff. Another thing, before you march off, Isaac's wanting to know how much you paid for that Empire living room suite?"

"Why, Rachel, price tag's underneath. Right underneath, tacked on that heavy oak piece." *Lord, Lord, chop off my tongue. Let her try and lift that couch.*

By now Susanna had wedged herself in the middle of a gaggle of church sisters from the three churches, the plain and the fancy. Her heart palpitated. She wiped sweat from her forehead. "Hello, Reverend Fry," she nodded to her own minister.

"A perambulator. Old wicker one. Would you look at that?" Clara Swick's coarse voice drifted in the wind.

Susanna glanced left to her John Better parlor table and saw Clara reach out and rock the old brown perambulator. Nausea hit her. Birds chattered in her head. She clutched her throat. What were those sounds, Timothy's and Aaron's cries--a child's words..."Mama, how much farther? Mama, can't we stop for a drink? Mama, please pick me up...."

Just when Susanna strolled past the table loaded with old picture frames and some of the hangings she couldn't use in the new house, a tall, slightly-stooped woman, black bonnet tied under her chin, turned to her, her kindly eyes twinkling through the creases. A thin hand lifted to the side of her face as she smiled. "You remember me, Susanna? Dorcas Hershberger's mother, Emma. Went to Willow Bend Church with you when you were a girl. Could we sit down somewhere, Susanna, there's something I must say to you." A slight palsy shook her head.

"Well, yes, Emma, over by the spruce trees, the lawn furniture. Could sit a moment in the shade by the everblooming rose. Surely."

Seated on a sturdy Adirondack chair, Susanna leaned forward, trying to ignore the dizzying buzz of the pressing crowd. "Yes, Emma, I know who you are." Susanna waited.

"Susanna, it was a terrible thing you went through back when you were eighteen--that experience with Reuben Maust." Emma found her handkerchief and wiped a tear.

Susanna's heart chilled. Why would she be bringing that Sweetbrier Creek thing up now?

"I have to ask you to forgive me, Susanna. I was wrong in what I believed about you and Reuben. I do believe what you said happened to you was true. I know it now. Such an awful thing, the way everyone blamed you and your name read from the congregation." Emma bent over and wept, her shoulders shaking.

All of a sudden, Susanna's eyes flooded with tears. Someone from *that* church asking for forgiveness? Saying, "I'm sorry. We made a mistake?"

"My own niece, Gretta Overholt, had an experience very similar to yours out in Ohio," Emma continued. "No one in the congregation or community believed her either. She didn't marry the man, though. She died. Terrible infection from a botched abortion." She whispered the word.

"Susanna, now I know all the men in power in our church stood against you--a lot of the women, too. But most of us recognized that Reuben Maust, whatever his problems were, got off too easy over at Edenvale Church. We'll have to work to change things, Susanna. We women have to be heard. Please, please, Susanna, forgive me."

A roaring like a whirlpool at floodtime on Sweetbrier Creek swirled in her head. Susanna clutched the arms of her chair to steady herself, and she drew back her feet. Forgiveness? One sister, one woman, after all these years?

"Daughter Dorcas wants to know if you'd let her come and see you. She wants to ask your forgiveness. Says she won't go another week."

"I do forgive you, Emma. I've forgiven the girls who were my age, too, though, sometimes, Emma, I have to admit, my anger spills over and I find myself thinking and saying things I should not. Yes, Emma, tell Dorcas she can come."

"Anyone would understand why you get angry and confused. Yes, I'll tell Dorcas and thank you. Maybe I shouldn't have approached you today, but I don't drive, and I seldom have a chance to come this way."

"I thank you for those words, Emma; I can't tell you how much it helps...."

"Susanna, I do hope to bid a high price on that wonderful walnut hall tree. You and Milton are fine folks and I want you to clear your debt and have plenty left over. Plenty." Emma Hershberger squeezed her hand.

***

Noon already? Thank God the sisters from Lynn Valley Sewing Circle were putting out a good lunch. Ham sandwiches, dill pickles, potato salad, hot dogs, hamburgers with onion slices, ham frying. Shoo fly, apple, cherry, gooseberry pie--what else? Homemade ice cream.

"The pi-anna. You selling the pi-anna?" a tall, plainly dressed woman from over east of the church called out.

Derstine, wasn't it? Louella Derstine, moved in from Lancaster. "No, Mrs. Derstine. Milton and I moved my piano to our new row house in Blessing." *Won't tell her I already have six young folks signed up for lessons. They allowing members to have pianos in their homes in the old church? Would've thrown me out if I'd a-tried it back when I was....*

The staccato of the auctioneer's singsong cadence carried in the wind above the murmuring crowd. A child with a bottle of grape pop bumped against Susanna's legs, a strange, woolly dog bounced after him. Odors of frying hamburger and onions caught in the wind.

"Here, Susanna. My," Elizabeth Histand, the Sunday School superintendent at her church, said, "you get to eat free. Sale makes money for our circle, no charge. Now, what kind of sandwich do you want?"

Thank God for the friendly offer, another sincere smile. "Why, thank you, Elizabeth. Yes, well, I believe I'll have that smoked ham, and a piece of apple pie."

"You sit right here on this end of the picnic table. Here comes that good-looking Aaron. My, don't these boys grow up and get out in the world before we know it? My Charles is down at Union Theological Seminary, looking it over."

"Well, Charles will make a fine minister. Yes, Elizabeth. The changes, they almost overwhelm one...." She bit into the tender smoked ham. She'd forgotten how hungry she was. "Elizabeth, could you kindly hand me a glass of that iced tea?"

"Mother, you saved a spot for me?" Aaron pulled up a nail keg and sat beside her.

"I'll have the ham, please, same as Mother," he called to Elizabeth.

Susanna wondered if she had the courage to ask him how much the teams brought. Even worse, who bought them? She chewed slowly as her eyes surveyed all the farm machinery down by the corncrib, the wheat drill, the cultivator, the hay rake, the.... Where was Milton? Wasn't he hungry?

WE HAVE TO FIND A PLACE FOR EVERYTHING

41

Following the lunch recess, the stray dogs, the shoving, hollering children, and at least twelve hundred bargain hunters bruised the grass with heavy boots, heels and toes as they gathered around to face the spacious porch on the dining room side of the house.

Sheriff Spengler rubbed his five-pointed star badge with the butt of his palm, cleared his throat and lifted his head, black eyes focused on the crowd of assorted Mennonites, plain and fancy, Brethren, and "the English," before him.

"Now this announcement." Spengler yanked a yellow paper from his hip pocket. "Might as well read it. What we're all waiting for."

Sheep bleated from the barnlot. Did they have water? Who bought them? Milton, standing by Susanna, gripped her hand in his calloused one. Sweat had broken through his chambray shirt. "Teams brought only half of what they were worth, Susanna. Pray the place'll bring...."

"Due to required amounts now overdue, indebtedness on the Milton and Susanna Leatherman farm, section forty-two, Sweetbriar Township, Aaron County, Pennsylvania, amounting to twenty-two thousand three hundred fifty-four dollars...."

Susanna lifted her hand and clutched Milton's arm. Her heart palpitated.

Spengler stared, turned his square face, and looked over the pressing crowd. "Now you folks know Mr. and Mrs. Leatherman have a foreclosure here...."

The word exploded and grated her heart as if it were rubbed over a rusty kraut cutter. Wind rattled the maple leaves. Her face blanched.

"We wanna make sure our friends and good neighbors, here, Milton and Susanna, receive a fair price for this showplace. Don't have to tell you it was written about in a national magazine. You seen the pictures yourselves."

Murmuring spread and folks nodded and smiled to each other. Rachel and Isaac Weaver elbowed their way through to Milton's left, near the azaleas by the porch, Isaac's face drawn as if he was reviewing his bank statement.

Suddenly Susanna felt a warm, soft hand clasp hers. She caught the scent of lilac. Della? Della Delaney? "Oh, Della," Susanna squeezed her hand. "I'm so glad you came. It makes the day easier." Susanna stared deeply into Della's rich brown eyes, noting also her fine ecru linen suit and wide straw picture hat.

"Susanna, when they start bidding again on furniture, I'm going to bid the highest for that splendid Empire living room suite. Just what I need for my big parlor. Sturdy, well-made, last for years."

"Suppose you folks with serious interest have already taken a tour of this mansion here," Spengler swung his arm backwards. “Really sumpthin, isn't it? Now let's show the Leathermans we mean business." Sheriff Spengler nodded to auctioneer Cobb who cleared his throat, spat, lifted his cane, eyes beading in on the gaggle before him and right past Bishop Solomon Weaver and his squat wife with the dried mustard at the corner of her mouth, clutching her purse.

"If I faint, I'll keep standing," Susanna whispered to Milton, as the crowd pressed closer. A big, empty truck backfired and raised dust as it pulled up the lane.

"Who'll gimme twenty thousand, twenty thousand, who'll...?" The cacophony began, like a stricken locust struggling to the top of the walnut tree, as the auctioneer stabbed the air toward the wide-eyed crowd.

Susanna turned as a Brethren farmer, standing on a wagon seat to raise his head above the crowd, bid "Twenty thousand."

"I got twenty, I got twenty, who'll give thirty? Thirty...."

"Milton, we have to have more than that, pay off the debts and secure that house in...."

Someone in the crowd behind Della Delaney yelled out, "Twenty-one."

"I got twenty-one, now twenty-two..."

Mercy, the measly upgrade by degrees. Why didn't someone call out a fair price? Susanna glanced over at Sadie Weaver who brought her purse to rest on her stomach and clutched it with both fat hands.

"Twenty-two."

That was Isaac Weaver's voice. Susanna tightened her grip on Milton's arm. Won't turn to look at him, though. Might have known. Why didn't they buy Reuben's old place? That funeral-parlor house the right challenge for them....

The auctioneer stopped, wiped sweat from his brow and tipped back his broad-brimmed straw hat. "Now you folks all know this is a fine place. Can't sink your money into better land and I don't care where you look you won't see finer buildings. Let's get serious."

A cloud drifted over the sun giving them restful shade. Children tried to shove through the crowd, spilling orange and grape pop.

"Twenty-five. Got twenty-five, who'll bid thirty? Who'll bid thirty? Thirty? Thirty? Thirty?" The words echoed like the knock of a red-headed woodpecker on a hard maple trunk.

Susanna heard Milton swallow. She knew figures were circling in his brain, like hers. Would they make it? Maybe they would have to take the Buick back to....

Then Susanna glanced again at Bishop Weaver and Sadie, whose eyes had now grown glassy and seemed to pop out of their sockets. Sadie licked her lips. Did she elbow Solomon?

Solomon Weaver's fat fingers unlocked from his opulent belly and Susanna saw his hand raise, one finger waggling in the air.

"I got thirty, Bishop of the big congregation over the hill bids thirty," the auctioneer stopped. "Now we got a bishop of the community here knows proper worth of a place. Better look again at all these well-painted buildings. House alone worth half of the bid, isn't that right, Mrs. Weaver?" Ted Cobb bowed toward Sadie to give proper deference. Sadie mauled her purse and beamed.

It can't be. No. Susnna's heart started galloping without thought of rhythm or pace. Blood thundered in her ears. She looked up at Milton's red face.

"Who'll bid thirty-two, thirty-two...?"

***

The last piece sold, an old trunk from the attic which brought fifteen dollars. Then the crowd milled, streams heading for wagons, trucks, and cars.

"It's not ours anymore, is it, Milton?" Susanna's fingers slid from Milton's arm.

"Not ours, anymore. Where you going, Susanna?" His eyes narrowed.

"Just up on the porch with Bishop Weaver and Sadie, that's all. Be back in a minute." Susanna's shoulders leaned forward as if she were twisting the tail of a recalcitrant calf. Her feet pounded the bruised bluegrass.

"Brother Weaver, Sadie..." the words seemed to come on their own. Her hard heels hit the broad porch step. Bishop Weaver turned his stodgy body, his heavy eyelids blinked. "Why, Susanna, why, Sadie and I were just thinking, where's the key?" He cleared his thick throat.

"The key? Yes. I left the key inside the cupboard silverware drawer. You'll find it, Sadie." Sadie beamed like a mother hen who noticed all her eggs had hatched.

"Brother Weaver, something I want to say to you." Susanna was surprised that her heart beat normally. Her legs ached from standing all day, but she never felt so centered in her life.

"Say? Some words for me?" Solomon slid on an unctuous smile.

"Someone from your church, an older sister, apologized to me today. Begged in tears for forgiveness for misjudging me all these years. You, Bishop Weaver, refused to hear me when I was in need of counsel and support. You sided with Reuben Maust, even though he violated me--"

"Now, now, Susanna, don't you think after all these years...that's in the past, isn't it?" His eyes widened. He locked his fingers across his belly. Sadie began to maul her purse again.

"Nothing is ever just 'in the past,' Brother Weaver. We have to find a place for everything that happens to us. I found a place for sorrow and bitterness and Sister Emma Hershberger helped me today."

"Susanna, you're just tired. Losing your place today and...."

"No, Sadie, God is giving me the words. You turned your back on me when I needed friends. I don't hold it against you anymore. I told you in Rosefield that I forgave you, even if you still believed me guilty."

A breeze blew Sadie's covering strings. Her brow wrinkled. She shifted her feet.

"You probably judged me, too, for joining the Lynn Valley Church where the old regulations aren't followed. What you have to realize is that that was the only church of our denomination that would receive me into membership without me lying. I found help and peace there, Brother Weaver."

"Why, Susanna, no. We wouldn't judge those who fell away from our ch--"

"They didn't fall away. They only wanted ordinary rules to do the church's business, have Sunday school, and support

Missions and church publications. Your church has all of those, now."

Solomon's eyes rolled. "Ahem. Susanna, why, the Bible is plain, though, about attire, worldliness--"

"Brother Weaver, I stand here to tell you that all that looks 'plain' and according to written rules isn't always Christian. I think you know that, but preachers sometimes forget, or may overlook the real fruits of the spirit: 'love, joy, peace, long-suffering--'"

"Mrs. Leatherman." Bishop Weaver's mouth twisted.

"Now, I wish you a lot of happiness here. Sadie, the porch is pleasant. Look at the sweep of the lawn--the spruce trees, I hope they nurture your heart like they nurtured mine." Tears crept to Susanna's eyes.

Sadie Weaver bent over and started to cry. "Oh, Susanna, Susanna, I never..." Then she turned and waddled into the empty house.

Susanna reached out her hand. "Permit me to shake your hand, Brother Weaver, and congratulate you on your fine purchase today. Milton and I hope you and Sadie love it as much as we did." She turned and stepped down to the sidewalk and headed toward Milton by the gate, his face strained in bewilderment.

***

Milton steered the shiny Buick down the road. Ahead loomed the bridge where the willows made a canopy over the road near Blessing, Milton, shirt drenched in sweat, smiled at Susanna who sat holding her sewing basket and her worn-edged Bible, her feet close together, face straight ahead.

"Could you stop the car by this creek, Milton? Believe this stream runs into the Sweetbrier." Susanna turned left to survey the clear water rippling over the rocks.

The car stopped. The sweet smell of alfalfa hay drifted in the window, the willow fronds waved and sank. The water murmured as if it were singing, gently singing. Susanna smiled and faced Milton, her eyes tired but luminous. "Now, Milton, aren't the sounds of that brook pleasant? Refreshing and pleasant?"

"It is a refreshing sound, Susanna. Someday lets walk out here and follow that path alongside, see where it leads."

"I can't think of a nicer person to take that walk with than you, Milton." She brushed his hand with her own tired one. "What is that bird call?" Susanna looked down into the willow bushes.

"Why, Susanna, don't you know? That's a whippoorwill calling to its mate. A love song." Milton's lips spread into a wide smile.

"Well, I never heard it quite like that before, but that's a very pretty bird call. Very pretty." Her weary hands rested peacefully in her lap.

Milton started the car and eased down the brick-lined street.

Susanna turned her head towards him. "I never even thought of it. But looking back, the pieces fit. Bishop Weaver and Sadie...moving into my house." A broad smile spread across her tanned face, her eyes brightened. "Work a lot of that weight off, won't she, Milton?"

"You mean Sadie Weaver? Yes, all those stairs. Six bedrooms, on her knees scouring the ring off the Bishop's tub. I declare, Susanna, and did you see Rachel's face? When the Bishop gave that last bid, she looked over at Sadie as one would look at a cockroach that needed stepping on."

"A project, Milton. Project for the benefit of their souls. God uses everything for our best...'All things work together for good...' That our street up ahead, Myrtle? It is a pleasant street, isn't it, Milton?"

Milton turned the Buick and headed past the tall chestnuts. "A right pretty street, my love. Now when we get to our place, won't you sit right down at the piano and play something for me Susanna?" He reached across with his hot hand and brushed her arm.

"Play the piano? Tonight, before we find a place to eat?"

"That's my request, my love."

"Well, my dear, then I'll stretch my fingers and play *Look For the Silver Lining*." Susanna chuckled.

"I'd be content to hear you simply play *Home Sweet Home."*

Milton flashed Susanna a bright smile as he guided the Buick into the driveway.

The End